W9-ASB-925

TEXAS JUSTICE

A Novel

by

Judith Groudine Finkel

Fireside Publications

Lady Lake, Florida, 32159

TEXAS JUSTICE

This book is a work of fiction. Names, characters, businesses, organizations, places, events and incidences are either the product of the author's imagination or are used fictitiously. Any resemblance to actual persons, living or dead, is entirely coincidental

Published by:
Fireside Publications
1004 San Felipe Lane
The Villages, Florida 32159

www.firesidepubs.com

Printed in the United States of America

Copyright © 2009 by Judith Groudine Finkel

All Rights Reserved. No part of this book may be reproduced, stored in a retrieval system, scanned, photocopied or distributed in any printed or electronic form without written permission of the author.

First Edition: February 2009

ISBN: 978-0-9814672-9-0

PRAISE FOR:

TEXAS JUSTICE

2008 CONTEST WINNER
MYSTERY / SUSPENSE / THRILLER

"Judith Finkel's writing is clear and crisp. This is the real thing, a disturbing story that moves with the grit of truth. Finkel feels her work. She owns it." – Peter Chilson

Peter Chilson is a nonfiction writer and author of the short fiction collection *Disturbance-Loving Species*, winner of the Bread Loaf prize in fiction.

"This chilling tale of a young man tried in the press as well as the courtroom will have you turning the pages far into the night." – Linda Jacobs

Linda Jacobs is a Spur Finalist and the WILLA award-winning author of the *Yellowstone* series of novels.

"*Texas Justice* tells the gripping story of a mother fighting to save her son from being convicted of murder. Award winning author and attorney Judith Groudine Finkel mixes mystery, murder and maternal love in this must read legal thriller." - Madeline Maxine Westbrook

Madeline Maxine Westbrook is the author of *The Ghostwriter and The Muse*.

Judith Groudine Finkel

DEDICATION

This book is dedicated to Howard, whose love and encouragement sustain me, and to Michelle and Eric, the joys of our lives.

ACKNOWLEDGEMENTS

Thanks to the late Venkatesh Kulkarni whose inspiration started in his Rice University Novel Writing Colloquium and continues to this day. I am also indebted to my classmates, in particular Linda Jacobs who edited the entire manuscript, Marjorie Arsht, Kathryn Brown, Bob Hargrove, Elizabeth Hueben, Joan Romans and Madeline Westbrook, for their suggestions and support.

Judith Groudine Finkel

HOUSTON, TEXAS

August, 2001

Her son on trial for murder.

Mara Levine took Ariel's new navy blue suit out of his closet. It was just what his defense attorney had recommended. The suit, a polyester and wool blend, was well made but not expensive, making Ariel look respectable but not rich. She selected a white shirt and blue and tan tie to complement it. Ariel's nearby desk sported a picture of him reading from the Torah at his Bar Mitzvah six years before. The outfit he wore that day was almost identical to the one she'd chosen for this first day of his murder trial.

She still couldn't believe it.

Mara looked again at the picture of the thirteen-year-old Ariel so eager to accept the spiritual responsibilities of an adult and wondered why circumstances had brought them to this place.

ONE

Only three cancer patients visited Lingerie for Life the day after Thanksgiving. They came to pick up the bras Herlinda Sorento had fitted them for and Claudia Luna had altered so they perfectly contoured the women's prosthetic breasts. At holiday times people wanted to be with their families to try to forget they had cancer, not shop for items that reminded them. So while other stores in the Houston shopping center, like Kroger, Discount Delight and Child Proud Photographers, streamed with customers, Herlinda should never have opened her store that day.

Fear wouldn't let her take a day off. When her husband Eduardo had died thirty years before, leaving her with a six-year-old son, a seven-year-old daughter and a meager life insurance policy, she'd used the money to open Lingerie for Life. At first it barely supported the family, and even though now Herlinda had more than enough for food, shelter and clothing, she still remembered all the times she hadn't.

But she expected no more customers today. So a little before four o'clock she left the showroom with its mannequin torsos displaying different styles of bras and went through an archway where Claudia, her long time employee and friend, worked at a refurbished Singer sewing machine. Shelves stacked with oblong boxes containing the store's merchandise surrounded her. The beat of soft Latin music played from a radio at her feet. Herlinda held out a cigarette and smiled. The women enjoyed sneaking a smoke whenever the shop was customer free.

Herlinda knew Claudia wanted to be home with her husband Henry, a nice enough man ten years her senior. "Tell Henry to come get you. We're closing early."

A few minutes later Claudia headed towards the showroom to find Herlinda. She wanted to share a joke she'd heard on the radio.

Outside the store, a man of medium build, wearing a dark jogging outfit and a baseball cap, looked in the window. The tinkling of the bell over the door announced his entry just as Claudia got to the archway.

She watched as he rushed to the counter, reached towards Herlinda and said something Claudia didn't hear.

"You must be kidding," Herlinda replied. She ran from behind the counter towards the side room, which contained the fitting areas.

The intruder was so fast he caught up with her as she crossed the threshold. He extended his arm.

At first Claudia thought she saw him punch Herlinda in the neck. But when her friend cried out and toppled to the ground face down, she decided he'd done something worse.

Claudia screamed and ran to a phone at the front of the store to dial 911.

With two jumps the intruder reached her and cut her wrist, making her drop the receiver.

She thought she heard someone on the line. "Help, help, help," she yelled.

The assailant grabbed her from behind in a bear hug, pinning her arms, his face so close she felt the heat of his breath. What she thought were the man's knuckles pounded her over and over, starting on her chest and continuing down to her lower abdomen.

Then came his whispers. "Do you like it?"

She feared her screams were exciting him so she forced herself into silence. He opened his fist, and Claudia saw the knife.

"I'm going to cut your nose." And he did - right down the middle. "I'm going to make you pretty."

Claudia felt something pointed touch the skin behind her ear, and then a ticklish sensation from one side of her neck to the other. She fell to the floor, consciousness ebbing.

The knife wielder crouched over her and raised his hand to strike when the door opened, revealing a man in his sixties, medium height and thin build. The man grabbed a mannequin of a woman's upper torso and flung it at the assailant, hurrying towards him at the same time.

The intruder rose and swung his knife so swiftly and effectively that he cut the webbing of the man's right hand and right side with the same motion.

The man fell to the floor, breaking his glasses, and scrambled to get up. As he stood, his assailant jumped away from him, turned and ran out the front door, its bell jingling.

Claudia opened her eyes. "Henry, thank God, it's you." Blood dripped onto her husband's shoes.

"Are you all right, Claudia?" he asked as he helped her up.

"Yes, but Herlinda . . ."

"I'll call 911."

Claudia followed him to the phone. Without his glasses he couldn't see the numbers, so she dialed.

The tinkling of the bell, and a man about the same size and age as their assailant ran in. "Is something wrong?" he asked.

Claudia screamed and ran through the store, a trail of blood following her.

The stranger told her to lie down and stay calm.

She slowed to a walk.

Henry and the young man turned Herlinda over.

Claudia lay down beside her and poked her friend in the side. "Come on, Herlinda, get up."

Herlinda didn't move.

The stranger shook his head. "It's too late. Her throat's been slit."

"Shush. My wife will hear."

"Laugh . . . Herlinda . . . laugh." Claudia spoke haltingly, finding it difficult to breathe. So she closed her eyes, and felt the stickiness of her friend's blood beneath her as it mingled with the blood from her own stab wounds.

***

Houston detectives Oracio Crawley and Glen Healy were just a block away when the call came. They sped to the shopping center, quickly exited their car and approached Lingerie for Life.

Oracio, stocky at five foot eight and one hundred and sixty pounds led the way with his younger, taller partner close behind. They followed the droplets of blood outside the door of Lingerie for Life into the shop where they grew exponentially until they pooled around the two bodies lying next to each other, both Hispanic women in their fifties. Oracio was sure the larger of the two was dead.

A man about a decade older than the victims stroked the arm of the smaller woman. "I tried to save them. He was younger and bigger than me."

"Your name," Oracio ordered.

"Henry Luna. Claudia's my wife. I think he killed Herlinda."

"Describe the attacker."

"About twenty, six feet, blondish hair, jogging outfit, baseball cap. Where's the ambulance?" he asked, his agitation so evident that Oracio decided to question Henry in depth later.

A much younger man rose from his crouched position over Claudia Luna. "I've done all I can for her. We need that ambulance now."

Before Oracio could ask him who he was, two emergency medical techs came in with stretchers. After a quick check of her vital signs, they ignored Herlinda and worked briefly on Claudia. They put her on a stretcher and took her to the ambulance.

"Let me ride with her," Henry cried.

"You need to have your hand and side taken care of," the younger man said. He turned to Oracio. "Should I ride in the ambulance? I'm a chiropractor. Dr. Andrew Block."

"Stay here, Dr. Block, and tell me what you know."

"I was coming out of Kroger when I saw someone running from the direction of the lingerie store. He immediately aroused my suspicions. Why was he in such a hurry?"

Oracio studied the witness. It was odd he found a man running in a shopping center suspicious. And it was uncanny the way he fit the general description Henry Luna had given of the murderer. Andrew Block was in his twenties, just under six-feet tall with dark blond hair. But rather than wearing a jogging suit, he was in khaki pants and a black shirt. After eighteen years on the force, Oracio considered all possibilities. Andrew could have quickly peeled off the jogging outfit, removed the baseball cap which would have partially obscured his face and run into the store, giving himself an excuse for having the victims' blood on him and his fingerprints all over the shop.

"It would help to establish the time," the detective said. "Do you have a receipt from Kroger?"

Andrew pulled the receipt from his shirt pocket. The time shown was 4:01, when the 911 call had come in. The date was illegible.

Andrew gave a general description of the suspect, which fit Henry Luna's.

"I jumped into my car and started following the guy's dark Land Rover out of the shopping center. That's when I saw his license plate and copied it down. It's on the back of the receipt."

Oracio quickly called it in. "PBD164." To make sure there was no mistake, he repeated it as "Paul, Ben, David, 164."

Before Oracio could get back to questioning Andrew, Glen Healy approached him. He reported that the crew which had entered the shop just after them had dusted for prints, used amido black to check for latents and had taken samples of blood from around the store.

"Is there anything else you want them to do?"

Satisfied with the work of the crime scene officers, Oracio rejoined Andrew. He jotted notes as his witness told him how he followed the dark Land Rover to the east exit of the parking lot and then decided his medical skills might be needed at the lingerie shop so he parked, ran in and found the victims.

"I knew right away it was too late for the one woman but I suspect I saved the life of the other, making her lie down so she didn't lose any more blood."

"We'll get all that down in your statement at the station. Give Detective Healy your phone number so we can reach you when we're back there."

That's when the call came. The Land Rover was registered to a Virginia Levine, who lived at 1700 Stanton, a few miles away.

Oracio's suspect was a man, but a woman owned the get-away vehicle. "Has the Land Rover been reported stolen?"

"No, but about six months ago, a Mitsubishi Eclipse was reported stolen from the same address. Complainant was Benjie Levine, seventeen years old."

Oracio couldn't believe his luck. He had a suspect, an address and lots of blood at the scene, which the killer would have transferred to the Land Rover.

He hoped Sissy Kleinman was the assistant district attorney assigned to the case.

She'd won so many hard ones for him that he wanted to give her this one as a gift.

***

All her life Sissy Kleinman had been plagued by people who asked, "What's your real name?"

"I was christened Sissy," she always responded firmly. And glowered in contempt at those who gave her a disbelieving look.

Then there was the matter of her last name. When Sissy told her father she was going to the East Texas High School prom with Dennis Kleinman, he'd said, "He's not some Jew-boy, is he?"

Sissy assured him Dennis came from good German stock. But once they married and she adopted that last name, people made the same mistake about her.

Undaunted by the holiday weekend, Sissy was in her Houston office the day after Thanksgiving when Reardon Jones, Harris County's longest serving District Attorney of twenty-two years, buzzed her on her intercom and asked her to come to his office. She assumed it was to congratulate her on her latest victory. Two days before the jury had convicted John Jamison of murdering his girlfriend. Sissy wasn't sure he'd actually committed the crime, but she did know from a couple of her detective buddies that the accused was quick tempered. So throughout the trial, whenever she glanced his way, she gave him a sly smile. His face reddened every time. Then when she and the jury were leaving the courtroom one day, she paused, looked him over and smiled broadly.

"Fuck you, bitch," he screamed. The jurors, not yet out of the courtroom, looked back in shock.

The judge refused the defense motion for a mistrial.

Sissy was dressed in her usual uniform, a navy blue suit with a sleeveless white shell underneath. Before going into Reardon's office, she applied enough concealer to hide the fine wrinkles on her thirty-nine year old face and brushed her medium length dark hair behind her ears, letting it flip up in the back.

She knocked on Reardon's door and followed his order to enter.

He sat behind his oversized mahogany desk, his shaved head reflecting the light coming in from the window above him. Always the gentleman, Reardon stood when she entered. "Good work on the Jamison case. I can't remember the last time you lost one."

Her boss was proud she'd sent thirteen killers to death row, the best record of any assistant district attorney in the State of Texas. Before Sissy could acknowledge the compliment, he went on,

"Except for my wife, you're the first person to know. I'm not running for a sixth term. I'm sixty-three and ready to rest."

Sissy's surprise mingled with excitement. She understood why she was the second to know.

"I want you to succeed me. And it'll be good for the Republican Party to put a woman in this office."

"I'm thrilled, sir, but I don't have the money to run a campaign," Sissy said.

"The party and some of my friends will take care of that. You just keep being the self-made gal from East Texas who wins all the big cases."

"A really big one sure would help."

"You've got it. A murder at a lingerie shop."

TWO

The black Land Rover sat in a carport at the back of 1700 Stanton. The two-story white brick was new as were about half the houses on the street. The rest were older one-stories which hadn't yet been torn down to make way for so-called progress.

Oracio Crawley went to the Land Rover and put his hand on the hood. It felt warm. He looked in the window on the driver's side and was surprised to see a spotless interior. No blood.

It was 5:30, which meant the killer had almost an hour and a half to clean it. His lab guys would find what the suspect had missed.

The killer was likely in the house so Oracio had Glen Healy call for reinforcements. But before the additional four police cars arrived, a dark complexioned woman in her thirties walked out. Upon seeing the two detectives, she opened her purse.

Oracio pulled his gun.

She dropped the handbag and started screaming. Glen ran up to her, and she collapsed into him.

The woman pointed to her purse. "Green card, green card," she said with a heavy Spanish accent.

"*No Immigracion. Policia,*" Glen responded.

This only made the woman look more frightened, so Glen went into her handbag and found a green card in the name of Consuela Blanco.

"*Seniorita Blanco, quien esta en la casa?*" he asked in his high school Spanish.

Consuela answered that no one was in the house.

Oracio decided she was too scared to lie.

"We need to get a translator before we ask her any more questions," he said. "Otherwise some defense attorney will say she didn't understand what we were asking."

Valentino Garza, driver of one of the newly arrived police cars, walked up the steps. "I'm an official translator."

After questioning Consuela, Valentino reported that Benjie Levine, stepson of Virginia to whom the Land Rover was registered, had not been at the house all day. His older brother Ariel, who was watching the house while his father and step-mother were in New York, had been there sleeping when Consuela arrived that morning. He'd left many times but always in his own car. She didn't know where either brother was now.

By the time Valentino finished questioning Consuela, she was shaking.

"Get her address and phone number and let her go home. But tell her we'll be calling to have her come in to give a statement," Oracio said.

From the porch Oracio saw a white Honda Prelude stop behind a police car. The driver, whose size fit the description the witnesses had given, walked over to Glen and said something.

Glen responded by slamming the kid against the police car, handcuffing him and pushing him into the back seat.

When Oracio got to the car, Glen was finishing the Miranda warnings and the suspect, whom Glen identified as Ariel Levine, was hyperventilating. Oracio grabbed the brown paper bag, which had once held his lunch but now was lying empty on the floor. He opened it and held it up to Ariel's mouth. "Breathe into it slowly."

While the suspect obeyed, Oracio studied him. He was close to six-feet, medium build and had brown hair with blond highlights. He wore a torn white tee shirt, black shorts and basketball shoes.

Ariel began breathing normally. "All I did was give the other officer my name and ask him what was going on. The house belongs to my dad and step-mom."

"There was a murder, and your step-mother's Land Rover was identified as the get-away vehicle."

"No one drove it while I was home. I don't even have the key to it on my chain. You can check," he said, twisting so that the right front pocket of his shorts pointed towards Oracio.

"Come with me." The detective pulled Ariel out of the car and led him to the Land Rover. When they arrived, he took off the handcuffs. "Put your hand on the hood. The engine's still warm."

The suspect complied. "Maybe someone stole the key from the candy dish and took it for a joy ride."

"Would it be okay if we went inside so we could see if the key's still there?" Oracio asked.

"Sure."

They walked through the hall into the high-ceilinged living room filled with furniture upholstered in gold damask. No knife or bloody clothes were in view. Oracio needed the kid to allow a search so, after seeing the Land Rover key, still in the candy dish, he invited Ariel to sit on the couch. With a few deft questions, the detective learned that the nineteen year old had been house sitting since yesterday, that he had an apartment a few miles away, and that, starting at 4:30, he'd been playing basketball on a concrete court next to it. Oracio excused himself, saying Detective Healy would stay with Ariel while he was gone for a few minutes.

Oracio called Sissy Kleinman's office, figuring she'd be working on the Friday after Thanksgiving.

"Grapevine says you got assigned the lingerie shop murder," was Sissy's greeting.

That was another thing Oracio liked about Sissy, the way she knew everything going on in the police department.

"I want to give you an easy one to win so I don't want to blow it."

He told Sissy he needed to search the suspect's folks' house and impound the stepmother's Land Rover. "If he's house-sitting, can he give me the okay?"

"He has custody and control of the house," Sissy answered. "What's his connection to the Land Rover?"

Oracio thought for a couple of seconds. "The key's in the house he has custody of."

"Good enough," Sissy responded. "I'm going to make a lawyer of you yet."

Oracio blushed. In part because someone that smart had complimented him and in part because he was picturing Sissy with her suit jacket off and her ample breasts outlined by one of those elasticized white sleeveless numbers she always wore.

He returned to Ariel. "I called downtown. We can straighten this out quick. I need you to sign some papers to let us search this house and your apartment and to take the Land Rover and your car to check out."

"How will I get anywhere?"

17

"I'll drive you down to the station. We'll clear the rest of it up there."

"I just need to go to the bathroom," Ariel replied.

"Glen will have to go with you."

As Ariel walked away, Oracio added, "I want the clothes and shoes you have on, and any dirty clothes you have here."

"They're in the hamper."

Ariel Levine's being so cooperative didn't fool the detective. He'd dealt with plenty of killers who thought they could outsmart him.

***

Sissy decided to stay at the office in case Oracio needed her again. She had nothing to go home to. Dennis and their two daughters were in East Texas celebrating the holiday weekend with family. She couldn't leave with them on Wednesday because the John Jamison jury didn't come in with their verdict until after they'd gone.

It was probably for the best. Sissy dreaded those trips home. She had nothing in common any more with her family or with Dennis'. She was always on guard around them, knowing they were looking for signs she was acting like she was better than they were. If any one commented on Sissy's success in putting away the bad guys, her father had a quick response. "She never was successful in giving me grandsons. Thank goodness, we have her brother Bart for that."

As if to confirm Sissy was better off in her office in Houston, her phone rang. She picked up the receiver and heard the West Texas twang of Norty Walsh, police beat reporter from the *Houston Post-Gazette*.

What perfect timing. She knew from Oracio that she had an almost sure winner in the lingerie shop murder. He had a suspect and the get-away vehicle. Once the lab boys went over it, she'd make mincemeat of the killer.

She just needed to convince Norty what a big case it was so he could convince the public.

"I hoped I'd find you in. Are you going to be handling the murder at that lingerie shop?"

"Don't call it 'that lingerie shop.' It catered to breast cancer victims. If any of them had been there, he would have killed those poor patients, too."

18

Sissy heard the rustling of paper, a sign Norty was taking notes.
"Do you have a suspect in custody?"
"If we did, Detective Crawley would be bringing him in now."
"Thanks, Sissy. I'm on my way."

***

On the ride downtown Ariel chatted amiably with Oracio and Glen, always referring to each respectfully as "sir." As in, "I hope you had a nice Thanksgiving, sir."

Oracio figured he was dealing with a sociopath in the mold of Ted Bundy, charming and polite. And, hopefully just a little too clever.

"Sir, I'd better call my mom. She's an attorney, just does divorces and stuff. But still she'd expect me to call her."

"Remind me when we get to the station," Oracio replied casually.

But he'd have to move fast. Even if he got the kid to delay the call for a while, there might not be time to get a statement and do a line-up.

As they left the police car, Oracio told Glen, "Go to the jail and pick ten guys. No one black, no one real tall or real short. Have photos taken of five of them, and videos of the other five."

Oracio responded to Glen's puzzled look by saying, "Since a prime witness is in the hospital, I want both a photo and a video line-up to take to her. And as for Andrew Block, even if you call him now, Levine may be gone before he gets here."

Oracio and Ariel entered the Houston Police Department headquarters and rode the elevator to the twenty-fifth floor. Instead of taking Ariel to the squad room, the area filled with the desks of homicide detectives, including his own, Oracio led him to a small one used for interrogations. A dark wood rectangular table stood with two armless chairs on each side. A beige blind partially covered one wall. If Oracio lifted it, someone standing outside could observe them through a one-way window

The detective closed the door. He took four sheets of paper and a small notepad out of the black metal file cabinet in the corner of the room, sat down across from Ariel and handed him a pen. "This is just a formality. You'll sign at the X's to okay the photo and video lineups, the fingerprints and the piece of hair for DNA testing."

19

"All right," Ariel said hesitantly. "I still think I'd better call my mom."

"There's no phone in here. When we finish, I'll find Detective Healy and have him call her. Just write the phone number on the back of my card."

When the fingerprinting was done, and he had a piece of Ariel's hair in a plastic bag, which Ariel initialed, Oracio flipped over the top of a small notebook. "Tell me about your day,"

Ariel reported being awakened at his dad's home a little before eleven by a call from his father in New York and finding Consuela at the house. He listened to CDs and then went to his mom's to eat Thanksgiving leftovers.

"My brother Benjie could get a better deal on speakers for his car if he paid cash, so I went with him to my bank to withdraw some money."

"Where's that?"

"Lone Star Savings on the feeder of the Southwest Freeway."

"What next?"

"I went to my dad's to get my swim trunks and used the pool at the West University Community Center. Back at Dad's, I walked the dogs and watched a video until about 4:15 when I left to play basketball with my friends."

Sweat appeared above Ariel's upper lip.

The kid must know claiming to be watching a video when the murder was committed was a piss poor alibi.

Glen walked in. "I picked the guys for the line-up photos and video."

"Maybe you can call my mom," Ariel said. "Detective Crawley has her number."

"You don't mind doing the line-up before she gets here, do you?" Oracio asked.

"No. That's fine."

Oracio handed his partner the card. "Give her a call, Glen."

***

It was almost eight thirty and Mara was exhausted. After Ariel and Benjie had left her townhouse, she'd gone to her office to meet a new client, then spent several hours preparing a divorce petition for her. Driving home, she turned on the radio to the all-news station.

20

"And so the murder of store owner Herlinda Sorento at Lingerie for Life has left customers and employees of other shops at the West Baylor Shopping Center stunned and frightened," the announcer intoned.

Mara turned off the radio and took a deep breath. She remembered her trip to that shop with her mother more than twenty years before. Nineteen and frightened of losing her, she'd insisted her mother go to Lingerie for Life. If she looked normal, Mara could pretend she was healthy.

When the owner stepped inside the fitting room, she'd told Mara's mother, "Turn towards the mirror. Even you'll forget about your surgery when you see how you look just the same as before."

Her mother had walked into the showroom smiling.

"I'll see you back when you're ready to buy some more."

But her mother hadn't returned. She'd died six months later, leaving Mara orphaned.

Now the kind woman who'd helped her was gone as well.

Mara passed blocks of brick bungalows, drove onto her street of narrow two-story townhouses and pulled into her drive. She entered her home, sat down and had just taken off her shoes when the phone rang. She was so tired she considered not answering it, but it might be one of her boys.

"Mrs. Levine, this is Detective Glen Healy of the Houston Police Department. Your son Ariel asked me to call you."

Mara's heart beat faster. "Oh, my God, what's happened to him? A car accident?"

"He's fine. We just brought him in for questioning."

"Questioning? For what?" Mara was on her feet.

"Well, there's been a murder . . ."

"You said Ariel was fine."

"He is fine," Glen assured her. "He's a suspect."

Mara's throat tightened.

"Did you just say my son's a murder suspect?"

"Well, yes, I guess he is," the young detective replied.

"That's ridiculous." Mara spoke with conviction even as her hands shook.

"You can come to 1200 Travis, twenty-fifth floor, and pick him up. He'll explain everything."

"How long has he been with you?"

"Since a little before six o'clock."

Mara slammed down the receiver and headed out the door. She got into her silver Honda Accord and grasped the steering wheel with her still shaking hands.

Her whole conversation with the policeman had been so preposterous she hadn't even asked what murder he was talking about.

She thought of the one at Lingerie for Life.

It was outrageous for anyone to consider Ariel capable of such a thing.

***

After Glen left to call Mara Levine, Oracio got up and motioned Ariel to follow him. They took the elevator to the sixth floor and entered the photography studio where Kenny Williams wore a disgusted look, indicating he was not happy to be working at eight thirty on the Friday night after Thanksgiving. His black pants and shirt made the slim dark skinned photographer blend into the background he had Ariel stand in front of. He first snapped photos and then video taped the suspect.

When Oracio and Ariel got off the elevator at the twenty-fifth floor, the detective noticed a woman pacing in front of the squad room.

"Mom."

The woman turned around, and Oracio saw the resemblance between mother and son. Both had high cheekbones, wide set eyes and curly hair. Hers was shoulder length and held back with a tortoise headband. She looked to be in her early forties and would probably be even prettier if she had on make-up.

She rushed to her son. "What have they done to you?"

"Nothing. There was a murder at a lingerie shop, and someone wrote down Virginia's license plate number. Detective Crawley's helping me straighten it out. He's been very nice to me."

"Nice to you? He's accused you of murder."

"He's sure everything will be okay after they check out the Land Rover and my car and the witnesses look at the line-ups."

"Your son agreed to everything," Oracio said.

"You accomplished that by waiting to call me." Mara looked at Oracio so intently that he glanced away. "I assume he's free to leave."

22

"He needs to stay in town. We'll want to talk to him after we get the lab results on the vehicles."

"Trust me. That's when you'll know you have nothing to talk to him about."

Mara put her arm around Ariel's shoulder and waited to enter an elevator while a large man, who looked to be at least six-foot-four and over 300 pounds, walked out.

"Oracio, I need a scoop on the lingerie shop murder," Norty Walsh said.

"What makes you think I have anything to do with it?"

"Someone with a sexy East Texas drawl told me."

Sissy was amazing, already generating publicity for the case.

"Just give me the suspect's name," Norty wheedled.

"You know I can't do that"

"That was him getting on the elevator, wasn't it?"

"Can't say."

"Give me the name of the woman he left with."

"Mrs. Levine."

"First name?" Norty asked, as he pulled a small notebook from the pocket of his green and red plaid shirt.

"Her son didn't introduce us."

"Now I'll have to look up every Levine in the phone book," Norty groused.

THREE

"Mom . . ."

Mara put her finger to her lips. There were police officers everywhere as they walked through the lobby and out to the parking garage.

When they were in the car, she said, "Please remember the police can twist what an innocent person says."

"You think I shouldn't have spoken to them?"

"It's done. But any other speaking will be through an attorney."

"When they have their lab reports back, won't that end it?"

"Hopefully. Now start from the beginning and tell me everything."

Ariel told his mother about his stopping at his father's house when he saw the police cars, and how he was pushed against one and put into its back seat. Enraged, Mara envisioned her son being slammed against the police car and thrown into its back seat. He confirmed he'd agreed to the searches of the two vehicles, his apartment and his father's house, and to being in a line-up.

Why hadn't he learned anything three years before when he was arrested by campus police at his high school for having beer in his car? Mara had told him after that experience not to agree to any police requests until he'd talked to her or his father.

Yet, Ariel had only followed her example in acquiescing. He'd watched her throughout her marriage always going along with whatever Simon wanted just to keep the peace.

"I guess Dad and Virginia are going to be mad at me for letting them take Virginia's Land Rover and searching their house"

Mara shook her head at his naiveté. Ariel thought dealing with his dad and Virginia was his biggest problem.

"I'll call them when we get home."

"Thanks, Mom."

"Did you drive the Land Rover today?"

"Virginia would kill me if I had."

Mother and son continued the ride in silence. Anything more Mara said would just upset Ariel. He was innocent so he hadn't been afraid to agree to everything the police requested. Surely they must understand no one guilty would have been so cooperative.

Mara almost missed her exit off the Southwest Freeway and heard the blaring of a car horn as she quickly moved over two lanes to make it.

They pulled into the driveway of her townhouse behind Josef Kessler's white Dodge van. He must be inside having used the key she'd given him.

Josef opened the door. "I was worried," he said with a hint of a German accent. "You told me you were going straight home from the office, but I kept calling and no one answered."

He put his arms around her. She briefly rested her cheek against his broad chest, gently pulled away and kissed him, feeling the tickle of his handlebar moustache.

Mara turned to her son. "Get me your dad's phone number in New York."

"Okay."

"You need to write down everything that happened tonight."

"Now?"

"Now. While it's fresh in your mind."

Mara and Josef sat down on a brown and white striped couch in the combination living and dining room. Like the other rooms in her home, it was small, but the townhouse served its purpose. Its three bedrooms gave Ariel and Benjie each his own space. She'd bought it after the divorce, using almost all the money she'd received to pay for it in cash. Deciding she wanted to go to law school, Mara couldn't be saddled with mortgage payments.

She told Josef about the evening's events, but before he could comment, Ariel returned and handed her his father's phone number with a trembling hand. Mara stood up and hugged her son. "Everything's going to be all right." Not knowing what else to do for him, she said, "I'll get you something to eat."

Ariel glanced at Joseph. "I'll help myself, Mom." He headed for the kitchen.

Though Ariel was out of earshot, Mara spoke softly to Josef. "The police scare me."

"It's the District Attorney's office I'm afraid of."

Mara's heartbeat accelerated. "Why?"

"Because of how they treated one of my charges."

Josef was more than the director of a residential facility for abused teens. He was also the children's advocate.

"One of our girls, a sixteen year old, ran away and within a day was arrested for shoplifting a jacket. I assumed the police would let her return to our facility. Even when the store owner pressed charges, I expected her to be tried as a juvenile first time offender and given probation."

"What happened?"

"Sissy Kleinman, the assistant district attorney, had her certified as an adult. She got a two year prison term."

"How could that be?" Mara asked.

"Kleinman did a hatchet job on the kid when she cross-examined her. Made it seem she ran away so she could start a life of crime."

Mara felt a mixture of pity for the girl and fear for Ariel. But once no evidence was found to connect her son to the murder, she wouldn't have to worry about the likes of Sissy Kleinman.

Mara patted Josef's forearm and got up. She couldn't put off calling Simon any longer. She pictured his square-jowled face and imagined the accusations, which would flow from his thin-lipped mouth.

***

Simon Levine was looking forward to making love to his wife.

Virginia prepared for the event the way she got ready for a party. She coiffed her sandy blond hair into her trademark shoulder length pageboy, deftly made up her face to camouflage its length and accentuated her full cheeks with an accent of coral.

But as Virginia entered their New York hotel room from the bathroom, Simon ignored those efforts, his attention diverted by her breasts bouncing with each step.

It was funny how things worked out. When he and Mara divorced, he'd assumed he'd wind up with a sweet young thing. But Virginia was forty-four and tough, which had helped make her wealthy. She'd started her own advertising agency at twenty-four, and sold it to a national organization when she was forty-one.

She had no children and didn't want any, but was good to Simon's sons, chauffeuring them around before they could drive or whenever Mara grounded them. Virginia clearly favored Ariel, the compliant one, failing to appreciate the spirited Benjie the way he did.

Before Virginia got into the king sized bed, Simon stroked her left breast, circled its nipple with his finger, and was startled by the telephone's strident ring.

Only Ariel and Benjie had the number. Something had happened at home.

Simon's right hand moved from Virginia's soft skin to the hard plastic of the telephone receiver.

"Simon." Mara's voice.

"Is one of the boys hurt?"

"No, thank God."

"Then what?" Mara had no right to bother him unless one of his sons needed him.

"There was a murder at a lingerie store. Someone gave the police the license plate number of a Land Rover the killer left in, and it matched Virginia's."

"That's crazy."

"I know. But when Ariel stopped at your house, the police were there, and he gave them permission to search it and to take the Land Rover to look for evidence."

"You couldn't keep him from letting the police search my home and impound my wife's vehicle?"

Virginia gasped. "What?"

Simon put his index finger on her lips to shush her. She bit his finger so hard he barely stopped himself from yelling.

Virginia walked away, her slightly rounded behind moving further and further from his grasp.

"No one called me until after the police questioned Ariel at the station," Mara said.

"Ariel certainly has no faith in you as an attorney, or he would have thought to have you involved immediately."

"He asked them to call but they waited so I'd arrive after he'd agreed to everything."

"As soon as I get home, I'll find him a real attorney." Simon slammed down the receiver.

"What's going on?" Virginia, now wrapped in a green silk robe, demanded.

27

Judith Groudine Finkel

When Simon told her, she turned indignant. "Ariel couldn't do anything violent. He doesn't even have a temper, the way Benjie does. And Ariel would never take my Land Rover without my permission. The police better return it undamaged."

As upset as Virginia was about her Land Rover being impounded, what ate at Simon was the search of his home.

It reminded him of the story his mother had told him about the police in their village outside Paris coming through her parents' home on the pretext of looking for an escaped convict. Wanting to be good citizens, the family cooperated fully but became suspicious when they discovered it was only Jewish homes being searched. It turned out the police knew the village Jews would soon be sent to concentration camps, so they were staking out what they wanted to pillage from the homes when the deportations occurred.

Simon had learned not to trust what the authorities told him and to expect them to harm others for their own good. So he'd take no chances. He'd get Ariel the best criminal defense attorney in Houston. If the police hadn't planted evidence in the house or the Land Rover, the lawyer's services wouldn't be needed for long.

But just in case.

Simon's thoughts went from his son back to his mother. He remembered her telling him how the family's neighbors, people they thought were their friends, had spat on them and taunted them as they were led away.

His mother had warned, "We never really know another person. Anyone is capable of anything."

28

FOUR

Glen Healy looked concerned when he walked into the squad room. "The ten guys are back on the cellblock, five photographed and the other five video taped." Glen handed Oracio the pictures along with the tape of Ariel and the five prisoners whose images had also been filmed.

"What's the matter?" Oracio asked.

"Most of them don't look much like our suspect."

"Don't worry. We've got the right guy," Oracio assured his partner. "And here's the witness who's going to prove it."

Andrew Block, dressed in a beige and brown striped silk shirt and dark pants, stood at the entrance of the squad room.

Oracio joined him. "Dr. Block, thank you so much for coming and for all you've done already." He watched Andrew beam at the compliment and knew he was on the right track with the young chiropractor. "Mrs. Luna was so fortunate to have someone with your medical knowledge on the scene. And your getting the license plate number is what led us to our suspect."

"Is the killer here?" Andrew asked in a tone that mixed excitement with fear.

"No, we had to let him go, but once you identify him—we have photos and a video tape—we'll be on our way to an arrest."

Andrew followed Oracio to the same room he'd taken Ariel. Once there the detective opened a cabinet in the corner of the room that held a television and a tape player and set them up to show the video. He sat down next to Andrew, putting the six photos face down.

"You're our most important witness." Oracio spoke in a confidential tone. "Maybe our only one if Mrs. Luna dies and her husband stays too emotional to help."

Andrew nodded.

Oracio turned the six photos over.

"He wasn't anywhere near that old," Andrew said, looking at a man standing under a sign with the number one on it. The second man fared no better. "No way the killer was Hispanic."

After studying the third picture, Block's voice had a questioning lilt as he commented, "Could be this one."

Oracio handed him the fourth photo.

"The guy's sideburns are too long and his complexion's too dark." Andrew looked at the fifth picture. "He didn't have a buzz haircut."

He ran his hand through his own short dark blond hair as he studied the sixth photo. "His nose is too crooked."

The witness glanced at the tabletop as though looking for more pictures. When he saw none, he said, "The only one it could have been was number three but . . ."

"The video line-up might help you make your decision."

Oracio pressed a button on the remote and six men appeared on the nineteen-inch television screen in front of them.

The man whose image was under the sign with the number one was a little taller than the two Hispanics who came next and broader than the two pencil thin men who followed. Number six had dark stubble on his cheeks and chin.

Andrew pointed at number one. "That must be the killer. And that means I was right when I thought it was number three in the photo line-up."

"How sure are you?"

"Well, he's the only clean shaven guy who's the right size and the only one in both line-ups."

"I mean are you eighty per cent, ninety percent, one hundred per cent sure?"

"You can never be 100 per cent sure." Andrew spoke slowly. "And I saw him for just a few seconds." He fingered Ariel Levine's picture. "Eighty percent. Yes, I'm eighty per cent sure. Is that good enough?"

The detective gave his star witness a thumbs-up.

***

Oracio walked into the squad room, sat down at his desk and took out a sheet of paper. He put a line down the middle. On one side he

30

wrote, "What I Have" and on the other, "What I Need." He would make the case against the killer. He owed it to the victims.

He listed the license plate and Block's identification. But he knew how they might play out. He could tell from the house the suspect's family lived in that they had money to hire the kind of attorney who could fool a jury. Convince them how easy it is to make a mistake when you jot down a license plate number in a hurry, how often an eye-witness identification is wrong.

Under "What I Need," he wrote, "Second identification." Mrs. Luna might not live to give one. Her husband was the key.

He wouldn't wait to see Henry Luna. If his wife died, he'd be in no shape to help.

So at 10:30 Friday night Oracio arrived at Ben Taub, Houston's yellow-bricked public hospital. It bordered the Texas Medical Center in view of the grassy inclines of Hermann Park.

Having called in advance, he knew Mrs. Luna was in surgery so he went directly to the fourth floor surgical waiting room. The plastic chairs, each sporting a primary color, seemed out of place in such a somber setting. They were bolted to the floor, the administration having learned that otherwise they'd disappear.

Henry Luna sat in a red chair, his nearly bald head hanging down. He looked up, revealing a face gaunter than Oracio remembered.

"I'm Detective Crawley. I was at the store . . ."

"Did you see the doctors when you walked in? Did they tell you how Claudia is?"

"I understand she's in surgery, sir."

"Of course, of course. We won't know anything until that's over. Maybe if I'd gotten there a little sooner . . ."

Oracio sat down next to the crying man. "You got there right when you should have, just before he went for the final blow."

"But she still might die."

Oracio retrieved a box of tissues from a chair across the room, brought them to Henry and waited until the distraught husband stopped crying. "I have good news. We have a suspect and Andrew Block, the guy who saw your wife's assailant run out of the store, identified him."

Henry Luna didn't respond. He stared straight ahead. Just as Oracio was wondering whether the victim's husband had heard him,

Henry spoke. "It's what was done that matters. Who did it won't change anything."

Oracio struggled to keep the anger out of his voice. "But surely you want the man who hurt your wife punished."

"Of course."

"The hard part is convicting him. Once we have your identification . . ."

"My glasses broke in the scuffle. I can hardly see without them."

"Someone may look familiar. I have six photos." He thrust an envelope at Henry, who put it on his lap and opened it slowly.

He took each picture out and went through the same procedure. He held it close to his face, squinting one eye closed, opening it, and doing the same with the other eye. Then he held each picture at arm's length, and went through the same eye maneuvers.

"I just don't know."

"Try again. You don't want to fail your wife."

Henry gasped. He looked at each of the pictures once more.

"If it's any of these, it's number six."

Oracio frowned at Henry's failure to identify Ariel. He took the pictures from the victim's husband.

Henry averted his eyes. "I'm sorry."

***

Henry deserved to have the detective look at him with disgust. He hadn't gotten to the shop in time to keep his beloved Claudia safe, and now he was doing nothing to help put her attacker away.

Claudia was already afraid of so many things. Henry took her everywhere because driving scared her. It was for the best they hadn't been blessed with children since thoughts of childbirth frightened her. She was able to work at the lingerie store because she could stay in the back away from the customers. He had loved being her protector, but had failed her today when it mattered most. Henry cried as he thought about how Claudia might not make it home.

A man in blood-splattered green, carrying a surgical mask, walked into the waiting room and called his name.

Someone that young couldn't have saved Claudia.

He introduced himself as Dr. Cruz and said something about blood in the sac around the heart.

"Will she live?"

"I'm very hopeful."

Henry sank back into his chair and sobbed. Somehow he would help put away the man Dr. Block had identified.

FIVE

Friday night, after Josef left, Mara called upstairs to Ariel to find out if he'd finished writing up the day's events. After learning that he was still working on it, she sat in her favorite armchair and rested her feet on its matching ottoman. She closed her eyes while she waited

Saturday morning she awakened to find sunlight slithering between the slats of the living room blinds. Mara vaguely remembered Benjie coming home and kissing her on the forehead before he went upstairs. She'd meant to get up and tell him what had happened, to spare Ariel that ordeal.

She glanced at the small end table beside her, saw Ariel's report and picked it up. Mara stopped when she read, "Detective Crawley asked me if I'd be in a lineup. I said sure. I thought I'd be on a stage with other guys, like on TV, but instead he took me to a room where the photographer first snapped pictures of me and then video taped me."

Why did Detective Crawley refrain from having the other men on stage with Ariel? Did they look so different from him that he would have protested? And why was Ariel in two line-ups?

Mara felt a throbbing at her temples and rubbed them. She walked slowly into the kitchen, poured cold water on a dishtowel and turned it into a compress for her forehead. Water touched her cheeks, as though the towel was dripping.

But they were tears.

Mara pounded her fists on the counter until the sides of her hands turned red.

She climbed the stairs, holding onto the rail, heading for Ariel's room, determined to make him understand he was to have no contact with the police unless she was present.

His door was ajar. Ariel had fallen asleep with his clothes on, on top of the still made bed. A poster of Hakeem Olauwon making a jump shot graced the wall above him.

Mara couldn't wake her son. He looked so innocent lying there. She left his room, walked down the stairs and went outside. She admired the blue cloudless sky before she picked up the *Houston Post-Gazette*. It was worth the oppressive heat and humidity of Houston summers to have such a beautiful day at the end of November.

Back in the house, she unfurled the newspaper.

"SUSPECT QUESTIONED IN LINGERIE SHOP MURDER"

Mara gasped. There was no way her son could have committed the violent crime being reported. The murderer had slit the store-owner's throat and stabbed another woman twelve times. Someone else had done this thing—someone on drugs or with a violent history or who hated women.

But the article described Ariel.

"Police were led to the suspect, a Caucasian male of nineteen, through a witness's report of a dark Land Rover along with its license plate. Police are waiting for the results of the search of the vehicle before releasing the suspect's name."

Mara sank into the closest chair. This was worse than she'd imagined. She could hardly breathe.

The phone rang.

"Mrs. Levine?" the unfamiliar voice inquired.

Instinct told her not to respond.

"I'm Norton Walsh of the *Houston Post-Gazette.*"

The reporter who'd written the article she'd just read.

"I figured you'd want to get your son's story out."

Mara gripped the receiver so tightly her hand tingled.

"I'm not Mrs. Levine. I don't have a son. What's the matter with you, calling a stranger at eight thirty on a Saturday morning?"

"I'm sorry. I'm trying to reach the mother of Ariel Levine."

"Never heard of him." Mara slammed down the receiver.

First thing Monday she'd get an unlisted phone number. And there must be other things she could do to protect her son. She looked up and saw Ariel standing at the bottom of the stairs. The lower half of his face was filled with the lopsided grin Mara usually found endearing. Today it reminded her of his naiveté.

"The phone woke me. Was it Dad?" Ariel's tone combined eagerness and dread.

She needed to tell him about the call and warn him away from reporters but she couldn't do it. He looked so vulnerable, his hands in the front pockets of his slept-in jeans, his cheeks drooping now that his grin was gone.

"No, it wasn't your dad. Let's eat breakfast. How about French toast?"

"Great. I'll get out the orange juice and make the coffee." Ariel kissed his mother on the cheek and walked past her into the kitchen.

Mara followed and sliced the challah, the braided bread she'd eaten every Friday night for as long as she remembered. It was an integral part of greeting the Jewish Sabbath. She thought of all the Friday afternoons she'd come home from school greeted by the aroma of the challah her mother was baking.

But when she was a girl, she'd always had to wait for Sunday to eat her challah French toast. Mara's mother, more observant of Jewish law than Mara ever became, had always refused to cook on the Sabbath. Except once.

When she was eight years old and had been ill for three days with a stomach flu, Mara was feeling well enough to eat again on a Saturday morning.

She stood in the kitchen, her pajamas, decorated with yellow-billed ducks, hanging from her tiny hips, her thick brown ringlets overwhelming her narrow face.

Her mother, though just over five-feet and thin, loomed large to Mara. She asked her daughter what she wanted to eat.

"Challah French toast."

The child saw on her mother's face the struggle within. Should she violate the Sabbath to make sure her recovering child ate?

When her mother said, "I'll make it right now," Mara was at first excited; somehow this meant her mother loved her daughter more than she loved God.

Then that thought frightened her.

"I changed my mind. I'd rather eat cereal."

Mara was rewarded by a look of relief on her mother's face.

She prepared the French toast for Ariel using her mother's recipe, mixing three eggs with a fork and adding cinnamon and milk

Next she sliced the challah, and dipped the first piece, turning it over to make sure the liquid mixture permeated it, then gently laid it in the melted margarine in the frying pan..

Ariel handed her a cup of coffee. "I made it the way you like, half a packet of Sweet &Low and just a tad of milk."

"Make mine black with lots of sugar, bro," Benjie ordered as he entered the kitchen. He wore boxer shorts decorated with hearts, a gift from a former girlfriend. "French toast, my favorite."

"This first batch is for Ariel," Mara said.

"What do you have to do? Murder someone to get food around here?"

Mara dropped the spatula into the frying pan where it spattered melted margarine. She grabbed Benjie by the shoulders. "How dare you say such a thing?"

"It's okay, Mom. He was trying to be funny, to cheer me up," Ariel said in a soothing tone.

Mara let go of Benjie and turned to Ariel. "You have to understand how serious this is. That was a reporter who called. The same one who wrote a front page article in today's *Post-Gazette* about how the police have a suspect and describing you and the Land Rover."

Ariel dashed into the living room and returned with the newspaper. "I can't believe it. How could some reporter know all these details and have my name so he could call here?" Then he answered his own question. "Detective Crawley. But I cooperated with him. He acted like my friend."

"Anyone who knows you understands you're incapable of harming another human being," Mara said. "But the police and the press don't know you. They want to get convictions and sell newspapers."

She turned away from her sons and removed a burnt piece of French toast from the frying pan.

SIX

The doorbell rang.

Mara stared at the front door, fearing it was the reporter who'd called earlier. She looked out the peephole and saw Simon. She let him in, hiding her surprise at how much his gray hair had receded and how he'd gotten so paunchy around the middle.

He'd been a slim muscular man with a full head of brown hair when they'd met, a little more than a year after her mother had died. Mara was twenty-one and Simon twenty-seven. He'd only been in Houston six months, the Israeli software company he worked for having sent him to set up an office, the one he was running now. At the time his take-charge attitude had appealed to her. She was orphaned, at loose ends and happy to take directions.

Perhaps if his company hadn't decided to send him back to Israel seven months later, they would have had more time to decide whether marriage was the right choice. But it had frightened her to have the person she thought of as her rock thousands of miles away, so she'd agreed to the wedding.

The years in Israel had been good. Both her sons had been born there and the country had seemed like one large family, the way everyone mourned each time a soldier or a civilian victim of terrorism died. And in the neighborhood where they'd lived, women filled their home with food when she had her babies or fell ill. Mara had the extended family she'd always dreamed of.

Problems had surfaced after their return to Houston ten years ago. Simon's assurance he was always right hadn't played well when he'd tried to dictate where they'd live, where the children would go to school, how Mara would spend her time. He'd refused to recognize she knew Houston and the American way of life better than he did.

"Is that one of my buddies?" Ariel asked as he hurried down the steps into the living room.

He stopped when he saw Simon.

38

"I didn't know you were back from New York."

"We shortened our trip when your mother called." Simon looked at Mara. "You don't have to stay while I talk to Ariel."

Mara put her arm around her son. "Of course, I'll stay. I'm his mother and an attorney."

"Neither of those roles helped him yesterday."

Mara glared at her former husband, determined not to let him provoke her.

Simon focused on Ariel. "Tell me everything that happened yesterday from about 3:30 on."

"I got in from walking the dogs around 3:45 and talked to Consuela for a couple minutes. Went to my room and watched a video while I changed for basketball. Left about 4:15 and was with the guys by 4:30."

Simon rubbed his chin. "The police would have to believe you drove to the shopping center, attacked three people, returned the Land Rover to my house and cleaned it, got rid of the knife and clothes you were wearing and then drove to the basketball game, all in under forty-five minutes."

"It's preposterous," Mara said.

Simon looked at his son. "Go on."

"After the game, I saw all these police cars, and stopped to find out what happened. I'm sorry I let them search your house and take Virginia's Land Rover, but they told me if I did and went to the station with them, everything would get straightened out fast."

Simon frowned.

"I let them take my picture and agreed to the video cause I figured it would clear everything up. How could anyone identify me when I wasn't there?"

Mara didn't want Simon to berate Ariel for his naiveté. She looked at her former husband and shook her head.

He opened his mouth and closed it, then admonished his son, "You are not to talk to anyone about anything you did yesterday until you speak with your attorney."

"Who's my attorney?"

"I'll let you know as soon as I hire him."

"There's a really fine criminal attorney who offices in my building," Mara said.

"I'm choosing someone from the big leagues—let the police know we mean business."

"I just thought . . ."

"Unless you plan to pay his fees, don't give me any advice."

Mara, seeing Ariel clench his jaw as he looked from one parent to the other, restrained herself from responding.

Simon headed for the door.

Ariel walked over to his father and hugged him. "Thank you for taking care of all this."

Simon patted his son on the back as they embraced.

As soon as his father closed the door, a grinning Ariel said, "Guess that's the most beautiful sight in the world to you, Mom."

"What?"

"Dad's back as he walks out your door."

Mara laughed, reached up and tousled her son's hair.

The doorbell rang thirty minutes later.

"Find out who's there before you open it," Mara instructed Ariel.

Shouts of, "Hey, dude, let us in," made it clear some of Ariel's friends had arrived.

Skipper Gutman, dressed completely in black, entered first, followed by Farrell Miller, his long blond ringlets hiding part of his face and all of his neck. Pat Patel, in a perfectly ironed white button down shirt and khaki pants, bowed slightly in Mara's direction.

"Take your friends into the kitchen and let them empty out the refrigerator."

"You are so cool, Mrs. L," Farrell said, already on his way to the food.

"It's Ms. L, you a-hole. She's an attorney," Skipper corrected as he followed his friend.

Pat bowed again as he passed Mara.

"So, dude, when is your fat ass going to jail?"

"Speaking of his ass, that's what he'll have to protect."

Laughter pealed from the kitchen.

"Lucky he's so ugly."

"But maybe his ass isn't."

"How does it look in your dreams?"

More laughter.

Mara's right temple throbbed. She sank into the lounge chair and rested her face in her hands.

"How'd you know what happened?" Ariel asked.

"Benjie called."

"Did the police beat you up or torture you or anything."

"Nah, they were nice as could be."

"That was to get you to talk."

"When did they grab you?"

"Right after we played basketball. I was driving by my dad's house, saw all those patrol cars and stopped."

Mara heard Pat join the conversation. "I'm sorry I couldn't play that day. My father said you called twice just before game time but I was out."

That's when the craziness of the accusation against Ariel again hit Mara. If true, it meant that he'd brutally attacked three people and then gone on to play a friendly basketball game.

And how was Ariel on the phone arranging a game while he was fleeing a murder? Mara wanted to question Pat about the timing of the calls and to ask Skipper and Farrell when Ariel showed up at the game. But her better judgment prevailed. She needed to pass on the information to the attorney Simon hired.

She went up to her bedroom and called her former husband.

"Are the police bothering Ariel again?" Simon asked.

"No, nothing like that."

"Then what?"

"I was wondering if you'd hired Ariel's attorney and when he'll be meeting with him."

"I've got Greg Dickson, and he's going to see Ariel and me tomorrow. Doesn't mind working on a Sunday."

"Okay. I'll be there."

"What could you add?"

"I've learned some information that could help Ariel once it's followed up, and I suspect I'll pick up some more as the weekend progresses."

Simon was silent for a few moments. "Tell Ariel to be at Greg Dickson's office at ten tomorrow. You can show up after we've gone over a few things—at eleven."

Mara was about to argue but hung up instead.

Simon would never change, always having to prove he was in charge. Maybe this was one time it would help. He'd quickly hired

Houston's premier criminal attorney, probably at a cost of $400 an hour. He'd always wanted the best for his boys.

As soon as Ariel's friends left, Mara went downstairs.

"Your dad got you the finest defense attorney in the city. You need to be at Greg Dickson's office tomorrow at ten."

"Are you coming?"

"I'll be along a little later."

"Dad's up to his usual tricks."

Mara suppressed a smile. Simon's power plays never escaped Ariel.

"I'm going to stick around the house tonight," Ariel said. "Go over my notes on what happened with the police. Kind of get ready to talk to the attorney."

Mara, noticing the halting way Arial spoke, became even more concerned about what this ordeal was doing to him.

"Don't worry, Mom. I'll give you and Josef some privacy." He winked at her before he left the room.

But even if Mara had been interested in an amorous evening, it was not to be. Josef called to cancel dinner. One of the teens at the residential center he headed had run away.

Wanting to reassure herself, as well as Josef, Mara shared the news she'd planned to tell him that night. "I overheard Ariel's friends talking. At the time of the murder, Ariel was arranging a basketball game and going to it."

"Did any of his friends say he was with Ariel when the murder occurred?"

"No," she whispered.

***

Victoria Goldman, red curls bobbing, opened her front door to loud banging from Skipper Gutman and Ferrell Miller.

"You know that murder at the lingerie shop?" Skipper said.

The teen nodded and motioned the boys to follow her into the living room where all three plopped down on the couch.

"Guess who's a suspect?" Ferrell asked.

"Ariel Levine," Victoria answered.

"Who told you?"

"No one. He's just so weird it figured."

"Man, that's our bud you're talking about."

"That guy scared me so bad when we were kids at camp that I pretended I was sick so I could stay home," Victoria said.

"What'd he do?"

"A robin was lying on its back and I asked Ariel if it was dead. He took a stick and stabbed it over and over until its insides were flying. I screamed, and he said, 'Now it's dead for sure.'"

"I ran to the camp counselor but was crying so hard, I couldn't talk. When she asked Ariel what happened, he told her I was upset because as hard as he'd tried, he couldn't save a hurt bird. When the counselor hugged him, he smiled at me."

Skipper grimaced. "Aw, shit, he was probably nine at the time. He's okay now."

"I'm telling you Ariel's weird enough to have done it."

"Done what?" Victoria's mother asked as she entered the room.

Ferrell hesitated. "Um, I don't think we're actually supposed to tell anyone."

Mrs. Goldman glared at Skipper who took his feet off the glass coffee table and mumbled, "I'm sure your mom can keep a secret."

"Ariel's a suspect in the lingerie shop murder," Victoria said.

"That's ridiculous. He's a wonderful, caring boy. The way he looked after Benjie, schlepping him everywhere, so Mara could go to law school. She said he never complained."

Victoria looked at her mom. "He complained plenty to his friends. He just puts on an act for you adults."

Ferrell shrugged. "Doesn't matter. He couldn't have done it. Paper said the murder was at four. He was with us at four thirty playing basketball, acting perfectly normal. No blood on him."

"It'll all be over when we testify," Skipper said.

Mrs. Goldman shook her head. "For Ariel's sake, you better hope it doesn't come to that.

***

Pat Patel's mother always addressed him by his given name. "Where have you been, Anjay?"

Pat, who'd just opened the door to his home, wondered why his mother was standing in the hall frowning. He'd cleaned the swimming pool and mowed the grass before leaving the house. He could think of no chore he'd left undone.

"My car battery's dead. I'd hoped to use your car but it was gone."

"I drove over to Ariel's home."

"How is that dear boy?"

Pat hated to be the one to tell his mother about the accusation against his friend but she'd be angry if she found out he'd kept it from her.

It was a worse shock than he expected.

She put her hands on her head. "This is awful, just awful. Oh, his poor mother."

"She didn't say much."

"She's always been kind and generous, just like her son."

Pat knew what was coming. His mother went into a monologue about how Mara and Ariel Levine had been the most welcoming people when the Patels had arrived in Houston from India eight years before. It had been a traumatic time for his mother, and Mrs. Levine had driven her to shopping malls and helped her select clothes. And Ariel, probably at his mother's behest, had invited Pat to join his group of friends.

"We must do something for them, Anjay."

"It'll work out."

"I hope so, but if not, your father and I will find some way to help. I can't imagine Ariel has ever had a violent thought."

Pat knew better. He'd been there the night Ariel, Skipper and Farrell had thrown darts at a picture of a naked woman with her legs splayed. Every time Ariel's dart hit the target, he'd yelled, "Slashed her again."

SEVEN

After an overnight rain, the sun shone brightly Sunday morning as Mara walked down the concrete path from her front door to pick up the *Houston Post-Gazette*.

"ARREST IMMINENT IN LINGERIE SHOP MURDER," blared the headline.

Mara felt a mixture of relief and gratitude. They'd found the killer. Ariel was safe.

She continued reading, and with every word her heart thudded harder. She tottered inside, and was so dizzy she had to sit down on the couch. According to an anonymous police source, a witness had identified the likely driver of the get-away vehicle. As soon as tests came back on evidence taken from it, the killer would be arrested. They had to mean Ariel. He'd allowed the police to impound his stepmother's Land Rover and had agreed to both a photo and a video lineup.

Mara's heart was beating so fast she wondered if she were having a heart attack. She heard Ariel's footsteps coming down the stairs in an uncharacteristically slow cadence. She placed the newspaper on the table with the front page face down. Her pajama-clad son, hair still tousled from sleep, looked young and innocent.

"I don't need to wear a suit or anything to meet with the attorney, do I, Mom?"

"No, dear, just stay away from jeans and tee shirts."

"It's silly for you to drive me there, go home and come back," Ariel reasoned. "But I guess Dad would get really mad if you showed up earlier than he wanted."

"Hey, he's always mad at me for something."

Ariel shrugged and bent down for the newspaper. Mara grabbed it.

"Don't let the article on the murder upset you. As soon as they see there's no evidence in the Land Rover, you won't be a suspect."

Her hands shaking, Mara handed her son the newspaper.

"What the . . ."

When Ariel finished reading, he spoke in a monotone. "I'll get ready to go to Mr. Dickson's now."

***

On the drive to Greg Dickson's office, Mara tried to cheer up her son, but to no avail. When she pulled in front of the Lyric Center, with its statue of a smiling man playing a bass greeting them, Ariel wiped away a tear. She stopped the car and hugged him.

"Why is this happening to me, Mom?"

"I don't know, hon, but we're going to get through it together." She took two tissues from her purse and waited while Ariel looked in the rear view mirror and satisfied himself that he'd hidden the remnants of his tears.

They entered the building, and a guard, who looked to be in his eighties, had them sign the visitors' log before they took the elevator to Greg's office. Ariel followed Mara into the attorney's rectangular shaped waiting room. Chairs upholstered in a calming blue greeted them. Magazines made neat piles on three centrally placed glass-topped tables and four large pictures, all of sea and beach scenes, graced the walls.

Before she could let anyone know they'd arrived, Mara heard the door open, turned and saw her former husband.

"What are you doing here?" he asked.

Simon's brown suit, crisp white shirt and silk tie made Mara feel inadequately dressed in her copper colored pants suit and short sleeved black jersey. The scent of his aftershave reminded her she hadn't put on perfume.

Ariel responded for her. "Remember the police took my car to search. I needed a ride, and it was silly for Mom to bring me and go back home for an hour."

"You should have called me. I would have picked you up," Simon replied.

The appearance of Greg Dickson silenced him. Just over six feet, the defense attorney had a sturdy, slightly muscular frame. The wrinkles on his square-jawed face confirmed he was in his fifties. The collar of his white shirt peeked out from under a light blue silk sweater, complemented by navy slacks.

"I'm Greg Dickson." He made eye contact with each of the Levines as he shook their hands. They followed him to a wood paneled conference room with a long mahogany table surrounded by twelve chairs.

When they were seated, he began, "Before you make a final decision about hiring me, and I about taking the case, we must all understand that I would be Ariel's attorney. As such, I will do whatever is best for him, even if it has adverse effects on anyone else, including you, his parents, or other members of his family."

Did Greg Dickson give this speech to everyone or was he implying he knew Ariel had a brother whose description also matched the killer's?

Simon jumped in. "No one in the family had anything to do with the crime or has anything to hide. Ariel, tell us everything you know so Mr. Dickson understands that."

"It doesn't work like that, Mr. Levine. Ariel must talk to me privately so that anything he says can be protected by attorney client privilege."

"But he's innocent," Simon protested.

"Even so, he could say something which makes him appear guilty, and we'd want that protected."

"What if a client tells you he's guilty, would you keep acting like he's innocent?"

"To a point. But I couldn't, for example, let him testify and proclaim his innocence, or I would be suborning, or encouraging, perjury."

"So a guilty client shouldn't tell you he's guilty?"

"There's no need. I never ask."

Mara took Simon's momentary quiet as an opportunity. "Ariel can give you the names of boys he played basketball with around the time of the murder and also of people he talked to then. How do you check that out?"

When Dickson turned to Mara, she noticed his eyes were such a deep shade of blue that they must be enhanced by colored contacts.

"I have an excellent investigator, Harry Manson. He'll have a lot of work to do, like interviewing people who were in other stores in the shopping center at the time of the murder."

47

Mara noticed Ariel using a tissue she'd given him in the car to wipe sweat from above his lip. The thought of this ordeal going on long enough to need an investigator's services must be upsetting him. "Surely if they find nothing through their searches to connect Ariel to the crime scene, they'll drop him as a suspect."

"That's likely true . . . unless the case is assigned to Sissy Kleinman."

When Dickson took Ariel to his office, Mara went to the waiting area. She didn't want to be trapped in the same room with Simon. She'd just finished reading *Newsweek* cover to cover without comprehending a word when the attorney appeared to bring her back to the conference room where Ariel and Simon were already seated.

When she and Dickson sat down, the defense attorney said, "I'm going to call Reardon Jones and let him know I'm representing Ariel. He'll advise me as soon as they get the lab reports on the Land Rover, Ariel's car, Mr. Levine's house and Ariel's apartment. I'll get back with you as soon as I have them. In the meantime Harry Manson will get to work."

In the car on the way home Ariel asked, "What's the deal with the reports?"

Hadn't Ariel understood the implications when he'd agreed to the searches?

"The killer almost certainly got the victim's blood on him. So traces of it would be in the get-away car."

"What do they think they're going to find in Dad's house or my apartment or car?"

"Blood, and since they took the clothes you were wearing when they saw you and some more from the house and apartment, they're hoping to find something to connect you to the murder scene."

Ariel didn't speak again until they were pulling into the driveway of Mara's townhouse. "You know what's weird, Mom? If it had been Benjie, instead of me, who was driving past Dad's house when the police cars were there, he'd be the one with you now."

***

It was almost midnight when Josef Kessler walked into the kitchen of his one bedroom apartment and turned on the light.

48

Except for a pop-up toaster, every surface was clear. He went to the cabinet next to the refrigerator and removed a bottle of Scotch from the shelf where a few bottles of liquor were lined up according to height. He reached to the next shelf for a glass, and noticing a speck of dirt on its lip, washed it before pouring himself a drink. Maybe it would eradicate unpleasant thoughts so he could sleep.

He was letting his dislike of the boy influence his thinking about the murder. Today's events compounded his ill feelings. When he'd called to let Mara know he wouldn't be able to come by, Benjie had answered the phone. "Maybe I'll remember to tell her," he'd said just before he'd slammed down the receiver.

But there were objective reasons for his concern. Benjie had a terrible temper. Any time Mara reminded him about some obligation, he'd turn scarlet and raise his voice. Mara might ground him but she stayed calm, excusing his behavior as a result of the divorce.

But the main reason Josef's thoughts had led him to a dangerous place was because he couldn't imagine Ariel as a killer. Yet there had to be some explanation for Virginia's Land Rover being identified as the get-away vehicle.

A few weeks before Josef had heard Benjie tell Ariel they could take the Land Rover for a joy ride any time they wanted since Virginia always left a key in the candy dish. Ariel had demurred, saying neither Virginia nor their father would forgive them if they did.

Benjie claimed he was at a car stereo shop at the time of the murder. He knew Mara wouldn't check his alibi. Nor would the police. They had their suspect.

What if without Ariel seeing him take the Land Rover, Benjie had driven it to the shopping center, committed the crime and returned it? The police weren't checking his clothes for blood, just his brother's.

If Ariel's clothes were free of blood but the Land Rover had traces, Mara's thinking would take the same tack as Josef's.

Then she'd face the worse choice any mother could make.

49

EIGHT

In her sleep-fogged state, Mara struggled to answer the phone. Her success subjected her to Simon's voice. "Who gave them Ariel's name?"

It was 6:55 A.M. Based on his past habits, Simon had been up for almost an hour.

"Haven't you read this morning's *Post-Gazette*?" he asked. Simon continued so loudly that Mara moved the phone away from her ear. "The son and daughter of the murder victim named Ariel as the prime suspect. They're demanding he be arrested."

Mara's breath quickened. Arrest Ariel without evidence? Surely it couldn't come to that.

"They're both in their thirties, and they lived with their mother. I bet he's a *fagela,*" Simon said, using the Yiddish term for a homosexual.

"Stop it, Simon. None of that matters. We just have to protect Ariel now that his name's out."

"He'll have to stay home from his college classes until the police's fancy tests clear him. I will not allow the life of my innocent son to be disrupted." Not wanting to give Simon a chance to argue, she quickly went on. "It had to be someone in the police department or the District Attorney's office who gave out his name. Dickson knows everyone Ariel spoke to Friday. Have him get on this."

Mara hung up the receiver and got out of bed. She'd been a fool not to see this coming, clinging to the hope the lab tests would clear Ariel so quickly the public would never know his name. Now even when he was exonerated, people would associate him with a heinous crime. It's a burden he'd always carry. He needed to learn not to hide from it.

Mara would wait to go to her office until she had a chance to discuss the newspaper story with Ariel, convince him to go to school despite it and prepare him to evade the press. Her first client appointment was at ten with Letty Klinger who wanted a divorce. Mara felt like telling Letty to stay married for the sake of her three children. Maybe if Mara were still married to Simon, none of this would have happened. There wouldn't be a stepmother who had a Land Rover that could ruin Ariel's life.

No, staying with Simon wouldn't have been the answer. Mara remembered how, just before their separation, when there was so much tension in the house, she'd taken both her sons to a psychiatrist. Benjie was acting out and Ariel was keeping all his anger inside. Her staying with Simon would have made things worse for the boys.

Mara entered the kitchen and smelled coffee. Benjie had a cup of weak looking instant next to him as he hunched over the newspaper.

He looked up, his faced flushed. "The bastards named Ariel."

"I know. Your father called."

"What are we going to do?"

"Continue as usual. That's what innocent people do."

"You are such a fool," Benjie said. "They'll be whispering about him all through class." He clenched his fists. "Reporters will chase him down. There's no way to continue as usual."

As always, Benjie's anger unnerved Mara. It would have been useful had it been he who stopped at Simon's house when the police cars were there. He fit the description of the killer as much as Ariel did so they would have treated him the same way. But Benjie wouldn't have allowed the searches or the line-ups. Once the police had verified he was at a car stereo shop at the time of the murder, they would have lost interest in him. By then it would have been obvious Ariel was the next suspect so Mara would have hired an attorney before Ariel spoke to the police, made sure the line-ups were conducted fairly, created a time line which showed he couldn't be the murderer.

Mara turned to her furious younger son. "Why do you want to let people you hate ruin your brother's life? If he becomes a prisoner in his own home, they've won."

Benjie's silence suggested her argument had affected him. He continued to read the paper, his shoulders straining his white tee shirt as he looked down at it.

Mara took the opportunity to slice and toast two cinnamon raisin bagels, spread margarine on them and put them on plates. She brought one to Benjie.

He looked up from the newspaper. "Let me be the one to tell Ariel about his name being in the *Post-Gazette*. Then we'll both remind him not to respond to any reporter."

Without touching the bagel, Benjie took the paper and headed up the stairs. Though Mara was concerned about how he'd break the news to Ariel, she was so pleased to have him as an ally that she decided to let him handle the matter.

Mara slowly chewed half her bagel and was staring at the other half when she heard her sons coming down the stairs.

Ariel looked pale and particularly vulnerable in his light yellow pajamas. "Do you think I should go to class?"

"I've already told you . . ." Benjie said.

"I want to know what Mom thinks."

"You should go," she assured him. "You're innocent. Act that way."

***

Starting at eight Mara's phone rang incessantly, bringing calls from true friends and false ones. The former called earlier, knowing Mara would be awake. Elyse Stein, who was principal at the middle school the Levine boys had attended, was irate. "This is crazy. I've known Ariel since he was twelve. He's a kind and gentle soul." As much as Elyse wanted to help, Mara knew there was nothing she could do.

Garrett Jenkins, who'd been Ariel's probation officer after his arrest for having beer on his high school campus, told Mara he'd been incredulous when he'd read Ariel's name in the paper. "He's the nicest, most cooperative kid I've ever worked with. I'll be happy to be a character witness for him."

Mara's gratitude mixed with fear. Ariel would only need character witnesses if he were convicted.

The gossip gatherers started calling at nine. Brenda Moore, whom Mara hadn't spoken to since they'd graduated from law school asked, "Just what evidence do they have against him? The police don't arrest someone unless they have something."

"My son has not been arrested."

Relieved to leave the house, Mara made the fourmile drive to the Chase Bank Building, which housed her law office, and walked through the waiting room. Letty Klinger hadn't arrived for her ten o'clock appointment. Maybe Letty and other clients wouldn't want the mother of an accused murderer as an attorney.

She passed the desk of Ann Wine. The sixty-year old legal secretary had come out of retirement just over a year ago, set up Mara's office and run it impeccably ever since. "Mrs. Klinger called to say she'd be a little late," the petite redhead said.

"Any cancellations?" Mara asked.

Ann hesitated. "One today and another tomorrow. I'm sure they'll reschedule."

Mara's eyes filled with tears.

Ann stood, put her arm around Mara's shoulder and guided her to her office. She closed the door behind them. The two women sat down on the plaid upholstered chairs in front of Mara's cherry wood desk. Ann retrieved a tissue from the box on top of it, handed it to Mara and sat with her while she cried.

"I have to be strong for Ariel . . . and Benjie . . . and everyone, and I'm afraid reporters are going to call here . . ."

"I'll screen the calls. It takes a lot to get anything by me."

Mara smiled, appreciating the accuracy of the statement.

"And stop putting all of this on your own shoulders. You have me and Josef and lots of friends. We'll be angry if you don't let us help."

"Thank you, Ann."

Minutes later Ann led a thin woman in her thirties with straggly dark blond hair into Mara's office. Letty Klinger sat down and looked at her lap. "Would there be a problem if I waited to get the divorce?"

"None at all. In fact, it should be something you're sure you want."

Letty raised her face, and Mara noticed a black and blue mark on the right side of her jaw. "Unless, of course, your husband is harming you or your children."

"But he's never been violent before. He's just mad about the divorce."

By the time Letty left, Mara had the added job of filing a temporary restraining order to keep Charlie Klinger away from his family.

During their divorce she and Simon had stayed civil. Ariel had acted like nothing was changing, but Benjie could hardly contain his fury. Once when screaming at his mother about how she was ruining his life, he'd hit his fist so hard against the kitchen table that he'd broken his little finger.

The intercom buzzed. "Josef's on line one."

"Those damn police are trying Ariel in the press. It's outrageous," were Josef's words of greeting.

"I've told Simon to have Dickson find out who's behind it and put a stop to it," Mara said.

"What if I come by tonight? You can tell me what's going on and how I can help."

Why didn't Josef understand she needed him now?

"I'm sorry we can't talk sooner but I have to go to the hospital."

"The hospital?"

"We found our runaway. He went home to his mother, who beat him."

***

Andrew Block spent Monday morning anxious to talk to Daryl Freed, the chiropractor who'd hired him five months before. They were both occupied with patients until lunch. Andrew found the older man in the physical therapy room, adjusting one of the bikes.

"Busy morning?" Daryl asked.

"Remarkable weekend." Andrew told Daryl about his role in the murder investigation.

"You saved a woman's life and identified a killer. You should be proud."

"The killer's name was in the paper today. Ariel Levine."

"I wonder if he's related to Simon Levine, the guy who sold me that financial software. He has a couple of sons about the right age."

"Levine's a pretty common name," Andrew said.

"He brought one of them here once. Stayed in the waiting room while Simon helped me with the program."

Andrew fiddled with one of the traction machines. "No one

introduced him to me. Maybe I wasn't here that day."

"Maybe not. Let's go. I'm buying lunch."

***

When Mara pulled into the driveway of her townhouse at 5:30, Josef's white Dodge van was parked in front. She walked into her home and was greeted by an amalgam of scents. In the kitchen Josef was cutting scallions while Ariel squeezed a lemon over a large piece of salmon. A garlic clove next to the wooden cutting board along with rejected romaine lettuce leaves, peels of carrots and tomato stems discarded in the sink provided evidence of a newly made salad.

"We wanted to surprise you." Over his beige shirt and brown pants Josef was wearing one of Mara's aprons emblazoned in red with "Kiss the Cook."

She did.

"Thank you, guys." Mara hugged Ariel. "Where's your brother?"

"Eating at Dad's tonight."

Another example of Benjie staying away from Josef. Mara blamed Simon. When the boys had told him about her significant other, she'd heard about his reaction from Ariel.

"Your mother goes from being married to the son of Holocaust survivors to taking up with a German. She'll do anything to get to me," he had said

Thinking of how she'd gone from a man who believed everything was about him to one who was so supportive of her, Mara put her arms around Josef's neck and kissed him again.

"We'll have to make dinner for her more often, Ariel."

"How was school?" Mara asked, when they were seated at the dining room table.

"I sat in the back of the lecture hall for history. When I came into the composition class, some of the kids were whispering, and the professor looked at me funny, but I managed."

"I knew you would."

She insisted that, since the men had made dinner, she'd clean up the kitchen. When she finished and joined them in the living

55

room, Benjie walked in. He waved at his mom, greeted Ariel with, "Hey, bro," and gave Josef a barely perceptible nod.

"Did Dad say if Dickson figured out who gave my name to the *Post-Gazette?*"

"Said it was a waste of time to try. But he did complain to the District Attorney."

"So now what does Dickson say we should do?" Ariel asked his brother.

"Wait for the lab results. They should be back tomorrow."

NINE

Tuesday morning Oracio Crawley arrived at the police crime lab, ready to pick up the report on the Land Rover. He watched for a moment as lab technicians looked through microscopes, put chemicals in droppers and rustled papers. Areas, where contamination had to be avoided, were sealed off with big signs reading, "Authorized Personnel Only." After gaining the attention of a middle-aged clerk with gray streaks in her blond hair, he handed her the case number.

"Jade Ng just finished her report." She buzzed the lab tech.

A pretty young woman with long dark hair appeared.

"What'd you find in the Land Rover?" Oracio asked.

Jade moved the report close to her chest. "There was a small amount of trace blood in the back near the portable dog kennel."

"Where else?"

"Nowhere," Jade replied softly.

"That can't be right. How long have you worked here?"

"Two months."

"I need to see Tim Wyeth."

Jade pointed the detective to an adjoining small room, containing a desk, two chairs and a three-drawer metal file cabinet. "I'll tell him you're waiting."

Oracio took the report from her and went into the office of the crime lab supervisor where he read the lab tech's conclusions. Her inexperience must have led to her inaccurate work.

He pictured the crime scene - footprints in blood on the floor, a bloody palm print on the counter, blood all around the victims. There had to be blood in the Land Rover, on the handle where Ariel opened the door, on the steering wheel, on the seat where his blood spattered clothes rested.

Tim Wyeth appeared, the shoulders of his small, emaciated frame hunched as usual. Rumor was that after forty years of

57

smoking, he was suffering from lung cancer. He slowly lowered himself into a wine colored Naugahyde chair behind his desk.

Oracio tossed the report at him. "You should have given this work to someone who knew what she was doing. Your new hire didn't find any trace blood in the front of the Land Rover."

"Why are you so sure she should have found something?" the supervisor asked as he took out a pack of Marlboro cigarettes and spun it around on the scratched top of his pine desk.

"The killer slit one woman's throat, stabbed another twelve times and cut her husband's hand. Blood had to have splattered on him and been transferred to the Land Rover."

Tim took a cigarette out of the pack and put it back.

"You need to go over the tech's work. She must have made a mistake."

"Either that or you've got the wrong vehicle."

***

There was no way he could have the wrong vehicle. Andrew Block hadn't made up the license plate number. He'd said it was on a Land Rover, and that's where they'd found it. And, on a dark Land Rover, just as he'd described. And driven from a house near the murder scene, quite convenient for the killer. It all fit.

Oracio walked into the squad room and saw Loretta Sanchez standing next to his desk, tapping a foot ensconced in a red patent leather shoe with a stiletto heel.

"Can't do a friend a favor? Have to feed everything to the *Houston Post-Gazette*?" she asked as Oracio motioned her to the chair in front of his desk.

"You're looking good," Oracio said. The twenty-something wore her black hair in a ponytail and had complemented her brown eyes with purple eye shadow and her full lips with mauve lipstick.

"No sweet talk. I'm here for a story. When are you going to arrest that creep who murdered Herlinda Sorento?"

Sissy Kleinman would want some physical evidence tying Ariel Levine to the murder scene before that happened.

Loretta took a notepad and pen from her large red purse and sat poised, waiting for the detective's answer.

"As soon as I know, I'll give you a heads up. You'll have a scoop for the *Weekly Bulletin,*" he told the reporter for the neighborhood newspaper.

"You don't have much time. Luis and Angelina, Mrs. Sorento's children, are impatient already."

Loretta told Oracio how brother and sister, both in their thirties, were devoted to their mother, even lived with her.

Oracio chuckled. "A guy in his thirties living with his mama. That tells me everything I need to know."

"It's not like that. He got into big gambling debts with Lucky Lazarus and sold his house to pay for them. That's why Luis had to move back in with his mom and sister."

The guy must value his life. Even though Lucky's gambling operations were centered in San Antonio, everyone knew that wherever you lived, if you owed Lucky, his henchmen would find you.

Loretta stood. "The paper comes out Friday. If I don't hear from you sooner, I'll be back Thursday."

Oracio owed her. Before becoming a reporter, Loretta had been his son Oscar's second grade teacher. She was the one who'd figured out that Oracio's first born had a form of dyslexia. Once she did, everything made sense—the way Oscar wrote 70 as 07, the way his Ps became 9s, the way he read dog as god. Thanks to Loretta, Oracio knew his son wasn't stupid, and they were getting him help.

Oracio's phone rang.

Sissy Kleinman's throaty voice. "Hey, buddy, what you got for me?"

"A solid identification from Andrew Block."

"I can always count on you."

Oracio smiled until he thought of how unhappy Sissy would be with his next piece of news. "We've got a problem at the lab. The only trace blood some young tech found in the Land Rover was in the back, near the dog kennel. So Wyeth's checking it himself."

"I need more soon. The victim's children are in Reardon's office, and he's siccing them on me."

"I'll get you something," Oracio promised.

As soon as he got off the phone, he called Ben Taub Hospital. Yesterday Mrs. Luna's condition had gone from critical to stable. It was time for her to identify Ariel Levine.

The doctor on the other end of the line resisted. "She's not up to visitors today."

"I'll be there tomorrow morning," Oracio said.

But he wanted to get something done now. He fingered his phone messages, rereading the one he'd put on the top of the pile. It was from Linda Smythe who worked at Discount Delight, two buildings from Lingerie for Life. She claimed a guy was acting so strangely Friday that she'd made him leave the store. It was probably nothing, but he needed to go back to the shopping center to see if anyone else could put Ariel Levine at the scene. He took the envelope with the photos from the top drawer of his desk.

***

Arms crossed over their chests, backs slunk into the wooden armchairs in front of District Attorney Reardon Jones's desk, Angelina and Luis Sorento, children of the lingerie shop murder victim, scowled.

Before sitting down in the third chair, Sissy shook Angelina's hand. She reached over to shake Luis's, but he ignored her effort. The two didn't look like brother and sister. Angelina had a thin face and a wide nose, and, except for a mole on her right cheek, an unblemished complexion. Luis had a narrow hooked nose on a full face that sported a bad case of acne. They both appeared to be in their mid- thirties. Sissy wasn't sure if Angelina was the older or if her gray streaked hair just made her appear that way.

Before Sissy could finish offering her condolences, Angelina interjected, "Our mother was a saint. Everything Luis and I have, we owe to her. She did it all herself."

Luis pointed his finger at Sissy. "When are you going to stop protecting the man who killed our mother?"

Sissy made an effort to keep a neutral expression and to speak in a quiet tone. No one worked harder than she did to put people behind bars. "When I have enough to make it stick, I'll have him arrested."

"The paper said there's an eye witness," Luis challenged as he pounded his fisted right hand into the palm of his left.

60

Reardon was watching her. She'd show him she could handle his job.

"A smart defense attorney can make a jury doubt an eye witness. The crime lab is putting your mother's case first. In the next couple of days I expect a report tying Levine to the scene."

Luis unclenched his fist and rubbed his hands together. "Will you arrest him then?"

"You have my word."

As soon as Sissy got back to her office, she called Tim Wyeth. "I understand that some young lab tech screwed up the trace blood evidence in the Land Rover, and that you're going to personally correct it."

Between hacking coughs, Tim said, "I'm getting ready to meet my Maker, Sissy. So I'm only going to correct that which needs correcting."

TEN

One look at Linda Smythe and Oracio suspected he was dealing with an attention seeker. The manager of Discount Delight, though at least sixty, was wearing her hair in blond ringlets, held back by a green headband. Her white slacks were so tight they showed the outline of her bikini underpants.

Her store was the size of a large barn, filled with shelves overflowing with merchandise—comforters, pots and pans, picture frames. He asked Linda if she had an office.

She led Oracio to the back of the store, fluttering her man-sized hands in bird-like movements as she walked. Her desk was in the storage area where returned merchandise peeked out of white plastic bags.

Oracio saw just one chair by the desk and motioned Linda towards it, saying he preferred to stand.

"I never guessed I was sending a murderer out of the store." Though the manager was a tall, broad shouldered woman, her voice had a chirpy quality about it.

"Tell me about him." Oracio took a notepad out of his back pocket.

"He walked up and down the aisles, touching everything he passed, all the while singing something about a fireman's ball. I figured he was on drugs."

That certainly didn't sound like Ariel, but Oracio wanted to be thorough. "What did he look like?"

"In his twenties, dirty blond hair, a little taller than you. Even taller than me," she added with a giggle.

The description fit Ariel.

"What was he wearing?"

"As warm as it was, he had on a brown overcoat."

That could have been covering the jogging outfit the killer wore.

"What time did you kick him out?"

"A little after two. He must have stayed around the shopping center for two hours, picking who to kill."

Ariel could have scoped out the shopping center and come back, but he seemed too smart to have brought attention on himself. Likely the manager was describing someone high on drugs who was unrelated to the murder. But just in case, he reached in his shirt pocket and took out the envelope with the six photos. Smythe probably wouldn't be able to identify Ariel, who was holding the sign stating he was number three, but there was nothing to lose.

"It's number six," she said without hesitation.

As he left the store, Oracio berated himself for having bothered to show a flake like Linda Smythe the photos. No harm done. The guy she picked had been plucked from a jail cell to have his photo taken so he couldn't be a suspect.

Oracio decided to deep-six the whole encounter.

When he passed the postal station located between Discount Delight and Lingerie for Life, he hesitated, trying to decide whether it would be a waste of time to look for witnesses there. A short, stocky African American woman, dressed in the garb of a postal clerk, stood outside smoking a cigarette. "Are you Detective Crawley?" she asked.

Not recognizing her, Oracio replied cautiously, "Yes."

"You sure got here quick. I just called the station a few minutes ago and they said they'd give you my message when you got back."

"You have information about the murder next door?" Oracio asked.

"I saw a young man in a jogging outfit running from that shop around four o'clock Friday."

"Is there somewhere in the post office we can go where I can show you some photos."

The woman's laugh had a tinge of bitterness. "Been working for the post office twenty-six years, and I don't have even the tiniest space to call my own."

Oracio took out his notepad. "Your name?"

"Mable Stower."

Oracio handed the witness the six photos. "Tell me which one of these you recognize."

She looked at them first in the order Oracio had given them to her. Then she closed her eyes, mixed them up and looked at them again.

"Nope. None of these." She handed the photos back to Oracio.

"Why don't you check once more?"

"No need," she said.

Oracio headed to his car, convinced he'd wasted his morning.

ELEVEN

When he arrived home from work Tuesday evening, Simon detected the aroma of chicken being fried in Cajun spices. He followed it into the kitchen which sported black granite counter tops, a hardwood floor and an island with a professional grade stove top where Virginia was working. Shannon and Duke, a mother and son Dalmatian duo, sat at her feet. Virginia tossed two pieces of chicken to the floor. Shannon ate one, and moved aside so Duke could have the other.

Virginia turned from the frying pan, revealing her butterfly decorated apron. "Some reporter from the *Post-Gazette* called. I told him he was scum for having published the name of an innocent child and demanded he not call again."

"I'll bet he won't," Simon replied before he kissed Virginia.

"Maybe. But since then someone has been calling and hanging up as soon as they hear my voice."

"That doesn't sound like a reporter's tactic," Simon said. A person who believed Ariel was guilty was likely harassing them.

"And look at these." Virginia picked up a bunch of dead daisies from the counter near the sink. "They were on the doorstep when I went out this morning."

Simon took the flowers and walked into the den. He didn't want Virginia to see how concerned he was. Could the dead daisies be a threat? If so, Ariel was the likely target, but he didn't live here. If they meant to do harm, it would be Virginia they'd find at home. He didn't want to frighten her, but he had to protect her. Maybe Greg Dickson would know what to do.

Simon grabbed the phone, called the attorney and told him what Virginia had related.

"This could be over soon," Greg said. "When I called the District Attorney about a report on blood in the Land Rover, he gave me a story about how they only had a preliminary report. Translation – the news is good for us, so they're redoing the tests."

"How do we make sure they don't change the results?" Simon asked.

"They're just trying to buy time to find some other evidence before they report to us," the attorney assured him. "But it seems they've been getting more bad news."

"What do you mean?"

"My investigator went to the shopping center this afternoon. He learned that a postal clerk who saw someone running from the murder scene didn't identify anyone from photos a detective showed her. And the manager of another store threw out a guy who was acting crazy about two hours before the murder."

Simon was so elated that when he called Ariel and Mara answered the phone, he blurted out the good news to her.

"I'll tell Ariel as soon as he gets here." Mara hesitated. "Did Greg Dickson mention which assistant district attorney was handling the case?"

"What does that matter?"

"Remember how Dickson said that Ariel would be in the clear if there was no blood in the Land Rover, unless Sissy Kleinman was the assistant district attorney."

Another example of why Simon was glad he and Mara were divorced. She took the happiness out of good news.

***

Josef picked up the phone after one ring.

"Just as we expected," Mara said. "The preliminary lab report shows no blood in the Land Rover."

"Great. When will they have the final results?"

"You don't think they'll be different, do you?"

"Of course not. It's wonderful. Both boys are in the clear."

"Both boys? Ariel's their only suspect."

"I . . . I know. But they could have come up with some excuse to go after Benjie."

After they hung up, Mara sat at the kitchen table. Going after Benjie made no sense. She'd told Josef that Benjie was buying car stereo equipment at the time of the murder. Had he thought that alibi wouldn't hold up if the police checked? She must be misconstruing what Josef said.

The man she loved had to believe in her sons.

67

***

"Mommy, Mommy, you're home." Six-year-old Paige Kleinman, arms outstretched and moving in imitation of airplane wings, ran in circles around Sissy.

"You'll get dizzy. Where's Daddy?"

"He went back to school for a teachers' meeting. Holly made me dinner, macaroni and cheese. Then she started studying and won't play with me."

Sissy sat down on the well worn sofa in the den of her family's four bedroom single story house while Paige chirped about her "so very good" day.

As Sissy pretended to listen, she thought about her own "so very bad" day. The lack of blood in the Land Rover was a huge problem. At her instigation Norty Walsh had described the bloody crime scene in great detail to the readers of the *Houston Post-Gazette*. That news coverage was supposed to educate a potential jury panel about the heinousness of the crime. Instead, she'd have to explain to a jury how the killer got no blood on himself or his vehicle.

There were still other lab results coming, but realistically, if nothing was found in the Land Rover, where the killer went first, it was unlikely anything would turn up any place else.

Sissy also had to contend with Angelina and Luis Sorento, the victim's children. If she had any physical evidence to tie Ariel Levine to the crime, their anger could help her persuade Reardon Jones to go with a quick arrest. The way things stood now, they were going to be a festering blister unless the police discovered something that would make an arrest imminent.

And she knew Oracio Crawley. If he'd come up with anything today, he would have been in her office, like a lap dog wanting its master's praise after performing a simple trick.

He'd been so sure he had the right suspect that he hadn't looked for any other leads. Now, with the murder four days old, the trail was cold.

There was no choice.

Ariel Levine had to be the killer.

68

TWELVE

Oracio Crawley, carrying a combination small screen television and video player, arrived at Ben Taub Hospital Wednesday morning at eight. When the elevator opened on the fifth floor, he was greeted by an antiseptic smell and moans from a patient lying on a gurney in the hall. He was about to enter Mrs. Luna's room when Dr. Nguyen, with whom he'd spoken on the phone, came out. Seeing how young the doctor was, Oracio was angry with himself for listening to his entreaties to wait to visit his patient.

"You must be Detective Crawley. Good news. Mrs. Luna should be able to go home tomorrow. You can visit her then."

"I'm seeing her now." Oracio walked past the doctor into the room.

He wished he'd knocked. Claudia Luna's hospital gown was almost at the top of her thighs. Henry Luna quickly covered his wife with the sheet that was resting at her ankles. The patient had bandages around the front of her neck and covering her nose, another that started just above the top of her green and white hospital gown and others that made bulges in the gown. Thinking of the twelve stab wounds that had caused the damage, Oracio was more determined than ever to bring Ariel Levine to justice.

Claudia, her face pale, whimpered when she saw the detective.

"It's all right," her husband reassured her. "He's come to help. He knows who did this awful thing."

Claudia raised herself on her elbows as Henry quickly put another pillow beneath her head. "Is he in jail?" she asked.

"Not yet," Oracio admitted.

"Then I'm not safe," Claudia wailed.

Henry looked at Oracio. He needed to say something to make Claudia feel better.

"We have one identification, and as soon as we get yours, we're on our way to an arrest."

"You already identified him, Henry?"

69

Her husband looked at the floor. "No, dear, remember he knocked my glasses off. Andrew Block, the young doctor who helped you, identified him."

Oracio put the small television with its compartment for videotape on the table next to the patient. He took out the envelope with the six photos.

"Your husband needs to leave while you make your identification. Otherwise, he could be accused of influencing you," Oracio explained.

Claudia grabbed Henry's hand. "No."

She must be afraid to be alone with him or any man except her husband. "What if I have a nurse in here with us?" Oracio asked.

When Claudia started crying, Oracio figured he wouldn't get his identification. But Henry came to his rescue. "What if I stand right outside the door?"

Claudia looked from Henry to Oracio and nodded.

Once Henry was out of the room, Oracio handed Claudia the pictures.

"I hope I can do this. It was like he had a nylon stocking over his face."

Andrew Block hadn't mentioned anything like that. Maybe Ariel took the stocking off as he ran out of the store.

Claudia sobbed softly as she looked at the pictures. "It's not one or two or five,"

Oracio took those photos from her. "I'd like you to watch this video tape and see if you recognize any of the men on it."

Claudia glanced at the pictures she was still holding as Oracio stopped the tape when each man appeared.

"Number one looks familiar. But I'm not one hundred percent sure."

"Are you ninety or eighty percent sure?" Oracio asked.

"If I am, you could arrest him, and then we could figure out if it was him, couldn't we?"

"You're exactly right," Oracio replied.

"Eighty percent." Claudia sank back onto her pillows and closed her eyes.

***

70

Oracio left the hospital and went downtown to the tall white brick building that housed the criminal courts and the offices of the District Attorney and his staff.

He knocked on Sissy's door and heard the familiar East Texas drawl invite him in. The assistant district attorney was sitting behind a large oak desk that would have made another woman of her size appear small. But Sissy's ramrod straight posture and the expansive way she moved her arms made her a match for the desk.

"What you got for me, buddy?"

"Another identification, by the stabbing victim Claudia Luna," he announced proudly. "I just got back from the hospital."

Oracio noted a brief look of concern on Sissy's face.

"She wasn't under the influence of medicines when you talked to her, was she?"

Oracio hadn't thought of that. But surely the doctor would have told him if she were. "No problem there," he assured her. "Do you think we can arrest Levine now?"

"I'm still waiting to see if the lab comes up with anything."

"Maybe they should test the trace blood found in the back of the Land Rover, near the portable dog kennel," Oracio said. "It could turn out to be human blood."

"That's unlikely, so I want to postpone that test until after he's indicted."

Feeling Sissy was disappointed in him, Oracio offered, "Just tell me what you need me to do."

"Levine's family hired Greg Dickson. That smells of money, but I need to know how much. Juries hate rich kids, especially those who attack working class women."

Back in the squad room Oracio went to his computer and got on the Internet. He tried Nexis first. It had news stories from the *Post-Gazette* as part of its base. He entered "Simon w/3 Levine." After wasting time on a Simon A. Levine and a Simon G. Levine, he came to two stories about Simon M. Levine. One from 1990 reported how the subject had been sent to the United States by the Israeli software company Compsware to head its Houston office from which all of its business in the southwest was conducted. With that kind of position the guy must be making several hundred thousand a year. The article mentioned Levine's Houston born wife Mara and his Israeli born sons Ariel and Benjie.

Simon was in the *Post Gazette* again in 1997 when he married Virginia Wallace and the *Post-Gazette's* society reporter took note of their celebratory dinner at Dominic's, Houston's poshest restaurant.

There was nothing on "Mara w/3 Levine" on Nexis so Oracio went to the Texas Bar Association web site. Ariel's mother had only been licensed as an attorney for a year so there likely was no big money there.

Oracio tried Virginia w/3 Levine and nothing about Ariel's stepmother appeared. But Virginia w/3 Wallace garnered what he wanted. In 1997 Virginia Wallace had sold her advertising agency for $3,000,000.

Rich people, Jews, foreigners.

Sissy would be pleased.

THIRTEEN

Thursday morning Mara tiptoed into each of her sons' rooms to kiss the sleeping boys goodbye. Benjie groaned when her lips touched his cheek and Ariel smiled when she did the same to him. She taped a note to the refrigerator letting them know she'd left for a 7:30 appointment at Babs' Beauty Salon.

Since she was nine, Mara had been coming to the shop to have her curly hair cut and shaped. Over the years neither the treatment of Mara's hair nor the salon had changed. The same brown linoleum floor went from the front of the store with its appointment desk, hair dryers and three cubicles to the small area in the back with its two sinks for washing hair. Babs still colored her hair coal black but now it surrounded a face sagging with wrinkles. Her walk was no longer brisk, arthritis in both knees having taken its toll.

Mara's first memory of Babs was when Mara was five, sitting on Babs' lap, her head resting on the then young woman's soft chest and people around them cried. "My Daddy died," Mara said.

"I know, sweetheart," Babs replied.

"Am I going to die now, too?"

Babs held Mara more tightly. "No, my little love."

Soon after Babs told Mara's mother Sondra, "My brother needs a secretary and you were the fastest typist in our high school class."

For the next fourteen years mother and daughter survived on Sondra's secretarial salary. Then breast cancer stopped her from working.

When chemotherapy robbed Sondra of her hair, Babs found an inexpensive wig and styled it every week. When Sondra was too ill to come to the shop, Babs came to their apartment. When Mara's mother died, a familiar scene repeated. With the sounds of crying people surrounding them, Mara sat next to Babs, encircled by her arms while Babs reassured her, "I'll always be here for you."

Today Babs greeted her with a hug. "This thing with Ariel is so unfair."

"If only it were me, instead of him."

Babs put her arm around Mara and led her to a cubicle. "There's nothing worse than watching a child suffer."

"Every day I wait for news they've found the real killer."

"I heard something from a client yesterday that might help," Babs said. "She told me her niece stopped dating Luis Sorento, the victim's son, after he sold his house to pay off his gambling debts. He still owed some San Antonio thug money, and the guy has a reputation for getting paid in full one way or another. That scared her niece."

"What's the thug's name?" Mara asked.

"Lucky Lazarus."

"Thank you, Babs. I'll have Ariel's attorney get right on it."

When Mara arrived at her office at nine, she called Greg Dickson. His secretary informed her he wasn't in but would call her back. At 10:30 she said he was in a meeting. Mara didn't have another client scheduled until 1:00 so she drove from her suburban office to Dickson's downtown office.

His secretary greeted Mara's request to see her boss with, "But you don't have an appointment."

"Mr. Dickson is my son's attorney. I have critical information which he needs to hear immediately."

The young woman left her desk and went into the attorney's inner sanctum. She returned with the message that Mr. Dickson could see Mara at noon. "Perhaps you'd like to get some lunch and come back in an hour."

"I'll wait in case he's ready earlier."

At twenty minutes after twelve Greg Dickson appeared in the waiting room, attired in a dark blue suit, a light blue shirt and a blue paisley tie. Mara suspected even his pajamas must be blue. She followed the attorney to his office, which had a huge globe in the corner and framed maps of ancient civilizations on its walls.

Greg sat down behind his large walnut veneered desk and motioned her to a blue pigskin chair in front of it. Instead Mara stood, gripping the chair's back.

After she related what Babs had told her, Greg looked at her as though waiting for more information.

Mara blurted, "You've got a criminal with a motive to kill instead of a motiveless non-violent teenage boy."

"And his motive is?" Greg asked.

"He had the mother killed so the son would inherit the business. Then the son sells and pays off the debt."

"You're assuming the business is worth something and that the son inherits."

"Your investigator can confirm that."

Greg put his elbows on his desk, clasped his hands together and rested his chin on them. "You need to understand that my investigator's task is to get information that will help me convince a jury that your son did not commit the crime. It's not to figure out who did. That job belongs to the police."

"But they're not trying to figure it out. They're just looking at my son."

"I'll pass the information to the District Attorney. Law enforcement officials all over the state are familiar with Lucky Lazarus, so it may pique his interest."

Greg fiddled with a pen. Then raised his gaze to Mara. "Mrs. Levine, I was wondering if your former husband knows you came to see me."

"No. What does that matter?"

"I charge him for my time. So in the future you might want to clear a visit with him."

***

Thursday morning Oracio Crawley walked into the bedroom his sons shared to tell them breakfast was ready. Oscar, still in his pajamas, was studying his spelling words. "Do you think I'll do okay on my test, Dad?"

"Just remember the tricks Miss Sanchez taught you last year, and you'll do fine."

His words reminded Oracio that Loretta Sanchez, Oscar's former teacher turned reporter, was expecting information from him today on the lingerie shop murder and the suspected killer Ariel Levine.

Less than an hour later when Oracio walked into the squad room, Loretta was sitting in front of his desk. Her long legs were crossed, hiking her red and white diagonally striped skirt to mid thigh level. Oracio chuckled to himself when he thought about how outraged the students' mothers had been and how appreciative their fathers, when she'd dressed and sat like that as a teacher.

"I have a ten o'clock deadline for tomorrow's paper," she said. "When are you arresting Ariel Levine?"

Oracio hated to tell her he didn't know. It made him look like a liar or an incompetent.

"I can't reveal that, but I can give you some information I've kept from Norty Walsh at the *Post-Gazette* so you'll have a scoop."

"It better be good, and you'd better not tell him until tomorrow morning, after our weekly's come out."

Oracio leaned over his desk, and motioned Loretta to do the same. She came close enough for him to smell the lavender scent of her perfume. "We now have two positive identifications of Levine. Mrs. Luna fingered him yesterday."

"Then why haven't you arrested him?"

Angry that Loretta wasn't grateful for the information, Oracio replied, "You're the reporter. Figure it out."

***

Sissy Kleinman spent Thursday morning preparing her opening statement in a murdered child case and presenting it to the jury.

During the trial's lunch break, she sat at her desk, taking bites of her sandwich while refining the questions she'd ask her first witness.

The phone rang.

Reardon's voice told her there was a problem. He emphasized the second syllable of her name and dragged it out.

"Luis Sorento called me."

From the way Reardon stressed "me," Sissy guessed he was angry she hadn't convinced Luis that his calls were to come to her, not her boss.

"Somehow he knew that Mrs. Luna had identified Levine," Reardon said. "Accused us of not arresting him because his family has money and influence."

Sissy couldn't let this case result in Reardon's deciding he wanted someone else to succeed him as District Attorney. "I'm sorry. I don't know why he bothered you when I told him to call me with any questions."

"Ah . . . seems there was a question about your ethnicity. He thought your last name meant you were Jewish, and that you were protecting one of your own."

It was an all too common mistake. One that could cost her votes when she ran for Reardon's job.

"Don't worry," he assured. "I straightened him out. But then I got a call from Greg Dickson claiming Luis owes Lucky Lazarus money, and that could be the motive for the murder."

"But the killer's license plate matched the one on Levine's stepmother's Land Rover."

"I reminded him, but still you need to mention it to Detective Crawley so Dickson can't say we ignored a tip."

"Sure thing," Sissy said.

She hung up and drummed her fingers on her desk. Reardon was asking her to step into quicksand. No one could ever pin anything on Lucky. And if word got out why they were trying, it would look like she was besmirching the murder victim's grieving son rather than arresting the real killer.

Everything would depend on how she handled Oracio.

"Hey, buddy," she said as soon as he answered the phone. "I need some information I'm sure you can give me."

"What?" Oracio asked, his tone filled with his usual eagerness to please her.

"Have you heard a rumor that Luis Sorento owed Lucky Lazarus on some gambling debts?"

Oracio spoke with such pride in his knowledge that Sissy pictured him puffing out his barrel chest and rising up to his full five foot eight inch height. "That's why Luis lived with his mama. He sold his house to pay off the debt."

"I was sure you'd be the one to know," Sissy said in her most drawn out East Texas drawl.

She let Oracio enjoy the compliment before she casually asked, "Then it's all paid off?"

Oracio hesitated. He didn't have an answer but, rather than admitting it, he'd give her the one she wanted.

Judith Groudine Finkel

"Sure is."
"Thanks, Oracio. That's what I needed to know."

FOURTEEN

Friday morning when Mara walked past her secretary's desk, Ann Wine opened her mouth slightly, then closed it and cast her eyes downward.

If Ann hesitated to talk to her, she must be planning to quit. Ann was a private person and all the publicity surrounding Ariel must have gotten to her. Mara didn't know how she'd manage without her.

"Is anything wrong?" Mara asked.

"Let's go into your office." Ann picked up something lying next to her computer.

It looked like a section of the *Houston Post-Gazette* but Mara had scoured the paper that morning. There was nothing in it about Ariel.

They walked through the reception area and passed the file room. Once inside the office, Ann closed the door. "I don't want to make your life any more difficult but this concerned me."

Mara, seated behind her desk, took the paper from Ann and motioned the older woman to sit down. To her surprise, the paper wasn't the *Post-Gazette* but a copy of the *Weekly Bulletin*, a free newspaper, containing numerous advertisements, which someone threw on her driveway once a week. Since its news stories were usually limited to where to avoid road construction, unusual hobbies of great grandmothers and neighborhoods experiencing break-ins, Mara always tossed it without opening it.

Today's front page article was entitled, "Children mourn while suspect remains free." In an interview of Luis and Angelina Sorento, son and daughter of the murdered owner of Lingerie for Life, Angelina related how their mother, widowed when they were in grade school, had opened the shop and worked long hours to support them. Her praise continued along with numerous mentions of how much she and her brother missed their mother.

Luis was quoted. "So you can imagine how we feel when a spoiled rich kid can get away with killing this hard working woman who sacrificed everything for us. If Ariel Levine lived in the barrio, instead of in a wealthy neighborhood near the Jewish Community Center, he would have been arrested by now."

"I don't consider the boys and me rich and Ariel has never lived near the Jewish Community Center." Mara looked at Ann. "You don't think mentioning the Center was an honest mistake, do you?"

"It is a way to identify Ariel as Jewish."

After Ann left her office, Mara thought of how ironic it was that the newspaper had put her family into a Jewish neighborhood when she'd grown afraid to live in one.

Her fear had come three years before, after the news of a bomb exploding in their old neighborhood in Israel, killing six of their former neighbors. A woman who appeared to be pregnant had walked into the café at the end of their block and detonated it.

Blood, bits of flesh and body parts of their dead and maimed friends had covered what was left of the café and the sidewalk beyond.

Half the face of Ariel's grade school girlfriend had been blown off, leaving her one remaining eye hanging from its socket. She'd committed suicide less than a year later at the age of seventeen.

It was safer to live where it wasn't easy for those who hate you to find you.

Mara studied the newspaper report again. Maybe she and Ann had overreacted. She'd call Josef, get his opinion.

She read him the article.

"Class warfare," was his immediate reaction. "A ploy used often in Germany."

"It doesn't help for Ariel to be viewed as a spoiled rich kid."

"That shouldn't influence a decision to arrest him," Josef said. "It could hurt in front of the wrong jury but we don't expect it to come to that."

Her discussion with Josef should have reassured Mara but she kept worrying during her meeting with a new client.

When he left Mara's office, Ann buzzed her on the intercom to say Simon was holding on line one.

"Do you know how much your visit to Greg Dickson yesterday cost me?" was her former husband's greeting.

"What's Ariel's life worth to you?"

"You didn't do any good," Simon said. "The police knew about Luis Sorento's gambling debts, and that he'd paid them off by selling his house."

"Babs told me about the house sale, but she heard he still owed money after that."

Simon laughed. "I have almost no trust in the police but even I believe them rather than a rumor at some beauty shop."

"Maybe you won't find this so funny," Mara replied.

She read the quote from Luis Sorento.

***

Simon's hand was shaking when he stopped gripping the receiver. They were trying to do to his son what they'd done to his parents—take him away because he was Jewish.

Sitting in his home office, Simon looked across his desk to the photos on his credenza. In the center was a picture of his somber parents on their wedding day, taken at the displaced persons' camp where they'd met.

Simon's father had told him that Europe's Jews had ignored the early signs. They'd viewed the anti-Semitic canards of Jewish wealth and power and influence as harmless talk. But the resentment it bred in their Christian neighbors had made it all too easy for them to acquiesce in the final solution.

Now Luis Sorento was using the same ploy to get the public behind him so the police would feel pressured to arrest Ariel.

Simon wouldn't let them take his son away. He picked up the receiver and called his sister Frieda.

***

Mara struggled with getting her key into the lock as she carried two bags of groceries filled with rotisserie chickens, salad fixings, potatoes, challah and baklava into her townhouse. She put her bundles on the white Formica topped kitchen counter where they partially covered a note from Ariel. When she retrieved it, she learned that he and Benjie were eating dinner with Simon and Virginia.

81

Though disappointed her sons wouldn't be joining her for Sabbath dinner, their absence would give her a chance to share some of her concerns with Josef, who arrived as Mara finished making the salad.

He walked into the kitchen and put his arms around her.

Mara rested her cheek against his broad chest and heard the steady rhythm of his heartbeat. She raised her face, accepted a long kiss and playfully tugged his blond handlebar mustache.

Josef smiled, recognizing this as Mara's signal she wanted to make love.

Afterwards, as she lay in her bed enveloped in Josef's arms, Mara stroked the fine blond hairs on his chest and remembered the time seven months ago when they'd first made love. She'd never before seen a naked uncircumcised man so she thought there was something wrong. Josef had noticed her look of dismay. "Don't worry. It works." So their first night of lovemaking had begun with laughter.

When they were back downstairs enjoying dinner, Josef asked, "How are things going?"

She told him about her frustration over her inability to get anyone to seriously investigate her theory that, because of Luis Sorento's gambling debts, Lucky Lazarus might be behind Mrs. Sorento's murder.

"I'm trying to figure out how I can investigate it myself."

"You can't," Josef responded. Mara must have looked as angry as she felt because Josef quickly added, "Even if you had the resources, you'd be endangering yourself, Ariel and Benjie. If your theory about him is right, Lucky goes after family members of those who cross him."

That thought frightened Mara, but so did the idea that she might not be doing everything she could for her son.

The front door opened. "Yo, Mom," Ariel said loudly. "Hope you and Josef are decent cause Benjie and I are coming in."

The two boys walked into the dining room, both dressed in jeans and Houston Rockets tee shirts. Ariel sat next to Mara while Benjie remained standing. They simultaneously helped themselves to baklava.

Mara noted Ariel's grin. "I'm glad to see you so happy."

"It's cause of Dad's great idea. Instead of my waiting until I finish college to go to Israel and join the Air Force, he thinks I should go now. Aunt Frieda said I can live with her in Tel Aviv until I get accepted."

Mara was stunned. As a dual citizen of the United States and Israel, Ariel was permitted by both countries to enlist in the Israeli Air Force. But she and Simon had agreed that wouldn't happen until Ariel graduated from college. Mara hoped by then he'd lose his enthusiasm for the plan, which would put him in constant danger.

"When Dad finished high school, he went on a six month backpacking trip and then began serving when he was nineteen, just like I am now," Ariel said.

"I can't imagine Greg Dickson thinks it's a good idea for you to go just yet."

"Dad talked to him, and he said once the final lab results are in, he'll confirm with the District Attorney that I can leave the country."

Mara was about to tell Ariel why the plan was a bad idea when Josef did it for her.

"Ariel, perhaps you need to wait a few months until everything dies down. Otherwise the newspapers may present your trip as fleeing, and since it would be to Israel, there'd be publicity about you being born there and being Jewish."

"Leave it to a German to be an expert on anti-Semitism," Benjie said.

"Benjie," Mara yelled.

"Don't give me any crap about Josef's being born after the war. We can all guess what his parents and grandparents were doing during it."

"You're no better than people who paint all Jews with the same brush. Apologize to Josef."

Instead Benjie left the house, slamming the front door.

Mara stood to go after him. Josef put his hand on her arm. "Leave it for now. We're all under a lot of strain."

Ariel sat hunched over, all the animation gone from his face.

Mara bit her lower lip. "I'll discuss a trip to Israel with your father after the final lab results are in."

FIFTEEN

Normally Oracio didn't work on Saturdays but he wanted to be at the interview of Consuela Blanco, who'd been cleaning the house of Simon and Virginia Levine the day of the murder. When the police had called her Monday, she'd begged them to let her wait until Saturday to come to the station so she wouldn't have to give up a day of work. She promised not to talk to the Levines, whose home she went to every other Friday, until after she met with the police.

Oracio had arranged for her to be questioned in the smallest interrogation room where she'd feel penned in, unable to escape any lies. He entered and found her and Lieutenant Sam Brown sitting next to each other at a rectangular table. The stocky balding officer was talking to the witness in Spanish in a tone, which indicated chit chat. Consuela wore a crucifix hanging from a gold colored chain outside her white blouse. When Oracio sat down across from her, she gasped and grasped the icon with both hands.

Sam chuckled. "Why does she think you're the devil?"

"I drew my gun on her the night of the murder. She was reaching for something in her purse. Turned out to be her green card."

"Let me explain and reassure her you're a good guy."

As he listened and tried to make out some of what Sam was saying, Oracio considered the irony of an African American cop being a Spanish translator while he, the son of a Mexican immigrant mother, could understand only snippets of his mother's native language. Things would be different if his American born father hadn't forbidden Spanish from being spoken in their home.

While Sam talked to Consuela, Oracio turned the witness information sheet towards him and learned that the Levines' maid was from El Salvador and was thirty-one. With her black hair pinned up in a bun and dark circles under her eyes, she looked years older.

When Sam finished vouching for the detective, Consuela removed her hands from the crucifix and rested them in her lap, but still averted her eyes from Oracio.

Sam's first few questions and Consuela's answers established that she was in the Levine house before Ariel woke up, and that he left numerous times in his car.

"Ask her where he was between 3:30 and 4:30," Oracio said.

He didn't like the answer Sam translated.

"The suspect came into the house about 3:45, after walking the dogs, and left in his car around 4:15."

"Where was he during those thirty minutes?"

Consuela glanced at Oracio as Sam spoke and then answered in a whisper.

"As far as she knows, he was in the house."

"Did she actually see him?"

Sam leaned close to Consuela whose answer was barely audible.

"No. She thinks he was in his bedroom. The door was closed."

"That's convenient. Did she see the Land Rover during that time?"

Sam asked the question, got an answer and asked a follow-up before translating.

"She never saw the Land Rover move all day, and she spent most of the afternoon in the laundry room which looks out to the carport where it was parked."

Oracio leaned across the table and shook his pointed finger at the witness. "Tell her that if she spoke to the Levines before she came here, she's going back to El Salvador."

Consuela burst into tears.

Sam pulled a handkerchief from his pants pocket and handed it to her. "That's enough translating for today."

Oracio stayed seated as Sam escorted the witness out of the room. Virginia Levine's Land Rover had to be the killer's getaway car. Its license plate matched the one Andrew Block had written down, and the engine had felt warm when Oracio put his hand on the hood a little more than an hour after the murder. Either the Levines had gotten to Consuela or she hadn't been paying attention when the Land Rover left the house. That's how he'd present the situation to Sissy.

Oracio smiled. His favorite assistant district attorney would make mincemeat of that scared woman on the witness stand.

***

Sissy tapped her fingers on her desk as she read the reports from the police lab. They'd still found nothing in either the Land Rover, Ariel's car, his father's house or his apartment to connect him to the crime scene. Even the small knife with the double edged blade found in the trunk of Ariel's car was no help. Mrs. Sorento was killed with a single edged blade. There were eight white fibers in the Land Rover. She'd have the lab run some tests to see if they were consistent with those from bras sold in the lingerie shop.

None of the fingerprints, footprints or blood in the shop matched Levine's. The scrapings from under Mrs. Sorento's fingernails were described as "inconclusive."

Something was missing. A palm print had been found on the counter near the cash register. There was no mention of it.

Sissy went to her Rolodex and found Tim Wyeth's home phone number. He'd likely be there on a Saturday.

"Hello, Mrs. Wyeth. This is Sissy Kleinman calling for Tim."

"He's feeling poorly. He may be asleep."

"I need to talk to him now."

After a few seconds Sissy heard Mrs. Wyeth put down the receiver. Two minutes later a coughing Tim Wyeth picked it up.

"Where's the report on the palm print from the lingerie shop?" she asked the head of the police crime lab.

"It's missing."

"I know that. It wasn't with all the other reports."

"I mean the palm print is missing."

"How could that be?" Sissy asked.

"I'll let you know when I find out," Tim responded between lethal coughs.

Sissy hung up and headed for Reardon Jones' office to give him all the bad news at once and in person. He needed to hear it from her if she was going to manage his reaction.

"Sissy, just the person I want to see," was his greeting. "Greg Dickson called. Ariel Levine wants to go to Israel to visit his aunt."

"He has joint Israeli/American citizenship, and not in name only. He's lived in Israel, and they don't extradite their citizens. If he's there after we indict him, we'll have to go to Israel to try him."

"Are you ready to indict him?"

"I've got two eye witnesses but still no physical evidence to tie him to the murder."

"Unfortunately the *Post-Gazette* has made a big deal about the bloody crime scene, so that really hurts us," Reardon said.

Did he suspect she'd fed that information to their reporter Norty Walsh?

Sissy had to regain her boss's confidence. "I'm waiting for the lab to find a bloody palm print. Just hold off until we get the test results on it."

"I'm sure it's been destroyed."

She must have looked surprised because he went on, "Remember the big rain the Sunday night of Thanksgiving weekend?"

She nodded.

He leaned over the desk and lowered his voice. "This is between us, but the lab roof leaks like a sieve. We've lost a lot of evidence that way."

About a year ago Sissy had heard rumors about roof leaks, but she'd assumed repairs had been made by now.

"There's nothing to wait for," Reardon said. "I'm going to tell Dickson his client can go. While he's out of the country, you need to figure out how to make the case."

***

Mara looked forward to Saturday morning services for the comfort of the familiar prayers. She walked down the long hallway of the Tree of Life synagogue, past the cases holding Jewish ritual objects—Sabbath candlesticks, ancient prayer books, Chanukah menorahs. Before going into the sanctuary, she stepped into the ladies' room.

Once inside a stall, she heard two girls talking. "I'm not surprised," one said. "Ariel Levine is so weird."

"Yeah, my mom said he reminds her of Eddie Haskell, some character on that old TV show *Leave it to Beaver*. He always sucked up to the parents but was really a bad ass."

"I know something worse. But you can't spread it around. I've only been telling a few of my closest friends."

"Don't worry. I only share secrets with a couple of people."

"When Ariel first came to Houston, we were at day camp together. He found a dead bird and took a stick and kept poking it so hard that all its insides flew out."

"Gross. It must have felt the same to him when he used the knife on those women."

The bathroom door closed and the girls were gone. Mara went to the sink and washed her shaking hands. They didn't understand how upset and angry Ariel had been about leaving Israel. And he hadn't killed the bird, just taken out his frustration on its corpse.

Is this what it had come to—people taking the most minor incidents and turning them into proof her son was a killer? Who knew how many people had heard the story and reacted the way those girls did.

What they didn't know was that this was the same boy who at the age of ten had found a sick kitten and offered his mother all the money he'd received for his birthday to pay the vet to cure it.

Mara needed to be with Ariel, not among people who could unfairly judge him. She walked past the sanctuary and out the front door.

When she arrived home, she heard rap music, with words she couldn't make out, blaring from her son's room. From his doorway, she smiled as she saw him barefooted and gyrating in time to the music. A half packed green suitcase rested on his unmade bed.

"What's going on?" she asked.

"Great news. The District Attorney said I have no travel restrictions. I'm leaving for Israel tomorrow to enlist in the air force."

"Tomorrow? That's ridiculous. You haven't even taken your finals."

"I can't concentrate. Dad's going to call the University of Houston Monday and try to get me permission to take them late, if I come back."

Mara's stomach clenched. "If?"

"It's a two year enlistment."

Mara left his room and rushed down the stairs.

"Mom, where are you going?" Ariel called after her.

She sped from her Houston neighborhood and headed on the Southwest Freeway towards Simon's. He'd gone too far this time —not consulting her, telling Ariel he could go to Israel, and before he'd even finished his college semester. Simon wasn't stupid. Yet, he was ignoring the publicity the trip would generate. She shouldn't be surprised. He'd acted the same way during their marriage. When he got an idea, he was like a dog with a bone, blind to everything else around him.

Mara saw a Ford Explorer pulled over for speeding and slowed down. She still arrived at Simon's white brick two-story house in record time, thirteen minutes after she'd left her own home. She pounded on the door until Simon appeared.

"Are you out of your mind?" she asked her former husband.

He looked puzzled.

"You can't send Ariel to Israel now. It'll look like he's fleeing."

"The District Attorney has given him permission to go." Simon shut the door behind him and joined Mara on the porch.

"The press will ignore that. They'll compare him to the kid from Maryland who held dual citizenship and really was a murderer. He fled to Israel so his trial would be held there and any jail time would be served there."

"It's a blessing Israel protects its citizens from other countries' show trials. Do you want your son to be another Dreyfus?"

"Your paranoia is going to be Ariel's undoing."

"Paranoia? You haven't been getting the hang-up calls and the dead flowers."

"At least wait until he finishes his finals. By then the police may have another suspect."

"Don't you understand? It's too late to have another suspect. That's why they've got to pin this on Ariel."

***

When Mara returned home, she went up to Ariel's room and found him pulling a second suitcase out of his closet.

"I'll help you pack."

"Then you're okay with me going?" Ariel asked.

"No, but I love you and want to spend time with you before you leave."

"Mom, I've tried not to let you know how hard this has been." Ariel's voice broke. "People whisper when they see me. They look at me like I'm a murderer."

What her son was going through was even worse than she'd imagined.

Ariel sat on his bed between the two suitcases. Though his eyes filled with tears, he smiled at his mother.

"Ariel . . ."

"I'll be okay, Mom."

Mara threw the empty suitcase on the floor, sat next to Ariel and hugged him to her.

SIXTEEN

Sissy Kleinman was about to leave her office to go to her daughter Paige's Saturday afternoon soccer game when the phone rang.

Sissy picked up the receiver and heard Luis Sorento. "When are you going to arrest Ariel Levine?"

If she told him in person about Ariel's trip to Israel, she'd have a better chance of influencing his reaction.

"If you and your sister come to my office now, we'll discuss it."

"Expect us in twenty minutes."

Sissy looked at her watch. It was 2:45 and the game started at 3:00. Maybe she'd make the second half. That possibility faded when the Sorento siblings didn't show up until 3:30. Sissy suspected they'd taken time to dress up for the meeting. Luis was wearing a sport jacket and tie and Angelina had on a brown pantsuit and heels.

Before Sissy could invite the brother and sister to sit down, Luis shouted, "You said you'd arrest him as soon as the lab results came in. He's still walking around while our mother lies dead in her grave."

"So far none of the lab results connect him to the murder scene."

Luis's mouth opened but no words came out. He and Angelina sat down.

"How can that be?" Angelina asked.

Before Sissy could answer, Luis did. "You know how smart those Jews are. He had this all planned so he left no trace."

"But I'll never figure out why he picked our mother. He didn't even know her."

"He's godless, he's evil," Luis boomed. "He didn't need a reason."

Angelina dabbed her eyes with a white linen handkerchief.

91

"What are you going to do now?"

"We're going to lull him into a false sense of security. That's when murderers make mistakes."

"I don't understand," Angela replied.

"Reardon Jones told Levine's attorney there were no travel restrictions on the kid. He's going to Israel to visit relatives."

"He'll stay there," Luis said.

"If we trick him into thinking he's not a suspect anymore, he'll come back. So we need to keep a lid on things, not go to the press or anything."

Sissy looked at the now silent Sorentos. "In the meantime, we'll figure other ways to make this case. When he's on trial, I'll make sure the jury knows he went to Israel, and you can guess what they'll make of that."

**

Luis and Angelina walked into the two-bedroom house they'd lived in since they were children. When Angelina was nine and her brother eight their mother had decided they should no longer share a room so Angelina had moved into her widowed mother's bedroom. When Luis returned to their home a few months ago, the two women had again shared a room. Angelina went into it and sat down on her bed. She looked at its empty twin, took a tissue from the box on the nightstand and wiped her tears.

She'd never planned to leave her mother, even looking forward to taking care of her in her old age—a way to compensate for how well her mother had always taken care of her. Angelina's one marriage proposal, when she was twenty-four, had come from a man who owned a souvenir shop in Padre Island where he'd met Angelina when she and her mother had taken their only vacation. If she'd married him, Angelina would have been a full day's drive from Mama.

"Think about his proposal some more," her mother had advised. "One day I'm going to die, and you'll be alone."

But Angelina had been sure a saintly woman like her mother would live such a long life that Angelina would only be alone a short time.

Ariel Levine had changed that.

If it hadn't been for Angelina's sin of gluttony, he wouldn't have succeeded. She'd eaten so much at their Thanksgiving dinner, obeying her mother's urgings to have second helpings of the fried turkey and corn bread stuffing. Friday when Angelina's stomach felt queasy, her mother had insisted she stay home from the shop. If she'd been there, she could have saved Mama.

The phone rang. Luis answered in his booming voice, and then spoke so quietly that Angelina couldn't hear even though the phone was in the living room, just outside her door.

The secrecy concerned her. Maybe Luis was involved with a married woman. That would explain why someone hung up whenever Angelina answered.

When she no longer heard Luis whispering, Angelina joined him on the plastic covered white couch in the living room. He sat with his chin in his hand and didn't look up until Angelina said, "Are you all right?"

"Sister, we need to be practical."

"Practical?"

"How long can we afford to hire a guard at the store?"

"We can stop once Levine's arrested."

"We got a lot of double talk from that lady lawyer today. She knows the bastard's in Israel and may never come back."

"God won't let that happen. Levine will be arrested. Even with the guard we can pay our expenses and have enough to live on."

"Just barely."

"There's no choice."

Luis took her hands in his. "We could sell the business."

Angelina jumped up. "Never. Lingerie for Life meant everything to Mama. She made a success of it by herself. She supported us with it. We can't be unfaithful to her."

"Do you really want to hold onto the place where Mama died?"

"It keeps me determined to see Levine punished."

***

Six-year-old Paige Kleinman, her fourteen year old sister Holly and her father sat around their kitchen table eating the ice cream sundaes he'd made them.

"Why didn't Mommy come to my soccer game like she promised?"

"Because she's a liar," Holly answered.

Dennis looked from Paige, face dirt smudged and pigtails askew to Holly, face made up with too much eye shadow and purple hair piece resting on her upswept dark hair. "What Holly means it that your mother wanted to come but she had to work extra to put some bad guy away."

"No, I mean she's a lying bitch who doesn't care about us."

"Holly, don't upset your sister."

Holly was undaunted. "It's going to get worse when she runs for District Attorney. She'll only be around when she wants our picture taken with her so she can prove she's a great mother."

Paige stopped licking her bowl. "Who's going to take our picture, Daddy?"

"No one, pumpkin." Dennis turned towards Holly. "I will not let your mother exploit you."

Holly stood. "The only way you're going to stop her is if you divorce her and get custody of us." She ran to her room and slammed the door.

Holly was right. But how had it come to this? A part of Dennis still saw Sissy as the classmate he'd fallen in love with at East Texas High School.

How he'd admired her spunk. At a time when girls were expected to hide how smart they were, Sissy flaunted it. He'd loved the challenge of trying to best her, though he almost never did. Yet, all her academic honors meant nothing to her father whose praise was limited to her brother's prowess on the football field.

And Sissy had never let her family's poverty stop her from doing what she wanted. When Dennis invited her to the senior prom, she'd worked extra shifts at the Dairy Queen to buy the material she used to make her dress.

But the past couldn't change the present, so, as soon as he finished loading the dishwasher, Dennis walked through the den and down the hall to the bedroom he shared with Sissy. He took out a three subject ruled notebook from its hiding place in a no longer used suitcase in their closet, sat lotus style on the floor and opened to the first blank page which was midway through it. He jotted the date and left a blank space for the time Sissy arrived home. Then he noted how upset Paige and Holly were about Sissy missing Paige's soccer game.

He replaced the notebook, his best hope of getting custody of his daughters when he informed Sissy he wanted a divorce.

He hadn't told Holly about it because he didn't want to get her hopes up.

As anyone who'd ever faced her in the courtroom knew, Sissy was almost impossible to beat.

***

Harold Miller and Kevin Gutman, friends long before their sons were born, finished their regular Saturday tennis game, poured themselves water from the pitchers located just outside the courts and sat at a nearby table.

Kevin put down his glass. "I think we were lucky that both Farrell and Skipper missed Detective Crawley's calls today. That gives us an opportunity to decide what the boys will say when they call him back."

"If they call him back," Harold said.

"I don't think we can mess with the police."

Harold wiped his pudgy face with a napkin. "I spoke to my brother, a criminal defense attorney in Dallas. He said it's dangerous for the boys to talk to him."

"Dangerous?"

Harold nodded. "What the boys know hurts the case against Ariel so they have to discredit them. If they talk to the detective now and then say even the slightest thing different when they testify, the assistant district attorney will make them seem like liars. Could even threaten to bring perjury charges against them."

"That seems farfetched," his balding friend replied.

"My brother's heard Sissy Kleinman's done it before."

"I wish our boys weren't involved," Kevin said. "Just their bad luck to be playing basketball with Ariel that day. If you believe he did it, you might think he'd planned it that way, so no one would figure he had time to attack those women."

Harold stared across the table. "But he didn't have time to do it."

"Daryl Freed, the chiropractor who hired Andrew Block as an associate a few months back, said that Andrew's a very careful person who would have gotten the license plate number down right, and who wouldn't have identified Ariel unless he was sure."

Harold snorted. "You're playing right into the prosecutor's hands. My brother said you wouldn't believe the number of innocent people who've been convicted because of mistaken identity."

"All right. The boys won't talk to Detective Crawley." Kevin gulped down the rest of his water. "I just hope this decision doesn't come back to haunt us."

SEVENTEEN

Monday morning Glen Healy's report was on Oracio Crawley's desk. Oracio had asked his partner to go to Mrs. Luna's home once she was out of the hospital and get her statement. The day she'd identified Ariel Levine, she'd been too frail to give one.

Two portions concerned him.

Officer Healy: Did your attacker say anything to you?

Mrs. Luna: He said something about making me pretty. And some other things I can't remember. Or maybe he didn't. Maybe I just dreamt them. I have nightmares all the time.

Mrs. Luna's confusion would make her a terrible witness.

Officer Healy: Had you ever seen your attacker before?

Mrs. Luna: I'm not sure. A couple of hours before a man his size, who kept his head down, came into the store singing. When I asked if I could help him, he left.

The man Linda Smythe had thrown out of Discount Delight had been singing.

Probably the crazy guy had gone to a number of stores in the shopping center. But that didn't make him the killer. He's not the one who fled in Virginia Levine's Land Rover. Yet, Consuela Blanco had denied seeing Ariel drive the Land Rover the day of the murder.

Oracio called Sissy.

"The key is how long it takes to drive from the Levines' house to Lingerie for Life," Sissy said. "If it's fifteen minutes or so round trip, it would explain why she never noticed the Land Rover was gone."

"I'll have Glen Healy drive it right away," Oracio replied.

"Not until next Monday. The road repairs that were going on around the shopping center when the murder occurred will be completed at the end of this week. I don't want anything slowing him up."

Sissy thought of everything.

Her instructions continued. "First drive every conceivable route between the store and the house in your own car. When you tell Healy to drive it officially, have him use the route that takes the shortest time."

"I wish I could arrest him now."

"You can't. The District Attorney let him go to Israel to visit family."

"He'll never come back," Oracio replied.

"We're going to lay low. Nothing to the press about him or the case so he gets a false sense of security and returns. Then we'll nab him."

So when Loretta Sanchez called a few days later, demanding to know when Ariel would be arrested, Oracio said, "It would help our investigation if you didn't print anything about the case for a while."

"What's going on? Luis and Angelina Sorento have stopped pestering me about keeping the story alive, and now you want me to downplay it."

Sissy had somehow gotten the victim's children to go along with her plan. And she must have convinced Norty Walsh to ignore the story for a while since there had been nothing in the *Post-Gazette* about it either.

"When this phase of the investigation is over, I'll call you with a scoop," Oracio promised.

***

Ariel had been gone one week and was following his usual pattern. He neither wrote nor called. Mara tried phoning him, but with Tel Aviv eight hours ahead of Houston, for six days in a row all she reached was the answering machine at his Aunt Frieda's home.

During that time Mara scoured the *Post-Gazette* every day but found no mention of Ariel or of the lingerie shop murder. Josef assured her he saw nothing either.

Certain there would be a story about Ariel's trip in the *Weekly Bulletin,* she opened that newspaper with trepidation on Friday but discovered no reference to Ariel.

Instead of feeling relief, she experienced a sense of unease.

On Saturday during dinner she shared her concerns with Josef.

"Don't you think it's odd that, after giving it so much publicity, the newspapers have been ignoring the lingerie shop murder?" she asked.

Josef put his fork down. "Maybe the police have a new suspect they're investigating so they're not feeding the papers information about Ariel."

Mara took her napkin and removed a tad of marinara from Josef's moustache. "I hope you're right."

Sunday Ariel answered the phone at his aunt's house and sounded ecstatic. "I've been visiting kids I grew up with. Some of them have just come home from backpacking trips. I even got to see Dov Lieberman. He was home on leave from the Air Force and was so happy to see me that he couldn't stop hugging me. I told him I'm gong to apply to the Air Force Monday."

When Mara reached her son four days later, he sounded dejected. "I failed the eye test so I can't be a pilot. If I join, I'll get some desk job. I don't think it's worth it."

Thank God, Ariel wouldn't be in danger. But didn't he want to serve Israel in some way?

Three days later he unexpectedly called. "I'm bored; Aunt Frieda's getting on my nerves; and I miss everyone in Houston. I'm coming home tomorrow."

Before she could ask if Simon knew about Ariel's decision, he said, "Dad told me the newspapers haven't mentioned me the two weeks I've been gone so he's okay with me coming back." Ariel laughed. "He can't stop bragging about how his plan worked."

EIGHTEEN

Mara and Benjie arrived at Bush Intercontinental Airport twenty-five minutes before Ariel's flight came in from Israel and waited an additional forty minutes while he cleared customs.

When Ariel released Mara from his bear hug, she looked up into his grinning face and noticed dark circles under his eyes.

"I was too excited about coming home to sleep on the plane," Ariel said as Benjie took his carryon bag.

"Wait. I want to give you your presents." Ariel grabbed the small green duffel bag from his brother and opened it while people walked around the family.

He gave Benjie a white skullcap embroidered in blue in Hebrew with, "If I forsake you, oh, Jerusalem."

He handed Mara a small charm—a hand with the palm facing out, fingers spread open. It was made of red glass with a gold loop on top for a chain to go through. "The saleswoman said it was a chasma which keeps away the Evil Eye."

"I'll wear it all the time," Mara said.

"The police dropped your car back at Dad's on Friday," Benjie told his brother.

"Let's get it now."

"You'll eat first," Mara insisted.

After dinner Ariel fell asleep on the couch and slept through the night.

The next day Mara dropped her son off in front of Simon's house and laughed as she watched him hug the hood of his three-year-old white Honda Prelude.

"I hung out with my buddies all day and tonight we're getting together again," he told her at dinner.

Mara was thrilled to see the old Ariel again, the carefree boy he'd been before becoming a murder suspect.

She touched the chasma, now on a gold chain around her neck, and hoped it would last.

***

Sissy answered the phone and heard Luis Sorento.

"He's back."

"How do you know?" she asked.

"He drove his car away from his father's house."

Sissy didn't like the implication that Luis had staked out Simon Levine's house. If he were discovered, it would generate unfavorable publicity, and she might somehow be associated with his actions. But this wasn't the time to challenge him. Instead she said, "We found eight white fibers in the Land Rover. The lab tech who can show they're consistent with fibers from bras in the shop will be back after the new year."

"I'm tired of your excuses. You're going to see just how tired."

***

Angelina placed the platter of meat loaf in front of Luis. Instead of taking any, he startled her by banging the table with his fist. "The bastard's back, and they still haven't arrested him."

"They can't wait much longer. Everyone knows he did it."

"We can't wait much longer. We need to sell the business while we still can."

"No."

"Sister, I want to leave Houston."

"I'll be all alone."

Luis left his seat, bent down next to Angelina's chair and put his arm around her shoulder. "You'll keep the store. Claudia will be back soon and the customers are crazy about you."

"But if you want to move . . . ."

"Just give me the house to sell," Luis said.

"You can't mean that. We've lived here all our lives."

"I need money to make a new start. It's too painful staying in Houston. The memories of what happened. Mama gone."

"Where would I live?"

"You'll rent a place, no upkeep like with a house."

"With paying the security guard, there's not enough money left for a nice place," Angelina said.

"You won't need the guard once Levine turns himself in."

"He'll never do that."

"He might, if he understands it's the safest thing to do."

***

Mara should have known it was too good to be true. Ariel was planning to resume his classes in mid January at the start of the winter semester.

But it all began again the first Friday of the new year.

The *Weekly Bulletin* had another interview of the Sorento siblings with Luis being quoted. "If you have money and influence, you can send your son to Israel and keep him out of jail."

He went on to say that the only reason Ariel came back was because he knew he wouldn't be arrested. "Certain kinds of people are protected in this city."

"It's just one article," she assured Ariel. "We should have expected that some note would be made of your having been away."

"I think it's going to get worse. My apartment manager said a huge guy came by looking for me, claiming to be a reporter from the *Post-Gazette.*"

"Give up the apartment and move back here until things die down," Mara suggested, and when Ariel immediately agreed, she realized how worried he was.

The crescendo continued. Monday the *Houston Post-Gazette* reminded readers how Israel can refuse to extradite its citizens and instead have them tried there. "Had Levine been indicted by a Harris County grand jury when he was in Israel, he could have stayed there and forced Harris County taxpayers to come up with the money to send witnesses and prosecutors to Israel for his trial."

"It figures each paper would have one go at it," Mara told Ariel. "Don't let it get to you."

But when Mara came home from work Wednesday, she found Ariel in his pajamas lying on the couch watching television. She asked if he'd visited any of his friends, and he said he'd been too tired. He ate just half a piece of lasagna for dinner.

Thursday Ariel stayed in bed all day. He refused to eat, saying he was tired and needed to sleep.

Mara could take him to a psychiatrist who'd likely prescribe anti-depressants. But if the newspapers found out, they'd present her son as a crazed killer in need of psychiatric help. Ariel would pull out of his funk if the publicity stopped.

Mara insisted Ariel go to Simon's for dinner Friday night. It would force him to leave the house.

***

Simon read the article in the *Weekly Bulletin* and then the one in the *Post-Gazette*. Mara was probably blaming him for the publicity and poisoning Ariel with that idea.

But he had something more serious to worry about. Tuesday when he walked out his front door, he found a purple daisy with its head sliced from its stem. It must be from the same person who'd left a bunch of dead flowers before Ariel went to Israel. But why had he resorted to just one this time? Unless it represented Herlinda Sorento's slit throat. Though the thought chilled him, Simon decided not to contact the police. They'd tip off the press.

Wednesday morning Virginia called him at work. "There were a group of purple daisies in a circle at our front door. Each one had a slice in its stem."

"Count the daisies," Simon ordered.

"Twelve."

The same number of stab wounds as Claudia Luna had received.

Simon stayed up Wednesday night, keeping the porch light on and sneaking glances out his living room drapes. He saw no cars stopping near his house and heard no noises on his porch.

There were no flowers waiting Thursday or Friday, but Simon had trouble relaxing.

When he arrived home Friday, he found the note Virginia had pinned to the brown cork bulletin board in the kitchen. She'd be home late so he needed to walk the dogs.

Though Simon had never had pets until he'd married Virginia, he'd become fond of her two Dalmatians. Duke was so patient with children that he'd stayed still for twenty minutes while their seven-year-old neighbor had tried to count his spots.

Simon walked out the laundry room door onto the carport and called the dogs who were in the small yard next to it.

They didn't come.

He heard Shannon whimpering, and found her standing over Duke.

"Let's go, you two. It's time for your walk."

Shannon continued whimpering, and Duke didn't move.

Simon bent over him.

White foam surrounded the Dalmatian's mouth and his eyes were closed.

Next to him lay the remnant of a piece of raw meat, its metallic odor wafting into Simon's nostrils.

NINETEEN

Simon threw what was left of the meat over the fence where it couldn't hurt Shannon.

But how could he protect his family? A restraining order against Luis Sorento who seemed the likely culprit? Simon couldn't prove it. And maybe it was someone else, a person with a vigilante mentality convinced by the newspapers that Ariel was guilty.

Whoever it was had provided a warning of what they could do to Ariel. Simon couldn't let his son come to the house.

Before he could go in to call Ariel, Virginia pulled into the carport in her Land Rover. She got out and headed towards her husband, her mouth open as though about to shout a greeting. She stopped. "What's wrong?"

Without waiting for an answer, Virginia ran to the dogs, Shannon still whimpering over the supine Duke.

"Oh, my God," she said as she sat in the grass beside Duke and cradled his head in her arms while Shannon rested her head on her mistress's shoulder.

"He's been poisoned," Simon said.

"Help me get him into the Land Rover. The vet will know what's wrong."

"It's too late."

But Virginia, her green silk pantsuit streaked with dirt, was crying and trying to lift the sixty pound dog. So Simon carried Duke to the back of the Land Rover where he gently put him inside. Before he could close the door, a car pulled up behind his wife's.

As Ariel got out, Virginia screamed, "Move your car. I have to get Duke to the vet."

"What's wrong with him?" Ariel asked.

"Your father thinks he's been poisoned."

"Oh, no," Ariel said. He ran over to the Land Rover and stared at the inert body of the dog who shared his bed when he slept over at Simon's and Virginia's. Ariel's face paled. He threw up on the concrete drive.

Simon removed a handkerchief from his pocket and wiped Ariel's mouth. "Go inside. I'll be right there." He took the keys from the teen and moved his car. Virginia sped away.

Simon went into the kitchen and found Ariel sitting at the table, his head resting in his arms. He lifted his tear stained face. "What kind of person would poison a dog?"

Simon didn't have an answer.

"They'll get me next," Ariel said.

"I'll never let that happen," Simon assured him. A plan for protecting Ariel came to him, but it would help to have Mara's support. "We're going to your mother's."

With Friday afternoon traffic, the trip took over half an hour. Ariel didn't speak, just stared straight ahead. A white Dodge van was in Mara's driveway. Simon, who still had Ariel's keys, used one to get into the townhouse.

Mara and Josef were in the kitchen, preparing a large salad, she in charge of tomatoes and avocados and he responsible for lettuce and purple onions. Mara was surprised to hear the front door open. Neither boy was due home, and no one called out. She looked at Josef who moved cautiously while she followed him to the living room. There she saw Simon leading Ariel to the couch.

"What's wrong?" Mara asked.

"I'll tell you as soon as he leaves," Simon replied, pointing at Josef.

"The hell he's leaving," Mara said.

Ariel gazed at his mother. "They poisoned Virginia's dog. There're going to get me next."

Mara suppressed a gasp. She didn't want Ariel to know how much that news frightened her. She sat down next to her son and hugged him protectively. "No one is going to harm you."

Simon looked somber. "There's been no threat against Ariel, but naturally he's worried."

"Maybe we can get him police protection," Mara said.

"We can't prove who did it. And telling them will only result in more publicity."

Ariel spoke in such a soft tone that Mara had trouble hearing. "I can't stay in Houston, Mom. They'll get me. I know they will."

"But where would you go? Another trip to Israel would feed the newspaper frenzy."

Simon had a ready answer. "He'll do the six month backpacking trip I did at his age, and his friends are doing now. It's a rite of passage for Israeli boys."

When Mara didn't respond, Simon went on, "Of course, I'll have Greg Dickson check with the District Attorney before Ariel leaves."

Mara looked at Josef, who was standing next to the couch, his arms folded over his chest. "I opposed the first trip," he said, "but if there's any question about Ariel's safety . . ."

Simon cut in. "Exactly. So I'll call Dickson, and we'll start making the arrangements." Her former husband's next comment reinforced Mara's fear for her son. "Meanwhile, make sure Ariel doesn't leave the house until I take him to the airport."

No sooner had Simon left her townhouse than Mara, thinking of all the problems that had resulted from Ariel's first trip, began having doubts about her decision to let him go again. But when Ariel sat listless at the dining room table, saying he was sure he would throw up if he ate, she realized that for the sake of his mental health, as well as his physical safety, he had to leave Houston.

"Where are you thinking of traveling?" she asked.

"A lot of the guys backpack in the far east. Thailand's really cheap. Maybe I'll start there and move on."

He could come back when all the publicity died down. Surely as time went on and Ariel wasn't indicted, the press would realize that credible evidence against him didn't exist. Mara fingered the chasma on the gold chain around her neck. With the way things had been going, she couldn't count on that.

Nonetheless, she put on a cheery façade. "Make a list of everything you need, and I'll go shopping this weekend."

When Ariel went upstairs to start his task, Josef looked at Mara. "I'm sorry I said anything."

"I hate it, but he has to go. I'd never forgive myself if anything happened to him."

***

A little after seven o'clock Friday evening Sissy Kleinman reached Sandy Turner at the police lab and asked for her report.

"The fibers found in the Land Rover are consistent with those found in some bras at the murder scene but they're also likely consistent with . . ."

"All you have to tell the grand jury is that they're consistent with bras in the shop. That's the physical evidence I need to get Ariel Levine indicted. Understand?"

"Yes," Sandy answered softly.

No sooner had Sissy hung up, than the phone rang.

Without identifying himself, Reardon Jones started talking. "Greg Dickson chased me down. Asked if Ariel Levine could leave Houston. Any reason I should have told him no?"

"Is he going back to Israel?"

"Doesn't seem so. Dickson mentioned a back packing trip, likely somewhere in the far east."

"No problem," Sissy said.

Here was her chance to indict Ariel when he was gone and make it look like he'd fled.

TWENTY

Saturday Mara bought Ariel a large red waterproof backpack. Sunday she joined him in his room while he packed but discovered he didn't need her help. All he could fit in it were one towel and two changes of clothes.

"Do you think you'll find washers and dryers often enough?" Mara asked as she snuck in an extra pair of underpants when Ariel was in the bathroom getting his toothbrush.

"It's normal to smell a little on this kind of trip."

"Maybe if I knew where you were going . . ."

"Part of it's how far my money will take me. Monday morning I'm cleaning out my bank account."

Mara bit her lower lip. That implied some sort of finality, almost as though Ariel wasn't coming back. She blamed Simon and Greg Dickson for the decision that Ariel would spend his own hard earned money rather than his father's for the trip. The attorney had told Simon that in case there was a trial, he didn't want Ariel to come across as a spoiled rich kid dependent on his father's largess.

"How will we reach you if you if we don't know where you are?"

"You can't reach someone who's backpacking. I'll stay in touch."

Mara stopped herself from reminding Ariel that typically he did no such thing. She wanted to keep the peace before he left, and she wanted him to enjoy himself his last night before the trip. "Invite your friends over tonight for a farewell dinner. I'll make whatever you want."

Ariel didn't speak for a few seconds. "I can't. Dad said not to tell anyone where I am."

Mara's breath quickened. She'd told herself that Simon's house had been the target of some crazy person because Ariel had been there before and after the murder. Her townhouse wasn't involved so she'd convinced herself he was safe with her. But now that Ariel was afraid to even let his friends know where he was, she wasn't so sure. Not wanting her son to pick up on her fear, she smiled. "I'll still let you choose tonight's menu."

So on Ariel's last night home, he and she and Benjie ate turkey and cornbread stuffing just as they had the day after Thanksgiving a few hours before the murder at Lingerie for Life.

After dinner Mara said she'd clean up so the brothers could have some time together. She refused Benjie's request to be late for school the next day to see Ariel off. She claimed it was because he had chemistry the first period, but it was so she'd have Ariel to herself in the morning.

She walked into the living room and heard Benjie say, "Every day you'll wake up and go wherever you feel like. I wish it were me."

"I wish it were you, too."

***

Monday morning Simon pulled into Mara's drive fifteen minutes early. She wasn't ready to give up her son. So when her former husband came to the door, Mara told him Ariel hadn't eaten breakfast and would join him at nine as they'd agreed.

Ariel walked down the stairs dressed in jeans, a black jersey and white high tops. Mara pulled her son to her and hugged him tightly. She felt a shudder pass through him.

"You don't have to go," she assured him. "We'll find another solution."

He gently broke from her embrace. "I can't stay here. I'm going to treat the trip like an adventure and try to enjoy myself."

"That's my boy," Mara said with an enthusiasm she didn't feel.

Mother and son went into the kitchen and tried to eat their French toast. Mara had trouble swallowing, each bite feeling rough against her throat. Ariel cut the fried bread into little pieces and spread them around his plate.

She poured him a second glass of orange juice, wanting him to have lots of vitamin C. He drank half.

At exactly nine, they heard Simon's car horn.

Mara followed Ariel into the hall where his bulging red backpack was waiting.

"God bless you, and keep you safe and well," she whispered as she stood on her tiptoes and kissed her son's cheek.

"I love you, Mom."

She hugged him one last time.

***

"All set?" Simon asked as Ariel tossed his backpack onto the back seat and sat down next to him in the front.

"Yep."

Ariel didn't look at his father but instead crossed his arms against his chest and stared out the side window of the Buick.

"Did I ever tell you all the places I saw when I did my trek?"

"Whatever," Ariel said.

When they arrived at the bank, Simon was about to get out of the car when his son said, "I can handle this myself."

As Simon explained how Ariel should carry just a little cash, and mainly Travelers Checks, his son left the Buick and slammed the door.

Simon rolled down his window and felt the warm breeze of a January day in Houston. He drummed his fingers against the steering wheel. What was wrong with Ariel? He never lost his temper. It had to be the result of misgivings about the trip–misgivings Mara must have fueled.

They traveled in silence to Bush Intercontinental Airport. When they arrived, Simon asked, "Have you decided where you're going? I need to know which terminal to drop you off."

"The international terminal, D. I'll decide when I get there."

"You're such a good son in all ways but one. You forget us when you're away. This time write, call."

"It's because I'm such a good son that I have to go."

"What do you mean?"

"I told you I didn't want to housesit. I said you should ask Benjie for a change. But you said I was the responsible one. He'd throw parties, he'd drive Virginia's Land Rover." Ariel shook his head. "It's amazing how Virginia has you pussy whipped while you treat Mom like shit."

"Ariel . . ."

"All those years I worked at keeping you and Mom together. Then after the divorce I helped her all I could. I took Benjie

111

everywhere while she was at law school."

Simon parked in front of Terminal D and looked at his son. His face had taken on a pink hue, and he was staring straight ahead.

"The psychiatrist Mom took me to just before the divorce told me it was natural to be angry, and that it was healthy to express that anger. Express it? If I had, I would have exploded."

The fury in Ariel's voice shocked Simon.

Ariel looked at his father, and laughed, an eerie sound, which reverberated in the car.

"What's the matter, Dad? Are you wondering if I exploded the day after Thanksgiving?"

Then he was out of the front seat, grabbing his backpack from the rear and running into the airport.

Simon opened the door to follow him and heard a loud voice. "You can't park here. Get moving, or I'll give you a ticket."

By the time he parked, it would be too late to find Ariel so Simon drove off, wondering if Mara had been right. He'd thought her idea of taking the boys to a psychiatrist was ridiculous. It was normal to be a little upset when your parents were getting divorced. Then when Mara had suggested Ariel see the doctor a second time because he was keeping his anger inside, Simon had told her she should be grateful for that and not try to change him.

Now Simon knew it wasn't just the divorce that infuriated Ariel. It was helping Mara with Benjie and him with his house, and who knew what else.

But surely that hadn't turned his son into a killer.

TWENTY-ONE

After ten days Mara hadn't heard from Ariel and had no idea where he was. So when his friend Skipper Gutman called, Mara thought Ariel had contacted Skipper who had a message for her. But his halting speech told her he was calling about something else.

"Ah . . . Ms. Levine . . . ah . . . I got this letter or notice or something that says I have to appear before a Harris County Grand Jury. Farrell Miller got one, too. His dad's going to call you. It's about Ariel and the murder at that shop."

Mara's stomach clenched.

But what she heard made no sense. Why would the District Attorney let Ariel leave the country if he were going to indict him for murder? Had Simon lied about Greg Dickson getting permission for Ariel to go? She had to stay calm while talking to Skipper, ask him pertinent questions.

He told her his grand jury appearance was a week from Monday.

"I guess they want to know at exactly what times you and Farrell were playing basketball with Ariel the day after Thanksgiving. Once they realize he didn't have time to commit a murder, all his troubles should be over."

She called Simon. "A grand jury is going to decide if Ariel should be indicted for murder. Tell your high priced attorney we're meeting him first thing in the morning."

***

Mara arrived at Dickson's waiting room to find that both she and Simon were wearing black suits, hers with a tailored white blouse and his with a beige shirt and black and brown tie. They looked like they were dressed for a funeral.

As soon as Greg Dickson ushered them into his office, Mara asked, "Who gave Ariel permission to go on his trip?"

"District Attorney Reardon Jones," Greg replied.

"What proof do you have?"

"I got his permission to tape it."

Mara looked at Simon who wouldn't meet her gaze. If Dickson had felt a need to tape the conversation, it meant he was concerned about Ariel taking this second trip. Mara suspected Simon had insisted, and Dickson had gone along with it.

The attorney took a small cassette player out of the middle drawer of his desk. Jones's words filled the room. "Unless you hear anything different from me by nine Monday morning, assume he can go anywhere he wants."

"You're sure the District Attorney didn't try to reach you?" Mara asked.

"Absolutely not."

Mara sat down on a blue pigskin chair in front of Dickson's desk.

"Then what do you make of this?"

"The good news is that our investigator interviewed the boys who said Ariel arrived at the game about 4:30 or a little before."

"You'll make sure they testify like that," Simon said.

"I won't be in the grand jury room. Even if Ariel were testifying, I could only wait outside in case he wanted to consult me."

"That's crazy," Simon shouted.

"It's the law," Dickson replied.

Simon spoke more quietly. "Then maybe it's better we don't know where Ariel is. He might get flustered if you weren't with him, get angry and say something stupid."

Simon wasn't making sense. Ariel never lost his temper, and his absence worried Mara. "Do you think letting Ariel leave was a set up so the District Attorney could indict him when he was gone?"

"Reardon Jones doesn't act that way, but . . ."

"But what?" Mara asked.

"That possibility exists with Sissy Kleinman."

***

As Sissy expected, Oracio Crawley, always anxious to please her, arrived at her office five minutes early. His blue blazer sported a polyester shine.

"You're a miracle worker," he said as he leaned over the desk and shook her hand, holding it a few seconds too long.

"Your hard work is more responsible than anything for getting us in front of the grand jury," Sissy replied.

Oracio grinned.

"But now we need to make sure we get our indictment," she added.

Through deft questions, she learned that Oracio thought Andrew Block would be a good witness whereas Claudia Luna would not.

"That's fine," Sissy assured the detective. "When I tell the grand jurors she's still too traumatized to testify, it'll remind them how horrific the crime was."

"And then when I describe the bloody crime scene . . ."

Sissy wished she were dealing with someone smarter. "Do you think that might be a problem, considering there was no blood in the Land Rover?"

Oracio blushed. "Good point, but how are you going to get around that?"

"No need to mention it. Instead Sandy Turner from the crime lab will testify that eight fibers found in the Land Rover are consistent with those in bras from the shop."

Oracio nodded but looked concerned.

"There's a problem?" Sissy asked.

"The kid claims to have an alibi for all but about thirty-five or forty-five minutes, but his friends refused to talk to me."

"That's why I summoned them before the grand jury, where they have to answer questions."

Noticing Oracio's slight frown, Sissy continued. "Don't worry. By the time I finish with them, they won't be able to say for sure when he arrived."

"I'd bet on you any time," Oracio said.

"You know the old saying, 'A Harris County Grand Jury will indict a ham sandwich if an assistant district attorney asks it to.'"

Oracio gave her a thumbs-up as he left her office.

The ham sandwich remark was true with one exception. One really strong willed grand juror could put a monkey wrench in her plans.

The phone rang. "Ms. Kleinman, this is Greg Dickson, Ariel Levine's attorney. I called District Attorney Jones with a question he said you could answer."

"Fire away," Sissy said.

"Considering there's no physical evidence to link my client to the murder scene, I'm wondering why you're taking the case before a grand jury."

Sissy waited a couple of seconds before answering. "I'm afraid your information is old, Mr. Dickson."

"What do you mean?"

"Eight fibers in the Land Rover are consistent with those in bras from Lingerie for Life."

"Consistent with and identical to are very different creatures."

"That will be up to the grand jury to decide."

***

The moment Simon got off the phone with Greg Dickson, he yelled for Virginia. Then he remembered she was walking Shannon. Once the vet had confirmed Duke had been poisoned, Virginia had insisted Shannon only be allowed outside when one of them was with her. Otherwise the Dalmatian had the run of the house. Simon couldn't object, considering that Duke's death had been an outcome of Ariel's troubles. He'd even gone along with Shannon sleeping at the bottom of their bed until the dog whined when the couple made love.

Simon paced in the kitchen in the space bordered on one side by the double ovens and stainless steel paneled refrigerator and on the other side by the granite rectangular island. When Virginia and the Dalmatian came through the door, Simon asked, "Have you bought any bras recently?"

"What?"

"Have you?"

"No."

"What about since you've owned the Land Rover?"

"Probably. What's this all about?"

"Eight fibers found in the Land Rover are consistent with those from bras sold at Lingerie for Life. But Dickson says it's likely they're consistent with fibers in most bras."

"Any bras I bought would have been in a bag."

"The bag must have been on the front seat and when you came to a sudden stop, the bras fell out."

"Don't raise your voice to me. I won't put up with anyone losing his temper."

"Has Ariel ever lost his temper with you?"

"Of course not. Why would you ask?"

"Crazy thoughts keep running through my head."

***

Virginia left their bedroom to the sound of Simon's snoring. Shannon padded down the hall from the kitchen and walked with Virginia into the den, where she put her head in her mistress's lap as soon as Virginia sat on the couch.

Virginia stroked the Dalmatian. "I can't believe how stupid I am."

She hadn't thought fast enough about why the police lab found bra fibers in the Land Rover or she would have accepted Simon's excuse that new bras had fallen out of a bag.

She couldn't admit how it had happened. Simon would leave her.

It had started so innocently.

Virginia had gone to a dinner for current and retired advertising executives.

They backed into each other during the cocktail hour. Virginia turned around about to admonish, "Be careful," when the vision of Myles Danforth's cocky smile, blue eyes and perfectly coifed blond hair greeted her.

He spoke in his deep baritone. "My fantasy come true. You're here."

Virginia caught her breath. "It's been years."

"Time doesn't matter."

"It does for me. I'm married now."

"I was then."

Virginia thought of Simon who'd told her he hadn't dated when he and Mara were separated because he was still a married man. He'd never understand how she could have had a relationship with Myles.

"Let's talk in the hall," she said. "You go first. I'll follow in a bit."

Virginia spent the next few minutes socializing and then headed towards Myles who stood at the end of the hall near the exit. She worried about where this meeting would lead but the closer she came the more his animal magnetism drew her in. He'd been the lover who'd pleasured her the most, sometimes by the force of his lovemaking and other times by his knowledge of every spot on her body that responded to his gentle touch. She suppressed a sigh.

He stroked the top of her hand. "I've missed you."

"You chose to move to California."

"I had to give my marriage another chance, and California's a gold mine for the advertising business." He paused. "But I never stopped loving you."

Virginia pulled her hand away. "I stopped loving you when I met Simon, my husband."

"I don't want to believe that."

"It's true."

"Okay. But we can still be friends, can't we?"

"I guess."

"After dinner would you drive a friend to his hotel so we can catch up like old friends do?"

Virginia didn't respond.

"It's the Ritz Carlton, just a few miles away."

"I don't want to start any gossip. We'll sit at separate tables. After dinner I'll pick you up on the west side of the building in my Land Rover."

Throughout the meal Virginia smiled and nodded at her dinner companions as though she were paying attention to their conversations.

Myles was waiting. He got into the Land Rover and kissed her cheek. Before Virginia could protest, he said, "That's how old friends greet each other."

"How's Gloria?"

"We're divorced. Tell me about your husband."

As Virginia said, "He's an Israeli software executive," she heard how boring it sounded.

"Must be a solid kind of guy."

"He's great."

Flustered by her need to defend Simon, Virginia took the

wrong driveway and wound up on the deliveries only entrance of the Ritz Carlton. She stopped for a moment to figure out whether she had to turn around or if she could go straight ahead. Myles leaned over and took the key from the ignition. "This is a perfect place. No one's here." His lips covered hers. His hands found her breasts. All the old excitement revived. But when he unbuttoned her blouse and put his tongue between her cleavage, Virginia struggled away from him.

"You want it," Myles murmured.

And she did.

But her survival instinct wouldn't let her succumb. Somehow Simon would find out, and she'd be alone.

"Get out now," she commanded.

"You're sure?"

"Yes," she whispered.

And then he was gone.

She couldn't tell Simon why the police lab had found bra fibers in the Land Rover, let alone testify about it in a public courtroom.

She needed to stop worrying.

Eight bra fibers weren't going to convict Ariel.

***

Mara heard the doorbell ring but didn't move from the couch. If it were Josef coming for the dinner she hadn't prepared, he'd use his key.

The front door opened. "Mara, what's wrong?" Josef asked.

"There were bra fibers found in the Land Rover, so they're going to say they came from those at Lingerie for Life."

Josef sat down next to her. "The grand jurors have to be smarter than to jump to that conclusion."

"The assistant district attorney you warned me about, the one Dickson was concerned about, too, is presenting the case against Ariel. I did some research. Sissy Kleinman has sent thirteen people to death row."

"She seems to be trying to be fair. Ariel's friends will be witnesses."

"Farrell Miller's father told me that neither his son nor Skipper Gutman would talk to the police. They'll have to answer questions before the grand jury."

"That'll help Ariel."

"Not if she twists their answers."

"Mara, perhaps you're being a little . . ."

"A little paranoid?" she asked.

"Well, perhaps."

"Easy for you to say. It's not your son whose life is in the balance."

"You know how fond I am of the boy."

"But you haven't raised him, so you can't be sure he's incapable of murder."

"I have complete faith in him. But I have the objectivity to judge the other side's tactics logically."

Objectivity? Logic? No. Mara needed to trust her instincts, and Josef's advice was always at war with them, making him an impediment, preventing her from doing all she could.

"I don't feel like eating dinner," Mara said. "Why don't you just go?"

TWENTY-TWO

Sissy Kleinman strode into the grand jury room in the Criminal Courts Building in Houston, Texas, and surveyed the twelve grand jurors and two alternates sitting around a horseshoe shaped Formica topped table. She noted seven Caucasians, four African Americans and three Hispanics. She smiled at them as she situated herself behind a blond wood podium. The court reporter, a woman who looked barely old enough to be out of high school, sat to her left and the witness chair stood to her right. Using her most pronounced East Texas drawl, the assistant district attorney said, "I'm Sissy Kleinman and I'm honored to be workin' with y'all. You're here because you're the cream of the crop."

Thirteen of the fourteen people returned her smile.

"Together we're going to perform a sacred duty. We'll decide whether to indict Ariel Levine, a fellow citizen, for murder."

An elderly African American woman bit her lower lip and a middle-aged Hispanic man stopped blowing his nose and looked up at Sissy.

"I'm sure you're thinking that the District Attorney's office wouldn't bring you this matter unless we believed you should indict. You're right. But remember you have the final say, and I respect that."

"Have you ever had a situation where a grand jury you thought should indict, didn't?" the man who hadn't smiled asked.

"Well, Mr. . . . ."

"Dr. Goldstein," he interjected, emphasizing his title.

"Excuse me, Dr. Goldstein, sir. That hasn't happened to me, perhaps because I've never brought a case unless I'm convinced there is enough evidence for a trial."

Thirteen grand jurors nodded approvingly.

"Now that I know Dr. Goldstein, let me meet the rest of you. As we go around the table, please introduce yourself and tell us a little about you."

Sissy learned the majority of the grand jurors were retired teachers, nurses and small business owners.

She reminded them where they could find the restrooms and coffee machines, and suggested a short break. Left in the empty room, Sissy tapped her fingers against the podium. Dr. Goldstein could pose a huge problem. With a name like Myron Goldstein, he was almost certainly a Jew.

She had no control over who was chosen for the grand jury. The judge in the court under whose auspices the grand jury served appointed citizens as commissioners, and they selected the grand jurors, almost always people they considered leaders in their respective ethnic communities or people like doctors, whom they held in high regard. So she'd wound up with Goldstein who likely was out to protect one of his own.

Sissy was in such deep concentration that she was startled by the hoarse voice of Myron Goldstein. "I need to talk to you."

She hoped he was going to tell her he didn't have time to serve on the grand jury. Sissy would do whatever she could to help him get off.

She motioned him to the corner of the room.

"When you said Ariel Levine is the guy who we'd be looking at, I wondered if I'm allowed to serve on the grand jury."

Dr. Goldstein explained that the company Ariel's father worked for had sold him defective software for his office computer a couple of years before.

"When I refused to pay, the bastards sued me, claiming I didn't know how to use it. They won. I even had to pay their attorney's fees," the doctor said, his face becoming more crimson the longer he talked.

"It's outrageous the way our civil justice system works. But none of what you've told me disqualifies you from deciding whether the son should be indicted."

"Good," Dr. Goldstein said, his heavily lined face breaking into a broad grin.

When all the grand jurors returned, Sissy wove the story of the crime for them in the same tone she used when she read to her younger daughter.

"You can imagine how Detective Crawley felt when he learned there'd been a murder at Lingerie for Life. He realized the victim

122

would either be a cancer patient or one of the women who offered them help at this terrible time in their lives."

Mrs. Arthur, an African American retired teacher, dabbed her eye with a tissue.

"Detective Crawley knew he was dealing with a monster. And he vowed to bring him to justice."

Sissy opened the door of the grand jury room and Detective Crawley, dressed in a neat brown suit and starched white shirt, which contrasted with his usual more casual attire, walked in. He looked each grand juror in the eyes as Sissy had instructed him and sat in the armchair to her right. Under the assistant district attorney's questioning Oracio told about his finding one woman dead, another near death and a man severely injured.

"What led you to Ariel Levine?"

"A license plate number taken down by Dr. Andrew Block, a witness at the scene."

"Did he later that day identify Levine as the killer?"

"Yes."

"Unless any of the grand jurors have questions for you, Detective Crawley, I'll let you get back to your important work and call Dr. Block as a witness."

When no one spoke, Crawley got up, smiled at the fourteen people in front of him and left.

Andrew Block entered and took the seat Crawley had vacated.

He told how he saw someone running from the direction of the lingerie shop, took down the license plate number of the Land Rover used for the get away and then went into the store.

"Detective Crawley believes I saved Mrs. Luna's life by the medical attention I gave her," Andrew said.

"What kind of doctor are you?" Dr. Goldstein called out.

"A chiropractor."

Goldstein shook his head.

Sissy quickly continued. "Did you identify Ariel Levine in both a photo and a video line-up as the man you saw running from the shop and getting into the Land Rover?"

"I did."

"If there are no questions from the grand jurors, you may leave."

When Block was out of the room, Sissy said, "Claudia Luna,

the victim who was stabbed twelve times, also identified Levine in both line-ups. She's still so traumatized that I didn't call her as a witness. She's just not ready to relive that horrible day."

Mrs. Arthur took another tissue out of her sturdy black handbag.

Sissy released the grand jurors for lunch, walked outside into a humid Houston day and found Norty Walsh leaning against the building.

"How's it going?" asked the reporter for the *Houston Post-Gazette*.

"You know grand jury proceedings are secret," Sissy said.

"Seeing Crawley and Block grinning as they walked out told me all I need to know." He paused. "There's a rumor the kid's left town."

"Bet your readers might take that as a sign of guilt, don't you?"

"Anything to keep the future District Attorney happy." Norty winked at Sissy and sauntered off.

After lunch Sissy introduced Sandy Turner to the grand jurors. The technician, wearing her white lab coat and reading from her notes, testified that eight fibers were found on the steering wheel and on the front passenger door handle of the Land Rover.

"Were the fibers consistent with those in bras from Lingerie for Life?" Sissy asked.

"Yes."

Mr. Cortez, whose family owned a hardware store, raised his hand.

"I'm no bra expert," he said to smiles from his fellow grand jurors, "but it seems to me that bras are bras so couldn't the fibers have come from any bras?"

Sissy replied, "But for there to be another explanation for where they were found, either someone was driving without her shirt on, or some contortionist found a way to make love on the front seat of a Land Rover."

When the other grand jurors laughed, Mr. Cortez blushed.

"Some of the confusion may come from the fact that we don't have the tests done on the blood found in the back of the Land Rover," Sissy said.

Mrs. Arthur gasped.

"So, of course, you can't consider that."

After excusing the grand jurors for the day, Sissy walked out the door into the hall and saw a boy dressed in Gothic black sitting on a bench beside a woman who might be his mother. Across from them a boy with blond ringlets sat next to a balding man who rose and spoke. "Are you ready for my son Farrell and his friend Skipper to testify?"

"Grand jury's been released for the day. They'll have to come back tomorrow."

"But the boys have already missed classes today," Farrell's father protested.

"I guess next time they'll speak to a detective when he calls," Sissy said as she entered an elevator.

The next morning when she exited the same elevator, the teens and their parents were there. "Are the boys next?" Farrell's father asked.

"Could be."

Sissy entered the grand jury room and found her fourteen charges dutifully sitting at the horseshoe shaped table.

"I hope y'all recovered from your hard work of yesterday."

Her words were greeted with smiles and nods. "Unfortunately," she went on, "today we're dealing with some unpleasant witnesses."

Mrs. Arthur and Mr. Cortez sat up straight.

"Ariel Levine's high priced attorney claims the poor boy didn't have time to commit the murder because he was seen by someone at his daddy's house at 3:45 and then was playing basketball at 4:30. Funny thing is his friends who could vouch for his playing basketball wouldn't talk to Detective Crawley. Well, they have to talk to you, so we'll hear what stories they've come up with to help their friend."

Skipper Gutman entered the room, wiping the palms of his hands on his black trousers. He fidgeted with the buttons of his black shirt, never making eye contact with the grand jurors.

"I understand you claim Ariel Levine was playing basketball with you the day after Thanksgiving," Sissy began.

"Right, starting at 4:30."

"You're sure of the time?"

"When I arrived the clock in my car said 4:25 and he came about five minutes later."

"About? You don't know for sure?"

"We don't wear our watches during the game. It's too rough. They'd get broken."

"So 4:30 is a guess. It could have been later."

"Well, maybe." Skipper replied so quietly that Sissy had him repeat his answer.

"You're excused."

Skipper stood.

"Let me remind you that grand jury proceedings are secret," Sissy said. "If you tell anyone what went on in here, you'll be here next as a defendant."

The teen looked at the floor as he walked out.

Farrell Miller, his blond ringlets covering part of his face, entered and was sworn in.

"Why did you refuse to speak to Officer Crawley?" Sissy asked.

Farrell wound one of his ringlets around his finger.

"Answer the question," Sissy demanded.

"My dad told me not to."

"Why?"

"He said the police were out to get Ariel so he'd twist whatever I said."

"Your dad wasn't trying to protect you from lying for your friend?"

"Of course not. Ariel got to the game right around 4:30."

"That's what your watch said?"

"I never wear my watch during the game. It's . . ."

"That'll be all. You're excused. And as I warned Ariel's other friend, these proceedings are secret. Do you understand?"

Farrell stood and mumbled his response.

"Speak up. The court reporter needs to hear your answer."

"Yes," Farrell said.

When he was gone, Sissy said, "I think their testimony speaks for itself."

Several grand jurors, including Dr. Goldstein, nodded.

"Since there are no more witnesses, it's time to vote. After all the good work our two alternates did, I'm sorry to tell them that since all the original grand jurors are here, they don't get to vote."

"It takes nine to indict. Let me see a show of hands."

***

When Mara arrived home Tuesday evening a patrol car was waiting in her drive. As soon as she stepped out of her car, two burly policemen, one African American and the other Caucasian left the front seat and accosted her. "We're here to arrest your son," the blond one said. "He's been indicted for murder."

Mara had expected this ever since Sissy Kleinman had brought the case before a grand jury so soon after Ariel left the country. But she wasn't prepared for it. She leaned against her car in an effort to remain standing and put her hands behind her back so the police wouldn't see they were shaking.

"He's on a trip the District Attorney approved."

"His father gave us the same story," the other officer said.

He looked toward her townhouse, making her wonder if they were going to search it. Instead, he said, "You know it's a crime to harbor a criminal."

"If I knew one, I wouldn't harbor him," Mara replied.

As soon as the patrol car drove away, Mara rushed for her townhouse, trying to get to a bathroom before she threw up. She made it as far as her front door. Even when the worst was over, she kept heaving. She went inside and was washing out her mouth when the phone rang. She managed to answer it on the fifth ring.

Simon's voice. "Meet me at Greg Dickson's office right away. Ariel's been indicted."

It took her over an hour in Houston traffic to make it downtown. She never put on the radio for fear she'd hear about the indictment. She arrived as Greg was ushering Simon into his office. She followed and sat in a chair next to the one Simon sunk into.

"What's most important is that we get Ariel back to Houston immediately," Greg said.

"Why? So they can railroad him some more?" Simon asked.

Mara glared at her former husband. "So it doesn't look like he's guilty. Now where is he?"

"He didn't tell me where he was going, and even if he had, we'd have to wait to hear from him. You can't reach someone who's backpacking."

Mara couldn't deny the truth of Simon's conclusion.

"He's been gone over two weeks. Surely you'll hear from him

soon," the attorney insisted.

"One summer he was at an overnight camp for two months," Mara said. "After a month we called his counselor to complain we hadn't heard from Ariel. The way they got him to send us a postcard was by refusing to let him into the dining hall without one."

"But under these circumstances . . ."

"What circumstances? His belief he wouldn't have been allowed to leave the country unless he was in the clear?" Mara asked.

When Greg didn't respond, Mara said, "He's been set up, hasn't he?"

TWENTY-THREE

The next morning a bathrobe clad Mara forced herself to walk out of her townhouse to pick up the *Houston Post-Gazette*. In the faint dawn light she saw a figure standing at the end of her front walk.

Frightened, she quickly turned around to go back inside when she heard the slightly accented voice of Josef Kessler call her name. She walked towards him and saw he was holding the newspaper out to her like an offering. They hadn't spoken since she'd asked him to leave after he'd downplayed the significance of Sissy Kleinman taking Ariel's case to the grand jury.

"You were right, Mara, and I'm sorry. I'm going to help you and Ariel get through this if you'll let me."

Mara hesitated and then motioned Josef to follow her back to the townhouse where they stood awkwardly next to each other.

"It's been awful," Mara said. "The police were here yesterday and I came face to face with the reality of Ariel's being arrested, taken to jail until he could be bailed out, maybe spending a lifetime there or . . ." She stopped.

Josef put his arm around her shoulder. "It's going to be all right."

"I should never have pushed you away," she said to the man whose blue eyes were looking at her so intently.

"I let you because I didn't know how much I could cope with. I was a coward happy to have an excuse to run. I'm going to make it up to you." He stroked her hair.

Josef believed he'd stay no matter what happened, but things might get so much worse. Taking him back could make losing him later all the more wrenching.

Mara opened the paper and found what she feared on the front page. "Levine indicted for brutal murder," was the heading of a story under the byline of Norton Walsh. The reporter informed readers that Levine hadn't been arrested because his family claimed he was on a trip. Walsh asked assistant district attorney Sissy Kleinman whether she believed Levine had fled to avoid arrest and quoted her response. "You can draw your own conclusion."

Mara put down the paper. "They're going to try him in the press."

"Have Ariel's attorney contact the reporter and let him know the District Attorney approved the trip," Josef suggested.

Mara went to the phone. "And how difficult it is to contact someone who's backpacking."

Because it was just a few minutes after seven, no one was in Greg Dickson's office so Mara left a message on his voice mail.

Benjie, dressed for school, came down the stairs. "How bad is the newspaper?"

"Awful, but we're going to have Greg Dickson give Ariel's side to the press."

Benjie looked at the front page for a few seconds and tossed it on the couch. "What a crock of shit." He picked up his backpack and headed out the door.

"I need your help to figure out how to contact Ariel," Mara shouted to her son, who was getting into his car.

Benjie turned back. "Can't you understand? There's no way to find him."

***

Later that day Mara called Greg's office, and his secretary assured her that the attorney had spoken to Norton Walsh for fifteen minutes about the circumstances of Ariel's leaving and why the family couldn't contact him. The next day on page three of the *Post-Gazette* Greg was quoted. "District Attorney Reardon Jones told me there were no restrictions on Ariel Levine's traveling so he went on a backpacking trip. The family hopes he'll contact them soon." The rest of the article dealt with how Claudia Luna said she wouldn't feel safe until Levine was in jail. "He's a monster who could come after me again if he's free."

With Ariel being presented as both a fugitive and a monster, Mara began to share Simon's fear their son couldn't get a fair trial. If they could reach him and bring him home, maybe the bad publicity would stop.

He just had to call.

Friday the *Weekly Bulletin's* headline read, "**LEVINE LIKELY IN ISRAEL.**" The front page story gave prominence to Luis Sorento's claim that the family, knowing Levine was about to be indicted, had sent him to Israel, where as a citizen, he wouldn't be extradited. "If you have money and foreign connections, you can get away with murder."

A story in the following Friday's edition proclaimed, "Levine still being hidden by family. Will justice be done?" Luis Sorento urged the public to put pressure on Ariel Levine's family to bring him home.

That day Mara's secretary Ann Wine came into her office. "Detective Crawley's in the waiting room. Should I send him in or get rid of him?"

Mara's first instinct was to refuse to meet with him. He was the man who'd decided her son was a murderer and who was doing anything he could to prove it despite the lack of any physical evidence tying Ariel to the crime.

But he might have some information about Ariel. He might even be coming to say her son had been found.

A scowling Detective Crawley walked into Mara's office and refused her offer to sit down. Though he was just medium height and build, his stance—legs apart and hands on his hips—made his presence threatening.

"You need to tell me where your son is."

"His father and I have both explained that Ariel went traveling with the permission of the District Attorney, and that since he's backpacking, we can't reach him."

"And he conveniently isn't reaching you."

Had she ever hated anyone as much as she did Detective Crawley? The only punishment painful enough for him would be for something terrible to happen to one of his children. But wishing anything bad on an innocent child shamed Mara. "We told the police he mentioned Thailand as a possible destination. We thought you were going to advise the American Embassy there."

"You know that does no good unless he contacts them."

"That's the best we can do. I'm sorry. I can't tell you how much I want him back home."

The next day the *Post-Gazette* quoted Detective Crawley.

131

"We're completely frustrated by the Levine family's refusal to reveal Ariel's whereabouts."

Monday morning Ann announced another unexpected visitor. "Shondra Nandagiri is in the waiting room. She said Showri Patel, Ariel's friend's father, suggested she talk to you."

A strikingly beautiful woman in her twenties with dark brown hair cascading to her shoulders entered Mara's office. At Mara's invitation, she sat in a chair in front of the attorney's desk.

"I'm a reporter from the *Post-Gazette*, but this conversation is off the record."

"I've learned not to believe anything anyone at the *Post-Gazette says,*" Mara replied.

"Mr. Patel, who's been friends with my father since they were boys in India, also feels the *Post-Gazette* has treated your son unfairly. He says there's not an ounce of violence in him."

"Then why . . ."

"Norty Walsh is the police beat reporter. As long as he tows the police line, they feed him information. I'm a features writer. I'd like to do a human interest story on the people who believe in Ariel, starting with you."

"How do I know you'll be fair?"

"Mr. Patel can vouch for me." Shondra hesitated. "But being fair means if I learn anything incriminating, that will be in my article, too."

"I need to talk to the Patels."

While Shondra sat in the waiting room, Mara called the Patels' home and was greeted by an answering machine. When she tried Mr. Patel's office, his secretary said he was out of town.

Mara didn't want to make a mistake but she didn't want to miss an opportunity.

She invited Shondra into her office and told her about Ariel.

When the reporter left, Mara called Simon and explained how they were finally going to get some good publicity.

"You shouldn't have agreed. What if she finds something incriminating?"

"How could she? He didn't do it."

Simon didn't respond.

"My God, you can't believe that's a possibility," Mara said.

"Of . . . of course not."

Mara knew Simon well enough to worry. If he thought Ariel couldn't get a fair trial and, if he had even the smallest crazy doubt about his innocence, he wouldn't want him back in Houston.

"Simon, if Ariel contacts you, you must tell me, and you must insist he come home."

"I'll do what's best for my son."

***

Sunday morning Mara brought the *Houston Post-Gazette* into her townhouse where Josef was waiting. They both sat cross legged on her bed as she read out loud the front page story by Shondra Nandagiri entitled "Saint or sinner?" It stated that while Ariel Levine had been indicted for murder, people who knew him as a non-violent young man believed it was a terrible mistake. And they denied that he'd fled to avoid arrest.

Mara was quoted. "After his father's dog was poisoned, we were concerned for Ariel's safety. Before letting him go on his trip, we called the District Attorney who approved it. We had no idea Ariel would be indicted." She went on to say that Ariel had never done anything violent. "It makes no sense that he would wake up one morning and decide to attack strangers."

Mrs. Patel vouched for Ariel's non-violent nature. "Ariel was the first of my son's friends to volunteer to work with me at the Special Olympics. There I saw what a gentle, patient young man he is. And I told the police my husband spoke to him on the phone right around the time of the murder."

Skipper Gutman commented that Ariel was such a non-aggressive basketball player that his friends only let him play because they liked him so much. "He arrived for our game at 4:30 and acted the same as always. Yet, he supposedly committed a horrible murder and got rid of all the evidence in the half hour before it started." When asked about the license plate number that led the police to Ariel, Skipper was convinced that Andrew Block either had written it down wrong or that he had something against Ariel and his family.

"Josef, Skipper could be right about Block having something against the family."

"Surely Ariel would have told you."

"It's Simon's company. They've sued or threatened to sue so

many customers over non-payment. Most of their software is for people in the medical field."

Though it was only 7:30, Benjie, who was spending the weekend at his dad's, answered on the second ring. "They finally got Ariel right."

Mara spoke to Simon and explained why she'd called.

"I don't remember Andrew Block as an account name," he said.

"He's so young he's probably an established chiropractor's associate. Check the names of all the chiropractors you've sold software to and find out if he works for any of them."

"That's a long shot," Simon said.

"We've got to think of everything."

Two hours later Simon called and said that Andrew Block worked for Daryl Freed who'd bought a lot of software from his company, had paid on time and been completely satisfied.

Mara felt deflated until Simon added, "One day when I was having lunch with Ariel, Daryl called because he needed a little extra instruction on the software. Ariel went with me to the office and was in the waiting room when Daryl and his new associate, who must have been Block, walked out with me."

"That's why Block identified Ariel," Mara responded excitedly. "He looked familiar because he'd seen him before."

"Exactly," said Simon. "I've left Greg Dickson a message."

***

Sissy Kleinman grabbed the Sunday *Houston Post-Gazette* and headed for her office. She put the plastic wrapped newspaper on the corner of her desk and picked up the Josiah Freeman file. Josiah had killed a man over a parking space, and Sissy looked forward to writing her opening statement. Unfortunately it was a black man Josiah had killed, and black on black violence almost never led to the death penalty. Sissy wouldn't ask for something she couldn't get. She wanted a perfect record.

She decided to take a quick look at the *Post-Gazette* before starting work. She removed the plastic wrapper and opened the paper to the front page. When she finished reading the article on Ariel Levine, she picked up her pen and stabbed the plastic wrapper over and over until it was in shreds.

"Norty Walsh should have warned me it was coming." First thing Monday she'd call Oracio Crawley and tell him not to feed even a tidbit of information to Walsh and to spread the word to the other detectives. The reporter needed to learn that if he didn't share information with them, they wouldn't share it with him.

The article could be a blessing in disguise. It gave Sissy insight into Levine's defense. She'd make the jury understand Mr. Nice Guy was another Ted Bundy, a sociopath who had everyone fooled. His cooperating so politely with the police was probably part of an act, which he'd perfected with his family and friends. And the phone call to Mr. Patel around the time of the murder just showed how clever he was, not that he was innocent.

But Skipper Gutman was still insisting Ariel had arrived at the basketball game at 4:30. Even if it were ten minutes later, it might be hard to convince a jury Levine had time to clean up the car when the crime scene was so bloody. She'd have to come up with some theory as to why he didn't get blood on himself.

And do it quickly. With this favorable publicity Ariel's family, who Sissy was sure could reach him, might encourage him to return to Houston, forcing her to try this iffy case before the election.

TWENTY-FOUR

Wednesday night Benjie stormed into Mara's townhouse grasping papers in his hand. "It's not just the Levine family. It's a Jewish conspiracy."

She took the papers from him. Each had a picture of Ariel with a caption reading, "Why Are You Hiding Him?" The following paragraph stated, "You should be ashamed for helping the Levine family hide this killer. Help bring him to justice. Call the police and tell them what you know."

Branding her son a killer, lying about him hiding. Mara tore the posters in half.

"They were on trees and electricity and telephone poles all around the Jewish Community Center," Benjie said. "My friends and I got down as many as we could."

And to so blatantly play the anti-Semitism card. It must be the victim's family. The police and District Attorney's office might secretly condone this tactic but they wouldn't want the publicity that would come of being part of it.

"You ought to apologize to Dad for acting like he was paranoid when he figured out those bastards were coming after Ariel because he's Jewish."

"You've spoken to your father?"

"I brought a bunch of the flyers to his house. He called Dickson. The wimp said there was nothing we could do."

The best thing was to not react. If the posters got any publicity, there might be people who believed their message.

The next morning the *Post-Gazette* ran a story about the posters including a quote from an irate woman who lived near the Jewish Community Center. "We Jews don't harbor criminals. Believe me, if I knew where Levine was, I'd go right to the police. The accusation implicit in the poster is no better than the Passover Blood Libel." Norton Walsh, the reporter writing the story, explained the woman was referring to the belief that Jews killed a

Christian child to use its blood to make unleavened bread for Passover.

"So much for no publicity," Mara said.

The next day the *Weekly Bulletin* had an interview of Luis Sorento in which he defended the use of the posters. "If they have nothing to do with hiding him, they shouldn't care. If they do, they should call the police."

That morning Mara's secretary Ann Wine looked solemn as she walked into Mara's office and slowly sat down in front of the attorney's desk.

"What's wrong?" Mara asked.

"I was at church last night for a Bible studies class. At the break people were talking about those flyers. Someone said it took courage to say what everyone knew about Jews protecting their own. People all around me were nodding in agreement until someone pointed at me to remind them I work for you. Then they all shut up."

Mara burst into tears. "How will we ever find an unbiased jury?"

***

His son couldn't get a fair trial. The publicity never let up. Every Friday the *Weekly Bulletin* ran an article about the murder. One was Loretta Sanchez's interview of Angelina Sorento in which she said she and her brother could barely break even keeping Lingerie for Life open. "Since Levine isn't in jail, women are afraid to come so now we have the added expense of a security guard. My brother says we should sell the business, but Mama wouldn't have wanted that."

The next week in a story graphically reporting Claudia Luna's injuries from the twelve stab wounds, the victim was quoted as saying that she couldn't return to the store even when she was better unless, "The monster is behind bars."

Then there were the attacks on the Levine family. Loretta Sanchez quoted Luis. "Simon Levine can travel out of the country any time he wants, claiming he's on business for that Israeli company that pays him so much. That's how he's getting money to his son."

Simon called Greg Dickson, wanting to sue Luis Sorento and the newspaper for libel.

137

"The publicity generated by you suing the murder victim's son will only hurt Ariel."

On top of that, Simon couldn't control Mara. She called his sister Frieda every week in Israel asking if Ariel was there, and she interspersed those calls with ones to the American embassies in Israel and Thailand. She refused to face the truth of what would happen to Ariel if he returned.

Simon became more and more angry as he sat in his study thinking about all this, so when the phone rang, he answered it gruffly.

"Dad? It's me, Ariel."

TWENTY-FIVE

Thank God, his son was safe. But would he be if he came back?

"Ariel, where are you?" Simon asked.

"Guatemala City. I want to come home. But I'm afraid."

Maybe Ariel had spoken to Mara who'd told him about the indictment.

"I think what happened to Grandma is happening to me."

Did his son finally understand he was being persecuted because he's Jewish?

Ariel's voice quivered. "You always said she had seizures because of things that happened to her in the concentration camp, but maybe it's hereditary. I've had two over here."

Simon's mother. Never recovering physically or emotionally from her time in the concentration camp. The same would happen to Ariel if he went to prison.

"When did you have seizures?"

"Two weeks ago at a youth hostel. Again yesterday when I was about to arrange my trip home. People in line broke my fall." Ariel starting crying. "I'm so scared, Dad."

"Check into a nice hotel. Call and give me the name and address. By then I'll know when I'm arriving. I'll find you a good doctor there."

"Once he puts me on some medicine, I'll be able to fly home, won't I?"

"Of course. In the meantime, there's no reason to worry your mother so don't call her."

Ariel hesitated. "I guess you're right."

He had to decide what was best for his son. Until he did, no one, except Virginia, would know where he was going. Simon couldn't give away Ariel's location until he determined whether Ariel was well enough to travel, and if his traveling should be back to Houston.

He needed to leave quickly but in a way that didn't arouse suspicions. Virginia could tell friends, and Mara, if she called, that he was on a business trip, and he'd inform his company he was taking some of his unused vacation time. While he threw some things into a carryon bag, Virginia could get him a ticket.

His wife was sitting on the couch in the den with Shannon's head in her lap, watching a <u>Law and Order</u> rerun on television.

When Simon revealed his plans, Virginia balked. "How will this look at a trial? Taking a pretend business trip to see Ariel just confirms what Luis Sorento has been saying."

"I'm not letting my son travel until he's well. My mother almost died when she had a seizure on a plane."

"At least let Greg Dickson know."

"He might have some legal obligation to tell the District Attorney who could force Ariel to come home before he's healthy."

"If you don't want anyone to know, does that mean . . ."

"What would you do if he were your child?"

Virginia nuzzled Shannon, gently removed the Dalmatian from her lap and stood. "I'll get you a ticket."

***

Simon grabbed the seat in front of him as The Holiday Inn courtesy van, on its way from La Aurora Airport to the hotel, swerved to miss a bus with live chickens sticking out most of its windows. The passengers put their heads next to those of their chickens as they screamed what Simon presumed were Spanish curses. The van driver took both hands off the wheel for emphasis as he retorted in a shrieking voice. Simon hoped he'd live to see his son.

The van pulled up to the hotel, and Ariel rushed from the lobby. Simon was barely on the sidewalk when his son grasped him in a bear hug. When Ariel released him, Simon noticed the teen's loose fitting jeans and the dark circles under his eyes.

"This is the fanciest place I've stayed since I left home. And the hundred dollars a night it's costing you is more than I spent in the past ten weeks on youth hostels."

"I hope you've been eating a lot and charging it to the room."

Ariel picked up his father's overnight bag as soon as the driver brought it out of the rear of the van. "My stomach was finally good enough yesterday that I could enjoy some food."

When they were in their room, Simon looked out the window. Guatemala City sprawled across a range of flattened, ravine-scored mountains.

"See all those markets, Dad? You can't believe the bargains you can get."

"We're going to see a doctor before we do anything."

Simon reached for the phone sitting on the table between the two double beds and dialed O. "Please connect me with the manager."

A man who identified himself as Jorge and spoke English with a penetrable Spanish accent assured Simon that he was recommending the finest doctor in Guatemala City, that he'd make the appointment himself and insist Ariel be seen right away.

Simon hung up the receiver and asked Ariel about his seizures.

"Two weeks ago I was about to check out of a youth hostel near Tikal, where the Mayan ruins are. I paid the clerk for two nights, and the next thing I remember is him standing over me."

"You're sure he didn't knock you down?"

"No, Dad. It was awful. I . . . I . . . even wet my pants. He pretended not to notice, told me to stay another night until I felt better."

Simon put his arm around his son.

"The day before I called you I went to a tourist office to arrange my trip home. I was standing in line, and then I was on the floor with all these people looking at me. They put me in a chair and told me not to leave until I was okay."

Maybe the emotional trauma the police had put Ariel through had caused his health problem. If so, telling him about the indictment would only make things worse.

Their conversation was interrupted by Jorge calling with the name of the doctor they were to see the next morning at ten. "I'll make sure the doorman has a cab waiting for you at 9:45."

Simon suspected the doctor was the manager's relative, that they'd wait for hours to see him and that the cab driver would take them to his office on a circuitous route. But this was the best he could do. He hadn't dared ask any Houston doctor to recommend one in Guatemala for fear he'd reveal where Ariel was.

The next morning Simon and Ariel entered a cab whose
interior smelled of cigarettes and whose floor sported a used
condom. The ten minute drive took them past sidewalks teeming
with people in bright multi-colored clothes walking in front of
modern hotels and colonial buildings. The driver spoke enough
heavily accented English to point out one museum housing Mayan
and Spanish colonial art and another, which displayed the
country's arts and costumes. As they passed market after market,
Simon saw women with babies on their backs wrapping their
purchases in swatches of red or blue material and putting them on
top of their heads.

The driver turned down a street of what appeared to be one
story houses and stopped in front of one.

"Medico?" Simon asked.

"*Si, si,*" replied the driver who double parked, almost got hit by
a truck as he opened his door and led his passengers into the gray
wooden structure.

Women holding babies or young children on their laps and old
men, all sitting on green plastic chairs, filled the waiting room. He
and Ariel could wait hours to be seen. Instead, when Simon gave
their name to a woman dressed in white, she immediately
motioned them to follow her into a room which barely had space
for an examining table, a stool on wheels and a small round table
that held a few metal instruments. She motioned for Ariel to get
undressed and handed him the thinnest paper gown Simon had
ever seen. It ripped as soon as Ariel tried to put it on.

A white jacketed man who looked to be just a little older than
Ariel and about a foot shorter walked in and thrust out his dark
skinned hand. "Ah, the Americans from the hotel. I'm Dr.
Castillo-Martinez. I just spent a wonderful year in your country
training at a hospital in Philadelphia. Are you from there?"

"No, Houston." Simon replied, relieved that the doctor spoke
English so well and that he had learned some medicine in the
States.

When the doctor asked Ariel for a history of his problem, he
related what had happened to him at the youth hostel and the
tourist office.

"Have you ever had seizures before?"

"Never."

"Then you're sure they're seizures?" Simon asked.

"We can never be sure unless we test the person immediately after he's had one. So we go by the description of the event."

"What can you do for him?"

"I'm going to put him on 100 milligrams of Dilantin, three times a day. I'll check his blood levels in a week to make sure that's the right dose."

"If it is, can I fly home?" Ariel asked.

"Yes, but, if not, I'll change your dose and check you again the following week."

"How long should I stay with him?" Simon asked.

"Perhaps a day to make sure he has no reaction to the medicine. After that, he can be around the hotel, so if there's a problem, help will be nearby."

"I'd like to talk to you privately, doctor," Simon said.

"Wait in my office while I listen to your son's heart and take his blood pressure."

The office, the size of a large closet, contained a small table and two chairs.

When the doctor entered, Simon asked, "What caused the seizures?"

"I don't know."

"My concern is they may have been brought on by some emotional trauma he suffered before he left on this trip. If so, there's some bad news I don't want to give him for fear it'll cause another seizure."

"That's unlikely. To be safe, tell him after he's been on the medicine for a day."

Simon's concern that Ariel would bring up the subject of the murder sooner abated when his son took his first dose of medicine, ate lunch and immediately fell asleep. But at dinner at the hotel that night Ariel asked, "Have they caught the guy who killed the lingerie store lady?"

"Not yet but the police are still looking," Simon lied.

Twenty-four hours after Ariel had taken his first dose of Dilantin, Simon suggested they go to their room.

When Ariel was seated in a chair with the remote control in his hand, Simon told him they needed to talk.

"There's some bad news from home."

"There's something wrong with Mom. That's why you told me not to call her."

"Your mother and everyone else are fine."

"Then what?"

Simon took a deep breath. "Shortly after you left a grand jury indicted you for murder."

"I don't understand."

"That means you're going to trial."

"I know that. But how could it happen when the cars and houses had no blood or anything in them?"

"It's because you're Jewish."

"That's crazy."

"All the newspapers keep mentioning it, and that you have Israeli citizenship. They've put flyers out around the Jewish Community Center telling people to stop hiding you and to turn you in."

"I can't believe this." Ariel brought his hands up to his head and cried until his breath came in gasps.

Simon reached for the phone.

"Don't call the doctor, Dad. I'll be okay."

"You'll be okay if you don't come home."

"That's even crazier."

"My mother's parents gave up an opportunity to send her to England before the Nazis got to France. If she'd left, she wouldn't have spent years in a concentration camp."

Ariel stood up and paced in front of the beds. "You think I'm going to spend years in prison even though I'm innocent?"

"Your grandmother was an innocent child, too."

"This is America you're talking about."

"You've been gone, Ariel. You haven't seen how much they hate you because you're Jewish. Why do you think things have gone this far?"

"I don't know." Ariel's eyes welled with tears. "Where would I go? How would I ever see you or Mom or Benjie again?"

"I'll figure out a way to get you to Israel without them knowing. Even if they find you, since you're a citizen, Israel would insist the trial be held there. No one who's fair would convict you."

Ariel was quiet. When he spoke again, he glared at Simon.

144

"Mom thinks I should come home. That's why you didn't want me to call her."

"She's misguided, naïve."

"You were the one who thought of this backpacking trip. Because I went, they're probably saying I fled."

"If you'd called . . ."

"You knew I hardly ever call when you told me to go."

"This isn't my fault, Ariel."

"Well, it sure isn't Mom's. I'm listening to her."

"I'm not leaving until tomorrow. Please think this over."

Ariel sat down, pressed the power on the remote and stared at the television.

***

Simon sat in the middle seat of the last row of a plane heading for Houston. Smells from the nearby bathroom assaulted him. The immensely overweight man sitting next to the window had fought him for space on the armrest and won. The teenage girl on his other side never stopped chattering with her friend across the aisle.

When the plane finally landed, Simon called home, but instead of Virginia's voice, he heard his own, asking the caller to leave a message.

He put his overnight bag in the trunk of his car and decided he might as well finish off the unpleasantness of the day with a visit to Mara. If he gave her the news about his hiding Ariel's whereabouts at her office, there was less chance she'd make a scene.

He entered the waiting room and saw only empty chairs. It figured. He never thought she'd make a success of her law practice. Simon was wandering down a hallway, unsure of where Mara's office was, when an older red haired woman got up from her desk and blocked his way.

"Do you have an appointment?"

"I'm Simon Levine, Mara's former husband."

The woman didn't move. "If you have bad news about Ariel, I want to prepare her."

"I just need to discuss some trial strategy with her."

The woman stared at him for a few seconds as if waiting for him to come up with a better story.

Simon looked away.

145

"Sit down," she said. "I'll let her know you're here."

Mara walked out of the third office and motioned him in. She closed the door. "Where's Ariel?"

"In Guatemala."

"That's where you've been?"

"I had to make sure he was all right. He called and said he was having seizures."

Mara gasped.

"The doctor there put him on medicine. He should be fine."

"Why didn't you bring him home?"

"The doctor has to check his blood in a week to make sure the dose of medicine is right."

Mara stepped closer to Simon. "I want Ariel's phone number now."

"He's going to call you tonight at home from a pay phone"

"You went there to convince him not to come back to Houston."

"If you care about him, you'll do the same when you talk to him."

"Call Dickson. He needs to arrange with the District Attorney to have Ariel turn himself in so things don't look worse than they are."

"He can't turn himself in until the doctor says it's safe for him to travel."

"I'll have Ariel contact me as soon as he gets the doctor's okay. Then if you don't call Dickson, I will."

"Mara, think about it. He can go to Israel."

"And when he's caught trying to get there, he'll convict himself."

"They've convicted him already."

***

Mara waited in her bedroom for Ariel's call, trying to read a novel but unable to concentrate. She jumped when she heard a knock on her door.

It was Benjie. She hadn't told him Ariel was in Guatemala. She couldn't take a chance he'd let the news slip out.

"Night, Mom. I've got to saw some logs. Track practice is at six."

146

Mara kissed Benjie on the cheek and shut her door as he left.

At eleven thirty Ariel still hadn't called. Mara considered demanding that Simon tell her how to reach their son. But if the police were tapping her telephone, she'd lead them right to him. He needed to call her from a pay phone.

Just before midnight Mara's phone rang.

"Sorry it's so late, Mom. I fell asleep after dinner. I think it's the medicine."

Tears filled Mara's eyes. "How do you feel?"

"No more seizures since I've been on the pills."

"Thank God."

But was he really okay? Until she saw him, she wouldn't know for sure.

"Do you still think I should come home?"

"Absolutely."

As soon as she spoke, she wondered if Simon could be right. If so, she'd always regret that one word answer.

"That's what I think, too. But Mom . . . "

"Yes?"

"I'm scared."

"We'll be with you. We'll get this straightened out."

She was glad Ariel couldn't see her hands shaking.

***

A week later Mara spoke to Simon. "Ariel called. The doctor cleared him to travel. Set up a time for us to meet with Greg Dickson."

The next day she and Simon sat in front of the attorney's desk as Simon revealed how he'd traveled to Guatemala City after Ariel called about his seizures.

"If you'd let me know before you left, I could have arranged with the District Attorney to have Ariel surrender after his medical problem was taken care of."

"I don't trust him. He would have had the police in Guatemala City arrest Ariel before he was treated."

Greg's brow furrowed. "The important thing now is to make sure Ariel's return is viewed by everyone as a voluntary surrender. Otherwise we'll have problems with bail, with publicity, with everything."

Mara nodded. "We'll contact him. Have him return immediately."

"He'll be frightened when the plane lands in Houston," Simon said. "He could have another seizure."

Mara gripped the arms of her chair.

Simon stood. "I'm coming back to Houston with him. He can transfer planes in Mexico City. I'll meet him there."

"Just so we do this quickly," the attorney said.

"He'll be here tomorrow," Simon assured Greg.

"I'll let Reardon Jones know."

***

The next day Simon picked up his overnight bag and was about to walk out the door to catch his plane to Mexico City when the phone rang.

Greg Dickson spoke in a monotone. "Don't bother going to Mexico."

"Why?"

"Ariel's been arrested in Guatemala."

TWENTY-SIX

Oracio followed a large, hulking, silent guard past the cells in the Guatemala City Jail. The first held three boys, elementary school age, lying on the concrete floor. The next contained a scar-faced man who held his hands over his ears and banged his head against the wall as his cellmate let out one high pitched scream after another. The third, with a pool of blood on the floor, was empty. When they came to the fourth, Oracio smiled. It was worth the trip from Houston to see Ariel Levine behind bars. He wished that rather than escorting him back to Houston, he could leave him here to rot.

"Detective Crawley, please have them give me back my medicine, or I could have a seizure."

The psychopath had come up with another ploy. He was going to claim he'd stayed in Guatemala because he was ill.

"I . . . I don't want to get sick on the plane."

So that was the creep's plan. He'd fake a seizure and blame it on the brutality of the Houston Police Department.

"I'll see what I can do," Oracio said.

The detective walked from the cellblock to an adjoining large room with benches filled by drunken men and provocatively dressed women. A female in a torn strapless black mini-dress stood up, shook her hips and motioned for him to join her. Among the nearby desks was one occupied by a secretary who was finishing the paperwork, which would allow Oracio to take his prisoner back to Houston. The typist, a woman about his own age, smiled, revealing three missing teeth, and said, "*Cinco minutos.*"

If she were right, they'd make the Continental non-stop which would get them in at 4:10 P.M. Some of the television stations could do live coverage for their five o'clock broadcasts. Oracio had alerted Loretta Sanchez, making good on his promise of a scoop.

The secretary took the document she'd been working on and

left her desk. Oracio followed her into an office whose door sported the nameplate Capitan Jesus Salvador. The police officer stood revealing a stomach, which lapped over his belt. He shook the detective's hand and spoke rapidly in Spanish.

"*No hablo Espanol,*" Oracio said.

The captain looked at the paper the secretary had brought him. "Oracio Crawley?" He emphasized the first name.

"Yes," replied the detective.

"No extradition *problema?*"

"They waived extradition."

The captain looked surprised.

"They're trying to pretend he wanted to come back to the United States," Oracio said.

The Guatemalan signed the document and handed it to Oracio.

As soon as the guard led Ariel to Oracio, the detective cuffed him.

"You don't have to do that. I'm happy to go home."

Oracio didn't respond.

Ariel shook his head. "It's only because I'm too friendly or too stupid that you had to make this trip. I had just walked into the airport when I saw this guy I knew from high school, so I smiled and waved. When he took off, I never guessed it was to get Airport Security."

Ariel's blathering infuriated Oracio, but he didn't want to do anything to discourage the little prick. He might say something incriminating.

Once they were on the plane, Ariel fell asleep. The kid looked like he'd lost weight. His belt, on the tightest hook, seemed about a size too large, and his face was thinner and paler. Fear had taken its toll.

***

Mara reached the airport two hours before Ariel's plane was due. Within an hour television cameras and reporters with microphones or notepads were jousting with her outside Customs to get the best position to see the prisoner arrive.

She heard a siren just before two police officers entered the building and ordered everyone to move back. Her first instinct was to protest, but she didn't want to bring attention to herself. The police might make her leave or the reporters might question her.

When Ariel walked through the door, Mara gasped. His hands were cuffed, his pants hung low on his hips, and he looked dazed. Cameras whirred and reporters shouted questions. Mara called her son's name but was afraid he didn't hear. He looked in her direction and smiled but before she could smile back a woman clad in a red miniskirt and holding a notepad pushed in front of her. Detective Crawley, his fist in Ariel's back, winked at the brightly dressed woman. "Why did you flee to Guatemala?" she yelled. "Were you going to Israel next?"

As soon as Ariel left the terminal, Mara rushed out and saw a police officer shove her son into the back seat of a patrol car. She hurried to the parking lot, waited in a long line of cars to pay and battled Houston rush hour traffic on her way to the Harris County Jail. Though she knew Simon was waiting there, and that it could take hours for Ariel to be processed, she cursed every slowdown and kept switching lanes in a losing battle to gain a few minutes.

She entered the anteroom to the jail, its seats filled with people of a conglomeration of races and ethnicities, all waiting to find out what was happening to their loved ones. She heard English, Spanish and Vietnamese and smelled cigarette scented clothes and alcohol laced breaths. Simon leaned against a wall, one of two men in suits. The other, Greg Dickson, was talking to a police officer at a desk behind wire mesh. When he finished, he motioned Simon and Mara to follow him outside.

"How soon can the bail bondsman get here?" Simon asked.

"Sissy Kleinman opposes any bail for Ariel. She insists he could flee again."

Simon clenched his fists. "She knows that's a lie. The District Attorney said he could leave Houston."

"We'll bring all that up in the bail hearing tomorrow," Greg said.

"You mean he has to stay here overnight?" Mara's heart raced. Her son might share a cell with a violent criminal who could beat him up or sexually assault him.

"I can't do anything until tomorrow morning," the attorney replied. "Get something to eat. It'll be hours before they finish processing him."

Mara and Simon went inside where they parted to sit in the only two empty chairs, which were on opposite sides of the room.

At eleven o'clock a police officer came to the door of the anteroom and called their names.

"Here are your son's personal effects," he said, handing Mara a brown paper bag with Ariel's wallet, watch and class ring inside.

"Can we see him?" she asked.

Ariel, in a prisoner's orange jumpsuit, his hands cuffed behind his back, was led to them.

Mara hyperventilated and willed herself to stop. She had a vision of Ariel on his first Halloween in a pumpkin costume the same color as he wore now. She noticed how pale Simon was and wondered if he were thinking the same thing.

"You have two minutes," the police officer said.

"Are you okay?" Mara asked her son.

"Don't worry, Mom, I'm fine. I love you both."

"If anyone tries to hurt you, keep yelling until a guard comes," Mara said.

When she saw a look of mingled surprise and fear cross Ariel's face, Mara was sorry she'd spoken. She put her arms around her son. "You're big and strong. No one will threaten you."

Simon's voice had a catch in it. "We're going to get you out tomorrow after the bail hearing."

"Don't count on it," the police officer murmured.

***

Mara arrived first at Judge Pressler's courtroom the next morning. She sat in the aisle seat of the front row bench. She heard a loud male voice, and turned to see a middle-aged man with an acne scarred face. He walked into the courtroom next to a woman with graying hair who looked a little older than he. Behind them was a man as tall as a basketball player and heftier than a football player. He was writing down the angry man's words in a notebook. "I told Kleinman my mother would turn over in her grave if Levine is allowed out on bail. If he's not in jail, he'll find a way to get to Israel."

When the three sat in the second row across the aisle from her, Mara opened her newspaper and brought it up to her face. She might have escaped recognition if Simon hadn't shown up and said, "Move over, Mara."

The woman pointed at her. "That's the monster's mother."

"Norty Walsh from the *Post-Gazette*," the large man called out. "Do you have anything to say to the victim's children?"

Before Simon could respond, Mara said, "We're sorry for their loss and hope the police find the person who murdered their mother. We have no further comment."

The courtroom was almost full when Greg Dickson walked in. Behind him came a woman about Mara's size wearing a navy blue suit and wheeling an oversized tan briefcase. She spoke with an East Texas drawl. "Hey, Greg, how you doin', partner?"

"Better when I have my client out of jail."

"Funny how you only defend the innocent."

"Miss Kleinman," the victim's daughter called out.

Sissy smiled and waved at her.

Mara fingered the chasma hanging from a gold chain around her neck. Her son's life was a game to Sissy Kleinman. She joked with the competition, put on a show for her admiring fans, cared only about chalking up another victory. The rules of decency meant nothing to her.

The bailiff intoned, "All rise," and Judge Pressler entered.

Mara studied the jurist, looking for any clue as to how he might treat her son. He had a square face, which looked too large for his thin neck. He was expressionless as he moved his hand over his gray crew cut.

The side door to the courtroom opened. Ariel, still in a prisoner's orange jumpsuit, his hands cuffed in front of him, entered with the bailiff, who led him to a seat at the counsel table next to his attorney. When he sat with the cuffs on, Ariel's arms spread from his body like chicken wings. He turned and smiled at his parents.

The judge looked at some papers and asked for confirmation this was the Ariel Levine bail hearing. Greg and Sissy stood and simultaneously said it was.

Sissy began her argument. "Your Honor, there's no way we can allow this brutal murderer out of jail. He's fled twice already."

"He's never fled, Your Honor. He left Houston with the permission of Ms. Kleinman's boss, the District Attorney," Greg responded.

"Even if that were so, he stayed away after he knew he was indicted."

"That's absolutely false, Your Honor. He was backpacking and couldn't be reached."

"The only reason he came back was because he was arrested in Guatemala."

"He was arrested at the airport on his way home to Houston."

"He was stopping in Mexico City where it's easy to get a visa to Israel."

"Your Honor, there is absolutely no evidence he had any intention of going anywhere except Houston."

"He has dual Israeli/American citizenship and two passports."

Mara had difficulty breathing. Her worst nightmares were coming true.

"Enough," the judge bellowed. "What does each of you want?"

"Remand to custody," Sissy demanded.

"$10,000 bail," Greg countered.

"That's ridiculous, Your Honor."

"I have a tape of the District Attorney allowing the defendant to leave Houston," Greg said.

When Sissy didn't immediately respond, Mara figured she didn't want her boss to be embarrassed.

Sissy quickly recovered. "If we were to consider any bail, it would have to be at least one million dollars, and the prisoner would have to be electronically monitored so he can't leave home."

"We can accept the second part of Ms. Kleinman's proposal but the first is outrageous for someone with no previous arrest for a violent crime."

Judge Pressler peered at the attorneys. "Electronic monitoring, surrender of both passports, $100,000 bail."

Greg nodded. "We'll post bail now."

"Where's he staying?" Judge Pressler asked.

"At my house," Mara called out.

When the judge looked at her, she added, "I'm Mara Levine, Ariel's mother."

"We should be able to have the electronic monitor set up by tomorrow," Sissy said.

Mara half rose and gripped the back of the bench in front of her. She didn't want Ariel to spend another night in jail.

Greg spoke. "Your Honor, the assistant district attorney is

being punitive, trying to keep the defendant in jail an extra day."

"I'm familiar with Ms. Kleinman's methods," the judge said. "The prisoner is out of jail today, with or without the monitor."

At six o'clock that night, after the police had put a receiver on a phone in Mara's townhouse, the judge's pronouncement came true. Ariel walked into the jail's anteroom, a black plastic box two inches square on his ankle, clinging tightly to his flesh. A thick elastic strap held it in place. The police officer, who escorted Ariel explained that the device continuously emitted signals to the police monitoring station via the receiver so the authorities would know if Ariel wandered from home or broke it off. The police officer said he'd have to follow Mara and Ariel in a squad car to make sure her townhouse was their destination. "After that if he goes further than a few feet from the perimeter of the house, we'll know and we'll be back to get him."

"Don't worry. I don't ever want to leave home again," Ariel said.

Mara hugged him and kissed his cheeks.

Once they were in the car Mara asked the question whose answer she feared. "Did anyone harm you when you were in either prison?"

"I was in a cell by myself in Guatemala. I shared a cell here with a drunk who threw up on his clothes and then fell asleep. The smell was awful. I called for a guard but none came."

Mara cried. The man could have been attacking Ariel, and no one would have helped him.

"I'm okay, Mom, really."

"Of course, you are. I've just missed you."

When Mara and Ariel walked into the house, Benjie ran down the stairs and hugged his brother. "I bet I weigh more than you do now."

Mara headed towards the kitchen. "I'm going to make you guys something to eat."

"No problem, Mom. Ariel and I will get some pizza."

Ariel held up his leg. "Can't. I'm being electronically monitored."

Benjie looked at the transmitter. "Those bastards."

"It's okay. We'll party here. Invite the guys over for tomorrow," Ariel said.

That night Mara walked into Ariel's room three times after he was asleep. It was a miracle to see him in his own bed.

The next day Skipper Gutman, dressed in his trademark black, and Farrell Miller, blond ringlets longer than Mara remembered, showed up at dinnertime. As Mara prepared lasagna for them, Skipper's voice drifted into the kitchen. "That assistant district attorney is such a bitch. When I testified before the grand jury, she tried to twist everything I said about when you arrived at the game."

"She tried to tear me to pieces," Farrell said. "Stay away from her if you can."

After seeing Sissy Kleinman in court, Mara was sure her son's friends were accurately portraying how she manipulated their testimony.

Who knew what she could make a jury believe when she cross-examined Ariel.

TWENTY-SEVEN

A few days later Mara opened the door to find a tall muscular young man whose thin face and jutting jaw looked familiar. "Dov Lieberman. I haven't seen you since the boys and I visited Israel four years ago. What are you doing here? I thought you were in the Israeli Air Force."

"I just finished my stint and came to visit my mom," her son's boyhood friend said. "She moved here after she and Dad divorced."

"Ariel's in the shower. Come in, sit down and tell me about your plans."

"I'm going back to school to major in criminal justice and psychology so I can be a profiler."

"I remember when you wanted to be a writer. Ariel acted in some of the little dramas you wrote for the neighborhood kids."

"After I solve a couple of big cases, I'll have quite a book to write."

"Who's there, Mom?" Ariel called from the top of the stairs.

Dov bounded past Mara up the steps. Once there he gave Ariel a long bear hug and the two went into his bedroom.

About half an hour later, Mara heard loud voices coming from behind Ariel's closed door.

"You must be out of your mind," Ariel shouted.

"I'm your friend. I want you to get help."

"No friend would think such a thing. Get out of here."

Dov ran down the stairs and slammed the door behind him as he left.

Mara went into Ariel's room where she found him sitting on his bed red faced. "What was that about?" she asked.

"Dov said he knows I slashed that woman's throat, that I need to admit it and get help."

"Why would he think such a thing?" Mara's voice quivered.

"Remember that horrible bombing a few years ago in our old

157

neighborhood in Israel?"

None of them would ever forget. Six of their neighbors dead, and all those horrendous injuries. Ariel had been so moved by the disfigurement of his first girlfriend that he'd written to her every week until she committed suicide.

"Dov told me about the terrible things he wanted to do to the Arabs. And I came up with worse ways to punish them."

Ariel averted his eyes from Mara's gaze. "He remembered me writing that I wanted to slit the throats of their women."

***

Sissy Kleinman sat in her office, drumming her fingers on her desk. The Levine bail hearing had been a disaster. She berated herself for being flummoxed by Dickson's announcement he'd taped the District Attorney's call allowing Levine to leave the country. It wasn't completely her fault. If she'd had a different judge, instead of no-nonsense Pressler, things would have gone better. His order even allowed the killer to leave his house to meet with his attorney once a week.

Well, she'd soon be rid of Pressler. He'd presided at the bail hearing because the Levine grand jury had been commissioned under the auspices of his court. There'd be a different judge at the trial.

That didn't solve her other problems like no motive and no physical evidence to tie Levine to the crime scene, expect for a few fibers that could have come from any bra. She couldn't lose this case and be elected District Attorney

Her intercom buzzed. "There's a Dov Lieberman to see you."

Dov sounded like an Israeli name. He could be another of Levine's friends trying to convince her of his innocence.

"He claims he has important information about Ariel Levine."

Could be a ruse but she couldn't take a chance. "Send him in."

Sissy was struck by how Semitic the young man looked with his dark complexion, black hair and hooked nose. If he were seeing her under false pretenses, he'd regret it.

Dov introduced himself and didn't sit until Sissy motioned him to a chair in front of her desk.

"You're a friend of Ariel Levine?" she asked.

"It's complicated. We grew up as young boys in the same

neighborhood in Israel." Dov shook his head. "Even then Ariel had this goody two shoes act that kept him out of trouble when the rest of us got punished."

Sissy was encouraged by the resentment in Dov's voice.

"Because I'm a couple of years older, he's always looked up to me, wrote to me after he moved back to the States, visited me when he came to Israel. After I got into the Israeli Air Force, he sent me numerous letters asking me to help him get in."

Dov hesitated. "They were weird. He kept assuring me he wasn't the nice guy everyone thought he was, that he was violent enough to fight for Israel."

Sissy's visitor took a deep breath. "One of the letters worried me so much that I kept it. Maybe if I'd told someone about it, that poor woman would be alive."

Dov was struggling with what he was about to reveal. Sissy cautioned herself to be patient and quiet so she didn't scare him off.

Dov stood and leaned against Sissy's desk. "I visited him a few days ago and told him he needs help but he refused to get it."

"Together we'll find a way to help him."

"I've been thinking that maybe you could encourage an insanity plea so he'd get treatment."

"Of course."

Dov sat down and took a folded piece of stationery from the inside pocket of his sports jacket.

As Sissy read the letter, she pictured just which paragraph she'd have enlarged as an exhibit for the jury.

I'm much more violent than you'd ever guess. If I was in Israel I'd slit the throats of their women. Maybe I'd better have a knife ready in case I luck out and find some sand nigger bitch here in Houston.

Sissy tried to hide her elation. "Does Levine know you kept this letter?"

"I told him I saved it but he probably thinks it's still in Israel."

"You've done him a big favor. I'll figure out a way to have this information help your friend."

***

159

As grateful as Mara was to have Ariel at home, his inability to leave the house was weighing on both of them. That first couple of weeks' visits from friends had tapered off. They were teenage boys, and as much as she tried to entice them with food and movie rentals, they had more fun places to go than her townhouse. She suggested Ariel work on his defense and bought him books by famous criminal attorneys to inspire him. They lay on top of his dresser where she'd put them. As often as she could, Mara arranged her office schedule so that she'd be home by three o'clock, figuring she could keep Ariel company, but for three days in a row, he was still asleep at that hour, claiming he'd been up late the night before.

She had to put a stop to it, so on the fourth day she went into his room and shook him awake.

Ariel sat up. "Don't ever do that," he said in a threatening tone.

Mara took a step back. "You can't spend your life in bed. From now on you'll be up when I get home."

Ariel's face reddened. He stood up, inches from his mother, and looked down at her. "You, Virginia, Aunt Frieda, always telling me what to do. Don't you think I'm tired of having a bunch of bitches trying to control me?"

He made a fist, brought it to his waist and swung his arm, knocking the clock radio off his nightstand.

"Ariel," was all a stunned Mara could say.

His breathing sped up, his chest heaved.

He closed his eyes tightly and took two deep breaths.

After a few moments Ariel opened his eyes, dropped his arm to his side and unclenched his fist. "This is really getting to me."

Mara put her shaking hands in her pants pockets. She tried to convince herself that the kind of frustration Ariel displayed was to be expected from someone whose life had been so unfairly and inexplicably torn apart.

Mara left her son's room, walked down the stairs and heard pounding on her front door. She looked out the peephole and opened the door for Simon.

"Where's Ariel?"

"In his room. What's the matter?"

Simon rushed up the stairs with Mara following. Ariel was

sitting on his bed, still in his pajamas.

"What's wrong with you?" his father asked.

"I'm tired. I hardly slept last night."

"I'm talking about that crazy letter you wrote Dov Lieberman."

Ariel blanched. "How do you know about that?" He looked at his mother, who sat down on the edge of the bed.

Simon glared at her. "You knew about this and didn't tell me?"

"Dov came here and reminded Ariel about a letter he'd written years ago. He understandably wanted to punish Arabs after they'd killed people in our old neighborhood."

"You're going to defend a boy who wants to slit the throats of 'sand nigger bitches.'"

"I'm defending my son who's incapable of such a thing."

"Why? Because he's so much like you? Always acting sweet and innocent while hiding his anger."

"Simon, you can't believe . . ."

"It's not what I believe. It's what a judge believes. Sissy Kleinman called Greg Dickson. There's going to be a hearing to revoke Ariel's bail."

161

TWENTY-EIGHT

The Levine bail hearing was a crapshoot. Since Levine's trial hadn't yet been assigned to a court, Sissy was still stuck with Judge Pressler. Winning with him was questionable but she could score points with the public.

She dialed Norty Walsh who answered on the second ring. "Hey, big guy, I've decided to forgive you for the Saint Levine article you didn't warn me about."

"I had no idea it was in the works. I explained that to Detective Crawley."

"To show you how magnanimous I am, here's a heads up. There's going to be a bail revocation hearing Wednesday."

"What have you got on him?"

"A letter that shows what I've always known. But you didn't hear that from me."

Wednesday Norty Walsh, notebook in hand, approached Sissy as she was about to enter the courthouse. As he talked to her, a photographer snapped her picture. "What new evidence led you to ask for this hearing?"

"A letter in which Levine plans to slit a woman's throat."

A few minutes later when Ariel walked by with his parents and attorney, the photographer took his picture.

As soon as Judge Pressler called the hearing to order, Greg Dickson stood. "Your Honor, the defense requests this hearing be closed. Ms. Kleinman is about to present information with no probative value, simply to inflame the public."

"Your Honor, when a murderer writes . . ."

"Not another word, Ms. Kleinman, until I decide whether to close the hearing. Up to the bench with whatever you have."

With Greg next to her, Sissy handed the letter to Judge Pressler who plucked his reading glasses from the pocket of his judicial robe. Sissy knew when he came to the significant paragraph because he raised his eyebrows and looked at defense counsel.

"Your Honor, check the date on that letter," Greg said. "It was written when Ariel was sixteen and was upset about a bombing in the Israeli neighborhood where he grew up. The press will ignore those facts and inflame the public from which we'll be selecting our jury."

Judge Pressler peered over his glasses at Sissy. "I don't want to give him an excuse to move the trial out of Houston. I'm clearing the courtroom. And both of you stay away from the press."

With just the judge, court reporter, Ariel and his attorney and parents present, Sissy said, "The letter shows the defendant planned the murder. Knowing this evidence will likely convict him, he'll flee if he's not in jail."

"Your Honor, Ariel was angry at the Arab woman who killed six people from his old neighborhood. This has nothing to do with the crime he's accused of. And with no physical evidence to connect him to the scene, he certainly does not expect to be convicted."

"No need for either of you to argue your case today," Judge Pressler said. "Bail is raised to $150,000."

As the judge left the bench, Sissy heard Greg say, "I had the bail bondsman here just in case. He's waiting for us."

Ariel wouldn't be in jail tonight, but Sissy vowed it would be just a matter of time before she had him there for good.

***

"Do you understand how close you came to winding up back in jail?" Simon asked Ariel who sat between him and Mara in front of Greg Dickson's desk.

Simon clenched his jaw when Mara answered for their son. "The assistant district attorney asked for the hearing to influence the public against Ariel. The judge must have known. That's why he kicked everyone except us out."

"But it was too late," Greg said. "I saw Sissy talking to Norty Walsh before the hearing, so expect some ugly publicity tomorrow."

Simon addressed his son. "When you testify, you'll explain what led up to the letter."

Ariel looked at the floor and then at his attorney.

"We haven't made a decision about whether or not your son

163

will testify, but I'm leaning against it," Greg said.

Simon jumped up. "If he doesn't testify, the jury will think he's guilty."

"The most damning evidence against Ariel is the perception he fled. If he testifies, Sissy Kleinman will deluge him with questions about his trip, and with each one, will convince the jury he did flee."

Mara bit her lower lip. "I heard his friends talking about how she twisted everything they said in front of the grand jury."

"Ariel's on trial for murder. He'll do what he has to," Simon said.

Greg cleared his throat. "We'll revisit the decision before the trial."

Simon glared at Greg who looked away. That's when Simon remembered what the attorney had said the first time they met.

If he knew a client was guilty, he couldn't let him testify.

TWENTY-NINE

The next day's front-page story was worse than Mara expected. It ran under the picture the *Post-Gazette's* photographer had snapped of Ariel who looked like he was baring his teeth. "Accused Killer's Letter So Damning That Judge Closes Hearing."

Josef didn't call Mara at her office or at home that night. Maybe he didn't want to speak to her because he had nothing encouraging to say or maybe he was no longer convinced of Ariel's innocence. How could she blame him when Simon made remarks about Ariel concealing his anger and questioned why he'd written a letter about committing such violent acts. Mara had taught English to teenage boys when the family lived in Israel so she knew how they said and wrote horrible things to prove their manliness without ever considering acting on them. Besides, Ariel was just like her. He couldn't murder anyone any more than she could.

When the following day's newspaper reported her son's trial would be held in Judge Denise Mason's court, Mara decided to call Greg Dickson to find out what he knew about her. As she reached for the phone, it rang. Mara heard Josef's slightly accented voice.

"Mara, I'm sorry I haven't called sooner. One of the children accused a staff member of fondling her. I've been dealing with the case worker, a vice detective and an assistant district attorney."

"Do you think it's true?"

"The staff member's on paid leave until the investigation's over. It's going to be in tomorrow's paper but in a back section. I don't know how you've lived with all the unfair publicity about Ariel."

Mara pursed her lips and squeezed her eyes shut. Josef believed in her son.

"When I read Ariel's case would be in Judge Mason's court, I

165

asked Jane Watkins, the assistant district attorney looking into our matter, about her. Jane's about to leave her current job, so she'll talk frankly with you."

"There's a problem?"

"I'm not sure. She'll be here this afternoon to speak to the child. If you can come around four, she should be finished."

At three forty-five the electric gate at the entrance of the Tumbleweed campus opened to permit Mara's car to enter. After she parked and was walking past the cabins where the teenage residents lived, she thought about the parental abuse, which had forced them out of their homes to seek refuge here. Had any of these children been accused of murder, she would have blamed the violence inflicted on them. What did people who believed Ariel was guilty think had turned him into a killer?

They probably blamed a bad mother.

When Mara entered the cabin, which housed Josef's office, his door was closed. His secretary said he was meeting with Jane Watkins so Mara sat down on a nearby bench. A few minutes later Josef exited his office with a very pregnant woman who had auburn hair and freckles to match.

Josef smiled when he saw Mara. She stood, and he walked over to her, close enough that she could enjoy the spicy scent of his aftershave. "Jane, this is my good friend Mara Levine. I will deeply appreciate any help you give her." As the two women shook hands, Josef added, "You can use my office."

After Mara closed the door, Jane slowly lowered herself onto the couch across from Josef's desk. Mara sat down at the opposite end. "I remember the last few months of my two pregnancies."

"You went through this twice? You're a real trooper."

"It's worth it," Mara assured her.

"You have quite a guy in Josef Kessler. He's helped a number of the children face testifying against their parents. He mentioned your son's situation, and when I told him I knew a little about the judge, he asked me to meet with you."

"Thank you."

"It's only right you know there's bad blood between Judge Mason and your son's attorney. She thinks she would have been a judge four years sooner if it hadn't been for him."

Mara had checked the Internet so she knew Judge Mason had

only been a judge for two years after having been an assistant district attorney for sixteen, but she had seen nothing about her running for judge before that.

"Six years ago Denise Mason indicated she wanted to be a judge," Jane said. "District Attorney Jones gave her a high profile murder case that should have been a sure winner for her. Instead, Greg Dickson won an acquittal for his client. In the process it was apparent that Denise hadn't done her homework. After the newspapers lambasted her performance, she dropped her plans to run for judge that year."

"It sounds like it was her own fault."

"It was, but she couldn't admit that her usual lazy work habits had done her in. I don't know whether Greg has any idea she blames him."

The information worried Mara, but what Jane told her was too tenuous to have Judge Mason removed from the case. "What should I do?" she asked.

"Watch Judge Mason's treatment of Greg and encourage him to challenge her if her antipathy towards him is obvious to the jury. Their verdict could depend on it."

"Thank you for your help."

"I hope you don't mind if I remind you of something," Jane said.

"What?"

"Sometimes the children here get in trouble with the law or, like now, accuse others. In either event it helps when Josef has a good relationship with the District Attorney's office. If he's associated with your son . . ."

"I'll tell Josef not to come to the trial." But the ordeal would be so much more difficult without him.

When the two women left Josef's office, his secretary said he'd gone to one of the cabins. Mara didn't wait for him. More frightened than ever that Ariel could be convicted, she wanted to get home to him. She was motivated both by a belief that her presence would somehow protect him and by the fear she might not have much more time to spend with him.

Mara walked in the front door a little after five o'clock and found Ariel sitting on the couch in front of the television, his eyes closed, snoring softly. She turned off the set and called his name.

He opened his eyes and yawned. "I'm so tired, Mom. Maybe it's the medicine."

Mara sat down next to him. "You might need a lower dose. I'll get you an appointment with a neurologist."

Ariel pointed to the black band on his ankle. "I'm not allowed to leave the house."

"Don't worry. Greg Dickson will arrange it."

But would Sissy Kleinman find some way to use the request against Ariel?

***

Sissy sat at her desk smiling at the prospect of Judge Denise Mason presiding at Ariel's trial. Denise had relied on her when they had both been assistant district attorneys. The future jurist had come to Sissy any time she had to brief a legal issue. Sissy had shared her research. The more people beholding to her, the better. Unfortunately for Denise, Sissy had been home, having just given birth to her second child, when Denise faced Greg Dickson in a case she botched when she had to go it alone.

The ringing of her phone interrupted Sissy's musings.

"Ms. Kleinman, Greg Dickson here. Seems we need a small change in the bail order Judge Pressler signed."

"That will go to Judge Mason now."

"I think you and I can handle it as an agreed order. It's a health issue. Levine needs to see a neurologist about changing the dose of his Dilantin."

"You're a sly one, Greg Dickson."

"What do you mean?"

"I'm not playing into your defense strategy that the poor sick kid stayed in Guatemala because he was having seizures."

"A doctor there gave him Dilantin. This is just to see if he needs a different dose."

"We both know how easy it is to buy drugs on the street in Guatemala. If there really was a doctor involved, bring him here to testify. Then Judge Mason can decide."

***

Monday afternoon Ariel convinced Mara to watch <u>Jeopardy</u> with him. "When we first moved to Houston, we never missed it. You knew so many answers I wanted you to be a contestant."

Those were the days right after the family arrived from Israel. Ariel, just nine, coming home from school insisting he learned so much from the show that it was like doing homework. Mara couldn't resist him with his imploring brown eyes holding her gaze and his lopsided grin making her smile.

She sat next to her son on the living room couch and tousled his hair. "I'm a regular receptacle of useless facts."

Mara had just correctly responded, "Who is Tricia Nixon?" to "This Presidential daughter got married in the White House in 1971," when the doorbell rang.

She opened the door for Simon, who walked wordlessly into her townhouse and sank heavily into the lounge chair diagonally across from the couch. He looked at the floor and when he raised his head, he addressed Ariel in a soft monotone. "I hope your memory is better than mine."

Mara turned off the television. "What do you mean?"

"Ariel, please tell me you remember the name and address of the doctor we went to in Guatemala City."

"Um . . . Costello-Martinez or maybe Martinez-Costello."

"I think it's something like that, too, but I have no idea about his address."

"Me neither, Dad. Both the time we went together and the time I went alone, the hotel manager had the cab waiting and had given the driver the address. The nurse called a cab when the appointments were over."

"What does all that matter?" Mara asked. "He's going to a doctor here."

"Sissy Kleinman's opposing it. She claims Ariel's seizures are a ruse."

Mara's throat tightened. "We're up against pure evil."

"Greg Dickson will fight, but he said it would really help if we had something from the Guatemala City doctor."

Mara jumped up and went into the kitchen where she took a phone book from a drawer in the built-in desk and looked up the number of a local Holiday Inn. After a few minutes they found the number for their sister hotel in Guatemala City. When she reached the operator there, she kept repeating "manager" as she didn't know the Spanish word. The second operator she spoke to connected her. The manager spoke English flawlessly. He told her that he was new but offered to check the records to find out who was on duty when Ariel was there. When he came back to the phone, he said, "That employee is no longer with us."

"How can we reach him?"

"He left town. There was a . . . a problem."

"He sent my son to a doctor whose name is something like Martinez-Costello or Costello-Martinez. We need to talk to him."

"I've never heard of him. He was probably the other manager's friend or relative."

"Can you check the telephone directory?"

"Of course."

Mara watched the clock. It was six minutes before the manager got back to her. "I'm sorry. I can't find any doctor with that name or one similar. Perhaps there's a listing under the name of a clinic."

While the manager held on, Mara spoke to Simon and Ariel. If there'd been a clinic name, neither of them had noticed it.

Mara resumed her phone conversation. "If the doctor's office hadn't been opened long, perhaps he's not in the phone book but directory assistance would have his number."

"I'll check."

Three minutes passed.

"I'm sorry."

"Thank you." Mara's eyes welled with tears but she willed herself not to cry. It would only upset Ariel. He and Simon were standing behind her waiting to hear the results of her efforts. "No luck locating the doctor."

Simon looked pale. "I can't believe how stupid I was not to write down the doctor's name and address."

Mara had never before heard her former husband belittle himself.

"We'll just have to count on Greg Dickson's persuasive powers at the hearing," she said.

The following morning Simon called Mara and told her Greg had him sign an affidavit swearing to the visit at the doctor's office in Guatemala City and his inability to reach the doctor now. His next statement surprised her. "He said neither of us should be at the hearing tomorrow."

"Why?"

"He's afraid Sissy Kleinman will try to call us as witnesses, and he doesn't want her to have a shot at us yet."

Mara had planned to be there, to observe the interactions between the judge and her son's attorney, but if she were trapped into testifying, it could hurt Ariel. She imagined the assistant district attorney asking her questions like whether she saw Ariel take three does of Dilantin every day. Since she was at her office when he took two of them, her answer would be "no."

The next day Simon's, "Hello, Mara," sounded so triumphant that Mara knew the judge had allowed the doctor's visit before Simon gave her the news. "There's just one thing," Simon said.

"What?"

"Dickson had to agree that Ariel would waive doctor-patient confidentiality."

***

Simon needed to pick his son's neurologist carefully. If he were someone who'd been influenced by the bad publicity to believe Ariel was guilty, he might write a report that Sissy Kleinman could use against the teen. He asked every doctor he knew for recommendations. A number mentioned Abe Cohen and Arnold Levy, who were partners. Their names indicated they were Jewish so they likely recognized the undercurrents of anti-Semitism surrounding his son's case and would be sympathetic.

Ariel grinned as he entered Simon's car. "I never thought I'd be happy to be going to the doctor's."

Simon had been so relieved his son wasn't in prison that he hadn't focused on how cooped up Ariel must feel being sentenced to his mother's townhouse.

As they passed a McDonald's, Ariel said, "What I wouldn't give for one of their chocolate milkshakes and an order of fries."

Simon pulled into the parking lot of the fast food chain but reconsidered. "We'll have to get it at the drive-by window. I only have permission to take you to the doctor's. If we screw up, they may not let you out again."

Ariel, who had just opened the car door, closed it. "I guess you're right."

When father and son arrived at Scurlock Tower, the professional building where Drs. Cohen and Levy officed, Simon drove into the indoor parking lot. Floor after floor was filled and,

171

as he made one sharp turn after another, he felt they were going around in circles rather than heading up. He found a space on the top floor, led Ariel to an elevator to the main floor and then another up to doctors' office. The waiting room was full except for two seats next to each other near the door.

Father and son sat down across from a woman with a toddler on her lap. Ariel waved at the little girl who waved back. Her mother stared at Ariel for a few seconds and then carried her child to the other side of the room. Ariel looked at his father who shrugged, trying to convey the message that the mother might be afraid of strangers in general, not Ariel in particular. Still the incident confirmed for Simon that he'd done the right thing making the appointment under the name A.Y. Levine. That's what the nurse called forty-five minutes after their arrival.

The thin dark haired woman led them to an examining room and motioned Ariel to sit on the examining table. "Do you go by your initials or by a first name?"

"Call me Ariel please."

"Ariel Levine," she responded as she studied him before taking his blood pressure. "Dr. Cohen will be in shortly."

A man in a white lab coat who was about Simon's age entered the room ten minutes later. His almost bald head made the wine colored birthmark which extended from his right cheek up to his forehead all the more prominent. "What sort of problem are you having, Ariel?"

The teen told Dr. Cohen the history of his two seizures and Simon chimed in about their visit to the doctor in Guatemala City.

"I remember you were in Guatemala," Dr. Cohen said.

"That doctor gave him Dilantin to stop future seizures and told him to take 100 milligrams three times a day. But Ariel's sleeping so much and has no energy so we wondered if that dose is too high."

Dr. Cohen wrote some notes on Ariel's chart. "I'm not sure he's had any seizures. The event in the tourist office was likely just a fainting spell. The only reason I suspect the episode at the youth hostel could be a seizure is the fact that your son reported he lost control of his bladder during it."

"But . . . but the doctor in Guatemala . . ."

Dr. Cohen moved the wheeled stool he was sitting on closer to

Simon. "It's a cultural thing, being deferential to Americans by over treating them or telling them what they want to hear."

"Then it's safe to take him off the Dilantin?"

Dr. Cohen made a noise that was halfway between a laugh and a snort. "After the history he gave me, I'd be asking for a malpractice suit if I did that. But I'll have the nurse take his blood. We may be able to lower the dose."

"And if not, what can we do for his tiredness?"

"It's probably depression. He'll need to see a psychiatrist."

Simon imagined a hearing to get permission for Ariel to visit another doctor and pictured a headline reading, "Parents recognize son is a psychopath, ask for psychiatric visit." So he implored, "But you would know what anti-depressant he can safely take with Dilantin. Can't you prescribe it?"

Dr. Cohen's birthmark deepened into a dark shade of purple. "I guess so."

While Ariel waited for the nurse, Simon went to the men's room. On his way back, he passed Dr. Cohen's office where the door was slightly ajar, and the physician was talking on the phone. Simon heard him say, "He's brought shame to the whole Houston Jewish community."

THIRTY

Judge Mason had given them just three months to prepare for trial. Mara sat with Simon and Ariel in Greg Dickson's office determined they do so well and immediately.

Ariel contributed little to their conversation and yawned frequently. After reviewing her son's blood work, Dr. Cohen had decided not to change his dose of Dilantin but had prescribed an anti-depressant. Ariel had taken his first dose that morning.

"Absence of blood is the key," Greg said. "Our blood splatter expert is Matthew Cavazos who worked in the San Antonio Police Lab for twenty-eight years before retiring a year ago. He'll testify that the way the three victims were attacked, the murderer would have gotten their blood on him."

"Wouldn't it help to have a doctor testify, too?" Mara asked.

Simon looked from Mara to Greg. "You'll have to forgive my former wife. She forgets she's only been out of law school for a year and has never tried a criminal case."

Mara took a deep breath. "I just want us to think of everything for Ariel's sake."

"With no physical evidence to connect Ariel to the crime, how do they plan to convict him?" Simon asked.

"In Texas it takes just one eyewitness," Greg said. "That is why it's so important to have an expert on the inaccuracies of eyewitness accounts. Dr. Patricia Lansing, the woman I've chosen, has written numerous articles on the topic and has testified for defendants so often she needs little preparation."

Mara had seen a newspaper article about prisoners released on the basis of DNA evidence in which Dr. Lansing had been quoted as saying that ninety per cent had been convicted because of faulty eyewitness testimony. But Mara had a concern. "Even if she gets the jury to doubt Andrew Block's identification of Ariel, there's still the license plate number he wrote down which led them to Virginia's Land Rover."

"Dr. Lansing is a memory expert so she's also going to testify as to how people writing down a string of letters and numbers tend to get the last few wrong."

So much hinged on Dr. Lansing. She had to be as good as Greg predicted.

"The current Mrs. Levine's car dealer sold five other dark colored Land Rovers around the same time she bought hers," the attorney said. "On their license plates the beginning letters are the same as hers but their ending numbers are different, yet close enough that Andrew Block could have written them down wrong."

"One of the owners or one of their family members could match Ariel's description," Mara said excitedly. "How soon can your investigator start interviewing them?"

"I've told you my job is to raise reasonable doubt with the jury, not search for the murderer."

"Can't you get the police to do something?"

"They're convinced they have the killer, and that he's about to go to trial."

Ariel shuddered.

"Give me the names the dealer gave your investigator, and I'll check them out," Mara said.

"My secretary has the list."

***

Back in her office, Mara wrote each name – Peter Yarborough, Mary Jane Logan, Leonard Gates, Sidney Elling and Thomas Denison – on a separate piece of paper in a spiral notebook. She took out the White Business Pages and looked up the phone numbers for each. Yarborough and Gates were listed as attorneys and Denison as a pediatrician. A Logan Advertising Agency could be connected with Mary Jane Logan but she saw no business with the name Elling in it. Mara turned to the Residential Phone Directory where she found a listing for Sidney Elling but none for Mary Jane Logan.

In the small law library she shared with two other attorneys, Mara went to Martindale Hubbell which lists attorneys nationwide and looked up biographical information on both Yarborough and Gates. The former, whose year of birth was shown as 1965, was in his mid thirties and so unlikely to either be mistaken for a man in his late teens or early twenties or to have a child that age. Gates' year of birth put him in his late forties. He could have a son the right age, so Mara tried him first.

She gave her name and told his secretary she was an attorney. A voice with just a hint of a New York accent identified the speaker as Leonard Gates.

"Mr. Gates, I'm Mara Levine, a fellow member of the bar, calling for a non legal reason. I'm thinking of buying a Land Rover and I wondered how you like yours."

"How do you know I have one?"

Mara had figured he'd ask. "When I was at the dealership, I heard another customer mention that his friend Leonard Gates owned one. Your name was familiar, probably because of some legal conference we'd both attended, and sure enough you were in Martindale Hubbell."

A few seconds of silence followed. Maybe Leonard Gates hadn't believed her. But then he spoke.

"It's my wife who loves the Land Rover. I bought it for her right after she gave birth to our twins. I was so thrilled we finally had children that I would have given her anything she wanted."

She shouldn't have expected success with her first call. Even though Peter Yarborough was the wrong age to be mistaken for Ariel, he might live with someone the right age, so Mara tried him next. When he came on the line, she went through the same script as she had with Gates. But instead of being wary, Yarborough immediately blurted out everything he loved about the Land Rover and added, "My partner bought it for me to celebrate our fifth anniversary together."

"Your partner likes driving it, too?"

Yarborough laughed. "No, he's fifty and going through a second childhood, so he'll only drive a sports car."

She had three more possibilities. When she tried Dr. Denison's office and the Logan Advertising Agency, she got recorded messages at both that their offices closed at five o'clock. She got no answer at Sidney Elling's home.

The next morning Mara called the Logan Advertising Agency and reached a man with a phony sounding British accent. He told Mara Ms. Logan was out for the day and asked if he could help.

"It's a personal matter," Mara said.

"If it were, you'd have her home number."

Mara called Dr. Denison's office. His receptionist said he was making rounds at the hospital and asked what the call concerned.

"I'm thinking of buying a Land Rover and wondered if Dr. Denison likes his."

"He did until he broke one of his rules."

"What do you mean?"

"He said he'd never let either of his teenage daughters drive it, and the first time he did, the older one totaled it. That car's so safe she wasn't hurt."

That night Mara went into her bedroom and shut the door. She didn't want Ariel to hear her call Sidney Elling. She wasn't going to let her son know what she was doing until she had some good news to report.

A woman with a high pitched voice answered the phone. When Mara asked to speak to Sidney Elling, she replied, "This is she."

Mara introduced herself with her usual lie about how she got Ms. Elling's name and then asked, "How do you like your Land Rover?"

"My children put you up to this, didn't they? They don't think a seventy year old woman had any business buying a Land Rover."

Mara apologized for bothering Ms. Elling and put down the receiver. Mary Jane Logan was her last hope.

The next day the same man as before answered the advertising agency's phone. Mara told him she was trying to reach Ms. Logan to find out how she liked her Land Rover.

"I don't know if you're a salesman or a stalker, but in either event, don't call again."

Mara held the receiver in her hand for a couple of seconds and then dialed Simon's number. Virginia had been in advertising. Maybe she knew Ms. Logan.

As soon as Virginia heard Mara's voice, she said, "Simon's not here."

Mara explained she wanted to speak to her because she might know one of the five other Land Rover owners.

"My husband told me how you keep coming up with hare brained schemes causing more work for Greg Dickson and his investigator which means more cost to Simon."

Mara willed herself to speak calmly. She needed this woman's help for her son. "I'm trying to do everything I can for Ariel who appreciates all of his father's support."

"Well, it's Simon's money. We keep our finances separate. And Ariel's a good boy. He always listens to me. But still, there's no reason for you to bankrupt Simon."

"I understand, but since I'm doing this on my own perhaps you can help me. I thought you might know Mary Jane Logan since you used to be in advertising. She owns a Land Rover with . . ."

"She saw me with mine at a meeting and went right out and bought one for herself. She was always one step behind me."

"Does she have any children?"

"Of course not. No successful professional woman does."

Mara hung up the receiver. How different her choices and those of Virginia had been. Virginia's had led to a successful career complete with financial security and the metamorphosis of Simon into a devoted husband. Mara's efforts to be the perfect wife and mother had resulted in her two sons still suffering the aftermath of divorce with a possible murder conviction hanging over the head of one.

And none of her efforts had helped him.

Completely disheartened, Mara called Josef. "Are you available for lunch?"

"How about Taco Delight?"

Mara arrived first and went to the flower-tiled counter to place their usual order of grilled fish tacos in corn tortillas. While she waited for her number to be called, she went to the condiment table and filled little white paper cups with *pico de gallo*, salsa and jalapenos, and placed them on a nearby table. As she was picking up their food, Josef rushed in, his tie askew and his sport jacket buttoned so that its right side hung lower than its left.

He took the tray from Mara. "Sorry I'm late, but I had to help break up a fight between two of our residents. Those girls were a lot stronger than I expected."

Mara smiled, took his plate of tacos off the tray and put it in front of him.

"What have you discovered?" he asked.

Mara related her failed efforts, ending with her call to Virginia. "The funny thing is they say a man keeps marrying the same kind of woman. But I don't think of myself as intimidating."

"Hardly." Josef squeezed her arm.

Mara, who was no longer hungry, put the last of her fish tacos on Josef's plate.

Josef hesitated. "There is another possibility."

"What?"

"Ariel may be lying."

Mara's chest tightened. She should have known it would come to this. She stood up, ready to leave, when Josef said, "Not about the murder, about the Land Rover."

She sat down slowly and waited for his explanation.

"You find Virginia intimidating, and you're an adult and an attorney. Ariel's a teenager who has to please her to keep peace with his father."

Mara looked at Josef. Where was he headed?

"Let's say, against all her admonitions, Ariel drove the Land Rover to the shopping center for some innocent reason. Through bad luck, he was there around the time of the murder, and the witness did see him drive off in Virginia's vehicle."

"His first instinct would be to lie about having driven the Land Rover so as not to get in trouble with Virginia," Mara said.

Josef nodded. "Since that's what he told the police, he'd be afraid to change his story."

Mara put her elbow on the table and rested her chin in her hand. She could picture Ariel getting into just such a predicament in the way Josef described. As a mother she wanted to rush home and ask him about it. As an attorney she knew she shouldn't. There was no parent-child confidentiality privilege in Texas.

So as soon as she got to her office, Mara called Greg Dickson. She stayed at her desk until he called back a little after six and shared her suspicion.

"You haven't asked Ariel about this, have you?"

"Of course not," Mara said.

"Good."

"If it's true?"

"It will be better for him if you never know."

THIRTY-ONE

His son's crying was a magnet attracting Oracio to the kitchen. Eight-year-old Oscar's head was bent over his cereal as in between sobs he kept repeating that he didn't want to go to school. Oracio didn't have time for this. He needed to get to work, and he didn't want his son acting like a wimp.

Oracio made an effort to keep the anger out of his voice. "Why don't you want to go to school?"

"The substitute teacher thinks I'm stupid because I keep getting my letters mixed up."

Oracio was furious, not at his son, but at this so-called educator, who couldn't recognize a child who was dyslexic.

"I'll drive you to school and explain it to her."

"It's a him, and he'll be angry."

"I know how to deal with angry people."

Oscar raised his head. "Can you arrest him?"

"If he doesn't shape up, I just might."

"I'll get my books." Oscar hugged his father's legs as he went past him.

At the school, Oscar jumped out of the car and took Oracio's hand as they walked down the hall. They came to room 103. "He's in there," the child whispered.

Oracio pointed to a bench. "Wait here."

When Oracio entered the classroom, the man writing "Mr. Davis" on the blackboard turned around and faced him. He looked to be close to seventy, with rheumy gray eyes in a thin face capped by wispy white hair. His black suit would have fit his small frame better if he hadn't been so stoop shouldered. It was funny how someone so unimposing could be so intimidating to an eight year old.

"Mr. Davis, I'm Detective Crawley. I've come to talk to you about my son."

The teacher motioned his guest to sit at a student desk. As soon as Oracio did, he regretted automatically obeying a teacher. The plastic chair might not hold his weight, and he didn't like Mr. Davis looking down at him. But he'd feel even more foolish immediately getting up.

"So your son is the boy who has trouble with reading, spelling and writing."

"The trouble's called dyslexia. It's a learning disability."

"During the forty years I taught full time, parents didn't make excuses for their children. They worked with them."

"I do work with him – the way Loretta Sanchez, his teacher last year, taught me to."

"There's no Loretta Sanchez teaching here."

"She's a newspaper reporter now."

"Ah, the one with the vendetta against that innocent boy."

Oracio needed to hold his temper. He could only make things worse for Oscar.

"So tell me, Mr. Detective, are you the one feeding her information?"

"It's public information that two witnesses identified Ariel Levine as the killer."

"And that there's no physical evidence, but she never mentions that."

"I came to talk about my son."

"You defend a boy who's guilty of using excuses instead of trying while you try to convict a boy who's guilty of nothing. You remind me of the police in Russia sixty years ago."

Oracio had to get away before he lost control. He stood up, knocking over the desk. Books and papers landed on the floor. The detective wanted to wipe the smile off the teacher's face but instead he strode out of the room.

As soon as he was in the hall, Oscar ran to him. "Did you arrest him?"

"Not yet. When will your regular teacher be back?"

"Tomorrow."

"Let's go. You're studying at home today."

***

In the squad room Oracio kicked his metal wastebasket. It landed in the corner, putting a dent in the wall. Davis could cause trouble for him, maybe going to his boss and claiming Oracio was feeding information to Loretta Sanchez. She'd always promised she'd refuse to name him as her source, but if her newspaper's editor insisted, who knows what she'd do. Then there was the way the teacher defended Levine. Davis could be a Jewish name so maybe he was sticking up for one of his own. Maybe he knew the family personally.

Yet, even some unprejudiced people might be influenced by the lack of physical evidence. The letter the murdering bastard had written to his friend would help. But Sissy wanted more.

Oracio was trying to figure out where to find it when a tall lanky African American with a shaved head and an earring in his right earlobe walked into the squad room. Oracio stood and shook his hand. "James, how can Houston's schools be safe if you're here?"

"The Houston School District's police force can do without me while I help a brother officer."

James relaxed into a chair, his long legs filling the space between it and Oracio's desk. "I have a piece of information which might help you with that rich little bastard you brought back from Guatemala."

Oracio sat down on the edge of his desk.

"Three years ago one of my underlings, Ava Branson, arrested Ariel Levine for having beer in his car which he'd parked in his high school's lot." James laughed. "The dumb fuck was cleaning out his car, throwing empty beer cans in a trash receptacle when she noticed him. Too bad for our future killer, two unopened cans were on the floor."

Oracio was sure a jury would see such a minor offense as meaningless.

"Sitting on the passenger seat was the kid's backpack which Ava took, figuring it might contain marijuana or hard drugs."

"Were there any?" Oracio asked.

"Nah. Just schoolbooks and a notebook. In the notebook she read what at the time she thought were rap lyrics, but now she's not so sure."

"What do you mean?"

"After she saw the newspaper story about how the kid wrote terrible things to his friend, she reconsidered. Maybe those were his thoughts and not rap lyrics."

"What kind of thoughts?"

"About killing a woman."

"Where's the notebook?"

"Ava gave it to the mother."

"Damn."

"But she still kind of remembers what was in it."

"Give me her phone number."

James jotted it down. "That rich spoiled bastard got probation for the beer. A kid from the hood would have his ass in jail."

As soon as James left his office, Oracio called Sissy. When the receptionist said she was in court, Oracio, noticing it was almost lunchtime, asked which one. He headed to the courthouse and walked into the 112th Criminal Court, hoping to catch Sissy when the judge called a break.

The courtroom was empty except for a lone figure sitting at a table in the front. As Oracio approached, he saw Sissy writing on a lined yellow legal pad.

"You never stop working, do you?" he said.

She looked up. "Preparation's the name of the game. Lucky for me most opposing counsel are too stupid or too lazy to play."

Sissy was amazing. So unlike his wife, who worked part time as a practical nurse, never thinking, just following other people's orders. Instead of wearing some ugly white uniform, Sissy was dressed in a high sheen navy blue suit with gold buttons. Oracio wondered what material it was made of, and, as he sat down next to her, he had to restrain himself from touching her sleeve to find out.

"I've been doing some preparation myself." He told her about James Underwood's visit, ending with, "Unfortunately Ava Branson gave the notebook to Levine's mother, so it's probably gone or she'll say it is."

Sissy tapped her fingers on the table. "Actually that could be quite fortunate for us."

Oracio didn't know what Sissy was getting at but he nodded, pretending he did. "I've got Ava's phone number for you."

He tried to hand her the paper James had written the number on, but Sissy put her palm up in a motion indicating he should stop. "You need to be the one to talk to her. When I have her on the witness stand, I want her to be able to answer 'no' if Dickson asks if she's ever discussed her testimony with me."

"What do you want me to ask Ava?"

"For now just whether she saw Levine's notebook with writing in it about killing a woman. Once we're sure the notebook doesn't exist, you'll have lots to discuss."

***

The doorbell buzzed just once, and then there was pounding on the door. As she got closer, Mara heard, "Open up, Sheriff's Department."

She had to hide Ariel. But that was crazy. No one had the right to take him away. He'd followed all the rules of his house arrest - only leaving to see his attorney once a week and going on the permitted trip to the doctor's. She opened the door determined not to let them have him.

A short, wide middle-aged man handed her a document and demanded she sign a paper he thrust at her confirming she'd received it. Although it was dinnertime, when he left, he said, "Have a nice day."

Mara sat down on the couch and opened the document, a subpoena for all of Ariel's high school notebooks. Why would anyone want them or think she'd still have them after all this time? She threw them in the recycle bin at the end of each semester, and Ariel had graduated a year and a half ago. Mara skimmed through the portion of the subpoena that defined terms like "notebook" and "Harris County District Attorney's Office" and came to the part, which stated that the subpoena specifically covered the notebook Ariel had in his possession at the time he was arrested for bringing alcoholic beverages to his high school.

Ariel walked in from the kitchen where he'd been helping Mara make dinner. "Who was at the door?"

Mara didn't want to alarm her son. Now that he was taking an anti-depressant he slept much less and made lists of questions to ask his attorney. "Do you remember anything about a notebook you had when you were arrested for having those beer cans in your car?"

Ariel looked puzzled as he sat down next to his mother. "There was probably one in my backpack."

"Did anyone make mention of it at the time? Maybe the principal or the arresting officer."

"Oh, yea. The lady who arrested me said the rap lyrics in my notebook were disgusting."

"Why was she even looking at your notebook?"

Ariel shrugged. "Don't know."

Mara stood. "Let's finish making dinner."

"Wait, Mom. What's the problem?"

"The assistant district attorney subpoenaed the notebook, but I don't have it any more, so don't worry about it."

"You'd better call Greg Dickson."

She did as Ariel instructed and was put right through to him.

"Your former husband's here," Greg said. "He brought his subpoena. I assume you got one, too. Let me put you on the speaker phone."

Mara wished Ariel wasn't standing behind the kitchen desk. She could speak more freely if he weren't listening. She told Greg and Simon what Ariel had reported about the notebook.

Simon's voice boomed. "What do rap lyrics have to do with anything? This is ridiculous."

"They're frequently anti-women," Mara said. "They sometimes even talk about raping and killing."

"Mrs. Levine, do you have the notebook?"

"No, it went into the recycle bin a long time ago."

"Won't that end everything?" Simon asked.

"Not with Sissy, it won't," Greg said.

***

Two days later as Mara sat in Greg's office with her son and former husband, she learned how prophetic the attorney's words had been.

When he'd advised the assistant district attorney the notebook had been destroyed, she said she wouldn't believe it unless Mara and Simon testified to that "under oath in open court," and that she was going to request a hearing for just that purpose.

"The purpose of the hearing is to generate more bad publicity," Mara said.

"Ariel, do you remember anything about the rap lyrics?" Greg asked.

"I don't even remember if I wrote them. We'd get bored in class and pass our notebooks around so anyone could have jotted them down."

"Did you deny you'd written them when the officer pointed them out to you?"

"No. I'd probably written some of them and, anyway, I wasn't going to argue with a policewoman."

"If she had no reason to look at the notebook, doesn't that constitute an illegal search which means she can't testify about what she read?" Mara asked.

"They'll come up with some excuse for why she read the notebook, and we'll fight it." The attorney was expressionless as he spoke, his usual reassuring smile missing.

"The important thing is to prevent a publicized hearing," Mara said. "The assistant district attorney let you use an affidavit from Simon about the doctor in Guatemala. Prepare affidavits for both of us about the notebook no longer existing and see if that satisfies her."

Greg sounded surprised and happy when he called Mara later that day to tell her the affidavits were acceptable.

But why had Sissy capitulated so quickly?

***

Oracio picked up the receiver of his desk phone and heard Sissy's voice. "I owe you, buddy. I have sworn statements from Levine's parents that the notebook was destroyed. Now it's your witness's word against theirs about what was in it."

Hopefully Ava Branson had a good memory.

"One other thing," Sissy said. "If Ava remembers things as we expect her to, call Loretta Sanchez and let her know about the notebook."

"Wouldn't it get more publicity with Norty Walsh at the *Post-Gazette?*"

"We have to teach him a lesson since he didn't warn us about the newspaper's favorable story on Levine. He'll be calling for more details after he sees the story in that suburban rag. That way we'll get double the publicity."

"Sissy, you're the smartest woman I know."

"You're a good match for me, aren't you, buddy?"

Determined not to let Sissy down, Oracio called Ava. They'd spoken once before when she'd confirmed she'd read Levine's notebook. He invited her to meet him for coffee near wherever she'd be at the end of the day.

Oracio arrived at Ike's Coffee Bar a couple of blocks from Lamar High School at four, fifteen minutes before their scheduled meeting. He stepped aside to allow two chattering teens clad in tennis outfits to leave, and sat down in a booth facing the door. When a woman in a French-blue shirt with dark blue pockets and epaulets walked in, he got up to greet her. Her matching trousers, set off by a double red stripe down the outer seam of each leg, hung loosely around her thin frame. She looked to be in her late twenties with straight brown hair, which, except for her bangs, was tucked behind her ears.

Oracio extended his hand. "Thank you for meeting me. What can I get you, Officer Branson?"

Oracio ordered two black coffees at the counter, brought them to their booth and handed one to Ava. "James Underwood regards you highly. Said you're the best team player he's got. You're the kind of police officer who moves up fast."

Ava blushed. "I do my best to get along with everyone."

"James is counting on you being a big help in the case against Ariel Levine, considering you saw the killer's notebook. That's about the most damning thing we've got."

Ava looked down at her coffee and stirred it. "Like I told you on the phone what I read might have been rap lyrics."

"Those are so disgusting. Only a woman hater would be interested in them."

Ava looked up and nodded.

"On the phone you mentioned Levine wrote about killing a woman."

"Yea, something about killing their bitches – like one gang planning revenge on another."

"Think carefully, Ava, could it have been slitting the throats of their bitches?"

"Well . . ."

"That's what Levine did, took a knife and slit one woman's throat and tried to do the same to another woman."

Ava put her coffee cup down. "You know there were doodles on

187

the page, and they could have been knives."

What a sick bastard. Not just writing about it, drawing pictures of it, too. And thinking about it for at least three years. They had to put the creep away, or he'd do it again.

"Then were his words that he planned to slit the throats of their bitches?"

"Yes, sir, I remember now."

***

Mara couldn't hide the *Houston Post-Gazette* from Ariël. He looked forward to reading it every day, doing the crossword puzzle and the anagram to help fill his time. But he paid no attention to the *Weekly Bulletin* so every Friday morning Mara scooped it from her front lawn and took it to her office. Her son didn't need to see any unfavorable story it might have about him.

On the Friday following the signing of the notebook affidavits, Mara sat at her desk and opened the paper to its front page. What she read took her breath away.

"High school notebook and letter to friend both show Levine's desire to kill."

Loretta Sanchez's article quoted an unnamed source. "This seemingly nice, polite, sweet guy from Israel fooled his friends and family while he fantasized about killing a woman. Unfortunately for Herlinda Sorento, Ariel Levine acted on it the day after Thanksgiving."

Mara forced herself to exhale, went to the waiting room, grabbed a copy of the *Houston Post-Gazette* and scoured it. She found nothing about Ariel. The *Weekly Bulletin* didn't have that large a circulation. Maybe the article wouldn't have much impact. She wanted to get Josef's reaction but he was away at a three-day conference. Instead, she called Simon and read him the article.

"Judge Pressler told the assistant district attorney she wasn't to talk to the press about the letter," he said.

"And she's too smart to disobey a judge's order. I'm sure it was Detective Crawley."

After Simon agreed to tell Greg Dickson about the article and to not mention it to Ariel, Mara cut it out, put in a file with other newspaper coverage, and tossed the rest of the paper in her wastebasket.

When she arrived home that night, neither Ariel nor Benjie

mentioned the article. If no one had brought it to their attention, maybe it hadn't been widely read.

Saturday Mara decided to take the occasion of Josef's being out of town to spend the evening with Ariel. She went to the video store and, knowing how he enjoyed the Three Stooges, picked Disorder in the Court, Heavenly Days and Curly Classics. Once home she found Ariel and Benjie sitting at the dining room table reading an early edition of the *Sunday Houston Post-Gazette*.

Benjie pushed his chair back from the table so quickly he almost knocked Mara over. He ran up the stairs and slammed the door to his room.

"What's going on?" Mara asked.

"Look at this," Ariel said.

Mara read the front page story under the by-line of Norton Walsh. She honed in on what made this article even more toxic than the one in the *Weekly Bulletin*. "When asked about rumors that in both the letter and the notebook Levine specifically fantasized about slitting a woman's throat, assistant district attorney Sissy Kleinman said, 'It would be improper for me to respond. But if that turns out to be true, a jury would have no choice but to convict.'"

That's why Sissy had Simon and her swear the notebook didn't exist. It gave her carte blanche to have her witness say anything she wanted her to about what the notebook contained. Even if Greg Dickson convinced Judge Mason the notebook couldn't be mentioned at trial because it was the result of an illegal search, potential jurors would have been influenced by Sissy's remarks.

Mara's office file was filled, with one exception, with unfavorable stories about Ariel.

"We need to move the trial from Houston."

* * *

Mara took the articles from her file and placed them on the long mahogany table in Greg Dickson's conference room. She faced the room's large picture window, which, instead of revealing a view of downtown Houston, was plummeted with sheets of rain.

She spoke to Greg, who sat across from her and Simon and Ariel. "I could read these thirty-eight newspaper articles to you but since we're all aware of what they say and what they've likely done to any Houston jury pool, let's save time and talk about moving the

189

case to another venue."

Greg went to the corner of the room and stood next to an easel holding a flip chart. He tore off the first page and revealed the work he'd done before they arrived. On one side the heading was "Advantages" and on the other "Disadvantages." The only advantage was "Possibly a fairer jury." The disadvantages fell under cost and convenience issues involving the family, the defense team and witnesses and included items like time and cost of travel and the expense of food and lodging. Greg pointed to the Advantages side. "As bad as the publicity's been, at least in Houston, you have a lot of immigrants and their offspring who can accept that someone was raised in another country like Ariel was. If we wind up in some outlying areas where anyone with a foreign background is viewed as suspect, we'll have bigger problems."

"There are other large cities in Texas," Mara said.

"Dallas is law and order and in San Antonio we'd wind up with a jury which is largely Hispanic, like the victim. Galveston is so close that the *Houston Post-Gazette* has a wide circulation there, and Kleinman will fight going to Austin, claiming its demographics are too different from Houston's."

"Is there no place Ariel can get a fair trial?" Mara asked.

"It's a crap shoot," Greg said. "You could wind up somewhere as bad or worse, and have significantly increased the costs of Ariel's defense."

Ariel turned to Mara. "I thought moving the trial was a great idea, but if it might not make any difference, I hate for Dad to throw his money away."

Simon put his arm around Ariel. "You know I'd spend my last penny to defend you."

Mara believed him. But he and Ariel were capitulating too quickly to Greg's arguments. Why was the attorney being so one sided? Did he want to stay in Houston because of his other clients?

Ariel had to be his priority.

"I can't believe there's nothing we can do to insure a fair trial for our son," Mara said.

"Our best bet is to get the trial delayed so that a lot of this publicity is forgotten," Greg replied.

"That won't do it," Mara insisted. "There'll just be more while we wait for a later trial date."

Greg tore off the sheet they were viewing and revealed one headed, "Path Forward." His proposal was to ask the judge to either move the trial out of Houston or to delay it. Since she would almost certainly pick the delay, the next step was to request a gag order so no one connected with the case could discuss it publicly.

Based on what assistant district attorney Jane Watkins had told Mara about Judge Mason's grudge against Greg, the judge wouldn't go along with either the delay or the gag order. As she listened to Ariel and Simon embrace Greg's plan, Mara decided to talk to Greg privately about her concerns. Ariel didn't need to add Judge Mason to his list of worries.

"Simon, could you take Ariel back to my house? I have to stay downtown to go to the courthouse."

Though her former husband looked surprised, he agreed.

When they left, Mara lingered in the conference room as Greg gathered the sheets he'd torn off.

"I'm sure you're aware of Judge Mason's ill feelings towards you," Mara said. "What are we going to do to make certain they don't play a role at the trial?"

"What are you talking about?"

"She would have run for judge four years earlier but you ended those plans when you defeated her in a case she should have won."

Greg crossed his arms over his chest. "Mrs. Levine, you don't do any criminal work so you don't understand how prosecutors and defense attorneys face each other all the time in the courtroom without feeling any personal animosity towards each other."

Mara felt her cheeks get warm. "According to what I heard, this was different. So please be on the lookout for any problems with her."

***

The first thing Mara noticed as Judge Denise Mason entered the courtroom and took her seat behind the bench was that she smiled at Sissy Kleinman. The smile did not improve a wide face with slack skin, the pallor of which was emphasized by hair dyed a deep shade of black. Mara knew from reading her biographical information that the judge was in her mid forties but she looked ten years older.

Greg Dickson's first request was that the hearing be closed. He argued that since the reason behind his request to move the trial was publicity, it would only add to the problem if this hearing generated more.

"Your Honor, this hearing was Mr. Dickson's idea," Sissy retorted. "He should have thought about the publicity before he asked for it."

"I agree with Ms. Kleinman," the judge replied.

"Then, Your Honor," Greg said, "I'm requesting you accept these thirty-eight newspaper articles as exhibits so I don't have to read them out loud."

"We'll take a short break while I look at them."

When Judge Mason returned to the courtroom thirty minutes later, Mara knew she hadn't had time to do any more than skim the articles.

"These seem to be a little worse than what we'd normally expect with such a ghastly crime," the judge said.

Sissy argued that "a little worse" couldn't justify the added expense to the State of moving the trial.

"But, Your Honor . . ."

"I agree with Ms. Kleinman," the judge said.

"Then, Your Honor, please postpone the trial until the fallout from the publicity has died down and impose a gag order so we don't get any more."

"Your Honor, consider the First Amendment implications of a gag order and the public's right to know," Sissy implored.

"The attorneys are not to speak to the press from now until the trial ends," the judge intoned.

Mara shook her head. That wouldn't stop Detective Crawley from feeding information to the press after Sissy fed it to him.

The judge stood.

"Your Honor, what about my motion to delay the trial?" Greg asked.

Judge Mason's gavel came down hard.

"Denied."

THIRTY-TWO

Greg Dickson leaned over his desk, cleared his throat and addressed Mara, Simon and Ariel. "At the pretrial hearing I went to yesterday I reminded Ms. Kleinman she had a duty to give me any exculpatory evidence, evidence pointing to Ariel's innocence."

The attorney explained that from reading witness interviews and lab reports he was aware Mrs. Luna thought the killer was talking to her as she dialed 911 and that the police had lifted a bloody palm print from the counter near where Mrs. Sorento was murdered and some skin from under her fingernails.

"If the killer's voice were on the call, I wanted to get a voice print to show it wasn't Ariel's voice, and, of course, the palm print and fingernail clippings could reveal the killer."

Mara jumped up. "We can prove Ariel's innocent."

"I'm afraid I have bad news," Greg said.

Simon closed his eyes. The moment he feared had arrived. The evidence showed his son was guilty. So sure was Simon of what Greg was going to say that when he heard something different, at first it didn't register.

"Sissy Kleinman claims all that evidence is missing."

Simon opened his eyes and saw Mara pounding her fist on Greg's desk. "It proves he's innocent. That's why they've hidden or destroyed it."

Simon marveled at how sure his former wife was of Ariel's innocence. He knew her well enough to understand she had to feel that way. If she believed Ariel were guilty, she'd want him to confess and get psychiatric care. Simon would fight for Ariel's freedom whether he was innocent or guilty.

Greg relayed Sissy's excuses. "911 tapes are routinely destroyed after thirty days, the police lab's DNA analysis of the nail clippings was inconclusive so they threw away the evidence and kept their report."

"That conveniently stops us from doing our own analysis," Mara said. "What about the bloody palm print?"

"Sissy has no explanation for why it's missing, but I've heard rumors there's a leaky roof at the police lab which has destroyed other evidence."

"How can everything we need be gone?" Ariel asked.

Mara pointed her finger at Greg, "What are you going to do about this?"

His former wife, who had never raised her voice during even the worst arguments of their marriage, spoke louder than Simon had ever heard her.

"The judge refused my request to have the case dismissed as a result of the missing evidence. When I cross-examine the police lab witness, I'll ask him about it so the jury is aware of what happened. Hopefully the jurors will react as you did, Mrs. Levine."

Simon bit his lip. What if they shared his reaction and figured the disappearance of the evidence could be a lucky break for Ariel?

***

Mara felt too disheartened to face Ariel so she claimed she had to drop something at her office and asked Simon to drive him to her house. She sat dazed in her car for ten minutes and then left the parking lot.

She drove home without seeing the cars on the freeway or the stop sign at the entry of her street. When she sat in her driveway, she still envisioned what was etched in her mind when she was on autopilot. Ariel in the defendant's chair, his jaw set while the jury foreman read the verdict. "We find the defendant *guilty* as charged."

Mara slumped over the steering wheel. Why was everything conspiring against them? The missing evidence that could exonerate Ariel. The judge so unjust she wouldn't drop the charges even though it was gone.

Ariel deserved better than this.

He was the caring child who at the age of seven had seen her crying on the anniversary of her mother's death and had run to the couch, put his arms around her and asked her what the matter was.

When she had explained she missed her mother, Ariel had said,

194

"Don't cry. I won't ever leave you."

"You're my sweet, sweet boy," she'd told him.

He'd remembered the praise. Later that day when she had two cookies and was about to give one to him and one to Benjie, Ariel had insisted, "But if I'm your sweet, sweet boy, I should get two sweets and Benjie none."

Mara felt as alone as she had that day she'd cried for the loss of her mother.

Josef. Maybe he could help her get through this.

Mara called and told him about the missing evidence.

"I can't believe this is the great American justice system that people in Germany and all over the world want to emulate. I don't know when I've ever been so disgusted."

"The trial starts tomorrow."

A few seconds of silence followed. "I'll be there as often as I can, in between my duties here at the residence."

"I don't think you should come at all. You can't be identified with Ariel. It could be a problem for the children under your care."

Mara had expected an argument, but instead Josef said, "We'll talk every night so I know what's going on. And there may be ways I can help even though I'm not at the trial."

Mara didn't respond.

"Thank you for understanding."

* * *

Henry Luna had become accustomed to Claudia waking up sobbing. He'd hold her until she fell back to sleep.

Now Claudia woke up screaming, and when Henry put his arms around her, she whispered, "Levine," and he had no response.

With the trial about to begin, Claudia had become more anxious. "What if he gets off? If he's not in jail, he'll come after me again."

"He'll be convicted. Detective Crawley is sure of it. He says Mrs. Kleinman always wins."

"But only Dr. Block and I identified him. That might not be enough."

If Levine were let go, it would be Henry's fault for not having identified him.

195

He left Claudia to answer the door for Mrs. Andrews, the Lunas' neighbor who came once a week and stayed with Claudia while Henry did the grocery shopping.

"Henry, take a little longer today. Visit some friends, go to a movie, whatever you'd like. Claudia will be fine with me."

Henry hadn't planned on taking advantage of the offer but on his way back from the super market he passed St. Teresa's Church. He hadn't been there since Claudia was attacked. She was afraid to go anywhere, even to Mass. The church had always given Henry answers. He'd dreamed as a young boy of being a priest.

But his family had needed the money a real job would bring so at eighteen he'd become a garbage man. The smells had stayed with him. They'd haunted him at meals so he ate little. They'd convinced him no woman would ever want to be around him. Claudia had changed that. And after they'd married, each evening she prepared a bath of soapy water and gently scrubbed him with a brush. Even after he retired, she continued the ritual.

Henry pulled into the church parking lot and saw Father Daniel's old Chevrolet Cavalier. A sign he should go inside?

Perhaps it was, for when he spied the large wooden crucifix over the altar, the pressure in his chest eased somewhat. To the right, footsteps on the stone floor announced someone leaving the confessional. Though there was nothing he wanted more than absolution for what he was considering, he hesitated.

Would God see that he only meant the best for Claudia or were His commandments set in stone?

Dragging his feet a little, Henry approached. On his knees, he found the grill that masked his confessor's face.

"Bless me Father for I have sinned. My last confession was eight months ago."

He had so many sins.

"I took the Lord's name in vain when I caught my hand in the door." He shouldn't have said it like that. God would think he was making excuses instead of confessing.

"I gossiped with one neighbor about another." He should have kept quiet when Mrs. Andrews talked about Mrs. Williams. He would the next time.

"I . . . I haven't been to Mass in eight months." He wished he could assure himself and the priest that he wouldn't miss any more but as long as Claudia was afraid to leave the house . . .

Henry hesitated. He took a deep breath. "I'm thinking of telling a lie."

"Why, my son?"

"To make sure a guilty man goes to jail."

"God never lets the unrepentant guilty go unpunished. If not in this world, in the world to come."

"But Father, if the man is guilty, and if my lying makes sure he goes to jail, has any harm been done?"

"It has. To your soul."

***

As instructed by Greg, Simon arrived at Mara's townhouse to drive her and Ariel to court. Greg wanted the public to always see the three of them together to show how both parents supported their son. They met the attorney in his office building's parking lot and rode to the courthouse with him. On the steps television crews shoved microphones and camcorders at them and reporters screamed questions. Mara recognized Norton Walsh and Loretta Sanchez. She suspected the new faces were from out of town. Bad publicity travels far. Greg's "No comment" and the snapping of camera shutters accompanied them into the building.

Once inside the courtroom Mara and Simon sat down on the bench directly behind Ariel and Greg at the defense table. The prosecutor's table was across the aisle to the right and the jury box, with two rows of seats, to the right of it. That gave the jurors a good view of the witness box, which was at the front of the courtroom just below the judge's bench.

Judge Mason entered. "You know better, Mr. Dickson. We have a jury panel of one hundred about to come in here to be voir dired. The parents need to sit in the last row."

Mara and Simon hastily moved. From her new vantage point Mara viewed those potential jurors as they walked in. About half were white and most of the rest divided between African Americans and Hispanics with a smattering of Asian Americans.

Judge Mason greeted them with a speech about their sacred duty. She read the names of the attorneys and witnesses and asked whether any member of the panel knew them. One was acquainted with Greg and another with Sissy.

The judge peered at the prospective jurors. "This case has

197

generated some publicity. How many of you have read about it in the newspaper, seen something about it on television or spoken to people about it?"

A sea of hands rose.

"It's good to have a jury pool that's up on current events. But to make sure the defendant gets a fair trial, I'm going to ask which of you have formed a preliminary opinion as to his guilt or innocence."

Mara counted twenty-one positive responses. After what they'd read, their opinion had to be that her son was guilty. At least they were honest, and would be questioned about their preconceived ideas later at the bench. But what about those who refused to admit they'd already decided?

When the judge finished her remarks, she said the attorneys would each have an hour to question the prospective jurors, and that the process would begin after the lunch break. Greg's secretary brought sandwiches and cans of soda into the courtroom so the Levines didn't have to face the reporters waiting outside. At the defense table Greg poured over the juror questionnaires. When Mara walked past, she noticed he was making notations next to questions about whether they or a family member had been the victim of or accused of committing a crime and the one about religious preference.

When the jury panel returned to the courtroom, Sissy Kleinman stood. "I need your help to make sure this trial is fair. I apologize in advance if some of the questions I ask seem silly or stupid. Will you bear with me?"

Her audience nodded.

Sissy asked whether anyone had ever been accused of a crime or been the victim of one. No one admitted to the former but fourteen had either been mugged or had their cars stolen or homes robbed.

"Now that that's out of the way, we can get to the important stuff." Sissy paused. "In Texas it takes just one eye witness to convict someone of murder. Is that a problem for anyone?"

A few people raised their hands.

Sissy acknowledged a man sitting in the first row.

"Well, you might have the real killer claim he saw someone else do it."

Sissy looked down at the juror sheets she held in her hand. "Good point, venire man number four. It's Mr. Alvarez, isn't it?"

He nodded.

"Let's say it's a witness you believe is reliable and honest and has no reason to lie. In that event is there anyone who would refuse to convict if there were no other evidence?"

A heavyset African American man wearing a bright orange sport shirt raised his hand. "You mean like no physical evidence?"

Mara wanted to hug him. Maybe his remark would get everyone on the panel thinking about the lack of any physical evidence to connect Ariel to the crime.

Sissy glanced at the paper in her hand. "Mr. White, you must figure what I used to - that a killer always leaves DNA. It turns out that's not true. Some killers are so smart they don't leave anything for us to run DNA tests on."

Or you get rid of it when they do, Mara thought.

Sissy looked at her audience. Though she was in the back row, Mara felt as though the assistant district attorney was making eye contact with her and suspected everyone in the jury pool felt that same personal touch.

"Some of you may be thinking, 'But if it's a stabbing, the killer must have gotten the victim's blood on him.' Come on, those who feel that way, fess up."

A woman two rows directly in front of Mara sat up straighter. "I'm a nurse so I would say, it depends on where the stab wounds occurred."

"You get a star Miss . . . Mrs. Cates. You're exactly right. There are areas of the body where a person could be stabbed and you wouldn't necessarily have any blood splatter on the killer."

When Mrs. Cates nodded, Mara's eyes welled with tears. Sissy was effectively making her case during voir dire.

"There's another common misconception I had until I became an assistant district attorney. I thought the State had to prove the killer had a motive. Why do you think the State doesn't have to?"

A man sporting a gray goatee and a suit of the same color raised his hand. "There are people who kill for no motive except the pure joy of being like Satan."

"I couldn't have said that better myself, Mr. Creider."

Creider was one juror Greg would have to strike.

Sissy ended her presentation by again asking whether anyone on the panel would refuse to convict if there were only one eyewitness and no other evidence. "If you can't convict under those circumstances, raise your hand now. If you don't raise your hand, I'll take that as your sacred word that you'll act as you're promising."

No one raised his hand.

The potential jurors were given a ten-minute break before Greg addressed them.

Greg stood and buttoned the jacket of his dark blue suit. "I'm Greg Dickson, Ariel Levine's attorney, and one thing Ms. Kleinman and I agree about is that we want a jury committed to a fair trial."

Greg paused. "A fair trial is one in which the defendant has no burden to prove his innocence but instead the prosecution has the burden to convince you beyond a reasonable doubt that the defendant is guilty. Otherwise you must come back with a verdict of innocent."

Greg looked out into the courtroom, and then at the sheets in his hand. "Mr. Hernandez, you look like something I said is bothering you."

"They must have some evidence or we wouldn't be here."

A lot of people must feel that way. At least the sentiment was out in the open.

"Actually, Mr. Hernandez, as Ms. Kleinman alluded to, they need just one little piece of evidence, just one person thinking he saw the defendant."

A few in the jury pool nodded.

"Has any of you ever been mistaken for someone else?"

A number of hands went up. Greg pointed to a middle-aged balding man wearing a tan sport jacket. "Tell us what happened to you, Mr. Pascal."

"I was in a restaurant with my wife when this woman came over and said, 'I'm going to tell my sister you're out with some hussy.' Then she looked at me again. 'You're not Keith.'"

Greg waited for the laughter to stop. "Poor innocent Keith almost got into big trouble."

Her son's attorney called on everyone who had a mistaken identity story. While none was as effective as Mr. Pascal's, the more incidents mentioned, the more doubt raised about the witnesses' identifications of Ariel.

"Let's assume you have a reasonable doubt about any identification of a defendant and there's no physical evidence to connect him to the crime scene, there's something else which might prejudice you against him, even though it's something you're not permitted to consider," Greg said.

Simon sat at attention. He probably expected Greg to mention Ariel's dual American/Israeli citizenship, but Mara knew what was coming.

"The defendant may not testify."

Greg wouldn't bring this up unless he had, despite his assurance that the decision would be reconsidered, firmly made up his mind to keep Ariel off the witness stand.

"Who can give me some reasons why an innocent person wouldn't testify?"

A man in the front row raised his hand. "Maybe he's innocent of a crime but guilty of something else. Like maybe if Keith had been with some hussy, he wouldn't want to admit that was his alibi."

Greg laughed along with the potential jurors.

"I'm a teacher," a woman said. "So I know teenagers who get confused when they talk to adults and don't look them in the eye so they seem like they're hiding something when really they're not."

Greg nodded. "Especially an adult like Ms. Kleinman. I'm older than she is, and I wouldn't want to be cross-examined by her."

"Your time's almost up, Mr. Dickson," Judge Mason intoned from the bench.

According to Mara's watch, Greg still had ten minutes.

"In closing, let me ask, is there anything any one of you thinks I ought to know about you or your attitudes or ideas which might make me wonder if you'd be an ideal juror?"

No one responded.

"Thank you for your time," Greg said.

"What happens next?" Simon asked.

Mara placed her mouth against her former husband's ear and cupped her hand around it. This was the closest physical proximity she'd been to him since the divorce. She forced herself not to pull away. "The attorneys will try to have some potential jurors removed for cause."

"Like those who've already decided?"

"The judge will call them up to the bench and ask if they can put aside their preconceptions and listen to the evidence with an open mind."

Most of the twenty-one would claim they could be fair, and with only ten pre-emptive strikes, Greg would have no choice but to leave some of them on the jury. After being individually questioned by the judge and the two attorneys at the bench, only four were dismissed. They smiled as they left the courtroom.

After the remaining seventeen went back to their seats, Greg and Sissy made notations on the sheets they'd held during the voir dire. They gave them to the clerk ten minutes later. He called out the names of the first twelve panel members who hadn't been stricken by either attorney, and said all the others were dismissed.

Though she'd anticipated Sissy would strike them, Mara was none the less disappointed to see Mr. White, who'd questioned the lack of physical evidence, and Mr. Pascal, whose tale of his own mistaken identity had resonated, leave the courtroom. All four women who'd noted on their juror questionnaires that they were Jewish were also among those dismissed. Mara was wondering whether she was being paranoid to think Sissy had struck them for that reason, when she heard Greg say, "Your Honor, prior to you impaneling this jury, I wish to make a Batson challenge."

"You'll do that at the bench," Judge Mason ordered.

"What's going on?" Simon asked.

"Kleinman isn't allowed to strike people because of their religion. If Greg convinces the judge that's what happened, everyone's dismissed and we start with a new jury panel."

But Sissy would likely come up with some excuse for striking every one of the four.

The attorneys returned to their seats and the judge impaneled the twelve people whose names had been called.

The jury consisted of seven men, four of them white, one African American and two Hispanics, and five women, two white, two African Americans and one Asian American, the twelve people who would determine Ariel's fate.

THIRTY-THREE

The courtroom seating reminded Mara of a wedding. Instead of the bride's family and friends on one side of the aisle and the groom's on the other, the victim's friends and family sat on the side behind Sissy Kleinman, and Ariel's supporters behind him and Greg Dickson. Norton Walsh, the *Post-Gazette* reporter, occupied a prominent place two rows behind the assistant district attorney.

All twelve jurors sat up straight and looked at Judge Denise Mason as she cautioned them not to discuss the trial with anyone or watch televised reports or read newspaper accounts. When she finished, she asked assistant district attorney Sissy Kleinman to read the indictment against Ariel.

Sissy rose. "That on or about November 24, 2000, in Harris County, Texas, Ariel Yitzhak Levine unlawfully, intentionally and knowingly did cause the death of Herlinda Sorento by cutting and stabbing her with a knife."

How could anyone believe Mara's sweet, gentle son could do such a thing? But, of course, none of the jurors knew him. Greg had warned her and Simon to hide any emotional reactions. If either seemed upset by something, the jury would read into it that the prosecution had made a point.

So Mara was determined to listen to the proceedings objectively, as though she were a juror, so she could judge how the case was going.

Simon shook his head. "You can guess why she included Ariel's Hebrew middle name in the indictment."

Mara nodded. Sissy Kleinman wanted the jury to remember her son was Jewish and born in Israel.

"How does the defendant plead?" the judge asked.

Ariel stood and looked directly at the jurors. "Ladies and gentlemen, I am not guilty," he said in a forceful tone.

Sissy, ready to make her opening statement, faced the jury.

203

"Ariel Yitzhak Levine is a murderer."

The assistant district attorney, her shoulders back, emphasized the viciousness of the killing, the knife wounds to Claudia and Henry Luna and the slitting of Mrs. Sorento's throat.

Surely the jurors had to wonder why with a crime scene so full of blood, there was none in the Land Rover.

"When Ariel Yitzhak Levine left Lingerie for Life, Mrs. Sorento was lying face down, blood pooling under her. The wounds inflicted on the Lunas had not yet begun to bleed. That occurred after they ran around the store trying to find a phone to call for help. So there was no blood for the killer to track into the Land Rover he used to get away."

It would be a stretch for the jury to believe that. Unless Sissy had convinced her witnesses to back up her theory when they testified.

In her friendly drawl Sissy told the jurors that both Mrs. Luna and Andrew Block had identified Ariel, that the license plate number Block had written down belonged to Ariel's stepmother's car and that Ariel had no alibi for the time of the murder.

Sissy turned towards Ariel. "You may look at the defendant and think he seems like some sweet non-violent kid. But one of his friends knows what he's like from a letter he wrote. Ariel Yitzhak Levine planned to slit a woman's throat."

An African American juror, Mrs. Gentry, put her hand up to her neck.

"And if that doesn't convince you that a murderer stands before you, remember that Ariel Yitzhak Levine stayed in Guatemala for months after he was indicted, only to be arrested at the airport there as he was about to board a flight, not to Houston, but to Mexico City."

When Sissy sat down, Judge Mason smiled at her. "Please call your first witness."

Greg stood. "Your Honor, I planned to make my opening statement."

"You want to do it now?"

Mara stared at the judge. She had no reason to act surprised. While Greg had the choice to wait to make his opening statement until just before he called his first witness, it made more sense for him to address the jury immediately so he could counteract what

Sissy had said. Judge Mason's acting like this was a mistake made Greg look incompetent.

Greg brushed an imaginary speck of dust off his sleeve and addressed the jurors. "This case was brought against my client because of misidentification."

He pointed out how there were people in the photo and video line-ups who didn't resemble the description of the killer and that despite the fact that Ariel was the only person in both line-ups, neither Mrs. Luna nor Andrew Block was more than 80% sure of their identifications.

Greg walked slowly from one end of the jury box to the other. "You're probably thinking of the license plate number Andrew Block wrote down. There are six dark colored Land Rovers, sold by the same dealer, with almost that exact same license plate."

He took a few steps and stopped. "Think of all the times you've written down a phone number or an address wrong. It's even easier to make that mistake when you've got almost no time to see and comprehend a license plate."

Sissy jumped up, attracting the attention of both the jurors and the spectators. "I object. It's argumentative to say 'almost no time.'"

The objection was so ridiculous that Mara was sure Sissy had made it to distract the jurors from the point Greg was making.

"Sustained," the judge said.

Jane Watkins had been right about Judge Mason's animus towards Greg.

He tried again. "Your Honor, Andrew Block's statement to the police shows . . ."

"Sustained," the judge repeated in a louder tone.

Greg turned back to the jury. "You'll see pictures of an extremely bloody crime scene. Yet, there was no blood in the Land Rover whose license plate number Andrew Block wrote down, and no physical evidence at the murder site connecting Ariel Levine to the crime."

Greg rested his hands on the front of the jury box. "That means in approximately thirty-five minutes from about 3:50 when he finished walking the dogs until around 4:25 when he arrived to play basketball with friends, he would have had to drive to the lingerie shop, attack three people, drive back to his father's house, clean up the Land Rover, change clothes, get rid of them and a weapon and drive to a basketball game. Our evidence will show that is not possible."

Greg, though doing well, had to handle the next part with skill.

"To try to make you believe that a young man with no history of violence is a killer, Ms. Kleinman is going to introduce into evidence writings which have nothing to do with the murder of Mrs. Sorento but instead have to do with Ariel's frustration at the killings of six of his former neighbors."

Greg walked to the other end of the jury box. "By the time this trial is over, you'll understand that the District Attorney approved Ariel's trip to Guatemala, and that he was on his way home to Houston to clear his name when he was apprehended."

Greg looked at each of the jurors. "Ariel Levine is innocent."

"Ms. Kleinman, are you ready to call your first witness?" Judge Mason asked.

Sissy stood. "I call Claudia Luna."

A petite, hunched woman in a gray shirtdress walked slowly to the witness stand. As she sat down, she looked at Ariel and recoiled slightly.

Mara glanced at the jurors but couldn't tell if they'd noticed.

Sissy asked questions which established Claudia's age as fifty-six, her husband of twenty years as Henry and her years of working at Lingerie for Life as nineteen. She talked about her duties at the shop and mentioned how their customers were cancer victims. "Even though they lost certain body parts, we can make them look good and feel good."

"I'm sorry but I'm going to have to ask you about that fateful day, November 24, 2000."

Claudia shuddered, and nodded. In answer to a series of Sissy's questions, she told the jury how a man of about twenty, wearing a dark jogging suit and a baseball cap ran into the store and reached towards Herlinda who was standing behind the counter. He said something to her that Claudia didn't hear.

"Herlinda said, 'You must be kidding', and ran for the side room."

Mara wondered what that statement could have been in response to. If she could figure that out, perhaps it would help find the actual killer.

Claudia continued. "He caught her, and it looked like he punched her in the throat. She screamed and fell over face down."

Claudia sobbed, barely able to catch her breath.

"Ms. Kleinman, I think this would be a good time to take a brief lunch break," the judge said.

When Claudia returned to the witness stand an hour later, she seemed composed. "I ran to the front of the store and dialed 911. The terrible man cut my wrist so I dropped the phone. He grabbed me from behind in a bear hug."

Claudia opened her right hand and revealed a crumpled tissue which she used to dab at her eyes. She took a deep breath. "I felt what I thought were his knuckles pounding me from below my neck to below my stomach. But it was a knife. I saw it just before he cut my nose. Then he put it behind one ear and brought it from one side of my neck to the other."

Mara's stomach clenched. What the witness had gone through was horrifying, but so was the thought that anyone could believe Ariel had committed such a heinous act.

"I don't remember anything else until I saw my husband bleeding. We called 911. A man came in and tried to help Herlinda."

Claudia sobbed.

"Is the killer in the courtroom today?" Sissy asked.

Claudia pointed at Ariel. "It's him. I'm 100% sure."

All twelve jurors looked at Ariel.

"No further questions. Your witness, Mr. Dickson."

Greg rose slowly from his chair. "Mrs. Luna, shortly after you were attacked, you were shown both photo and video line-ups. How sure were you then of your identification of Ariel Levine?"

"Eighty per cent."

Greg entered the photo and video line-ups into evidence.

"Was your attacker Hispanic?"

"No."

"How many Hispanics are in the video line-up?"

"Two."

"Is there a different Hispanic man in the photo line-up?"

"Yes."

"Did your attacker have sideburns?"

"No."

"Is there a man with sideburns in the photo line-up?"

"Yes."

"Is Ariel Levine the only person in both line-ups?"

"Yes."

"Did your identification come after seeing one line-up or both line-ups?"

"Both."

"So after seeing two line-ups in which Ariel Levine was the only person in both, you were still only 80% sure of your identification?"

"Objection. Leading the witness."

"Sustained."

"After seeing two line-ups, how sure were you of your identification?" Greg asked.

"Eighty percent. That's why I wanted to see him in person, and if they arrested the one I thought it was, then maybe I could know for sure. Now I do," she said, pointing at Ariel.

Mara looked down at her lap. She couldn't let the jurors see how close to tears she was.

"Let's talk about why you might be more sure months after the attack than you were directly after it happened," Greg said.

"It's because I kept seeing his face in my dreams."

"Did you have these dreams in which Ariel Levine appeared before or after you saw the photo and video line-ups?"

"After."

"Did you have more dreams after you saw pictures of Ariel Levine in the newspaper?"

"Yes, after I saw him in handcuffs when the police brought him back from Guatemala."

"So it was after having dreams and after seeing a picture of Ariel in handcuffs, that you became more sure he was your attacker?"

"Yes."

"No further questions."

The jurors must recognize how unreliable Mrs. Luna's identification was. But three in the front row looked quizzical and two in the back were yawning.

"Redirect, Your Honor," Sissy said.

"Mrs. Luna did you want to see the defendant in person so you'd be 100% sure of your identification?"

"Objection. Leading the witness."

"Overruled. You may answer the question."

"Yes."

"Now that you see Ariel Levine before you, are you 100% sure he was your attacker?" Sissy asked.

"Yes."

Norton Walsh who had written nothing during Greg's cross-examination now jotted down notes.

"I call Henry Luna," Sissy said.

A bald man, with a face so gaunt his black-rimmed glasses dominated it, walked to the witness stand.

Sissy's questions established that Henry was sixty-seven and had come to Lingerie for Life on November 24, 2000, to pick up his wife Claudia.

"Tell us what happened when you arrived."

"I saw a man with a knife crouching over Claudia. I grabbed a mannequin, threw it at him and ran towards him. He cut my hand and my right side, and I fell to the ground. My glasses came off and shattered. Before I could get up, he ran from the store."

"What happened after the attack?"

Henry related how he and Claudia called 911, and how Andrew Block came into the store and turned Herlinda over.

"Was there blood pooled under Herlinda?"

"Yes."

"Did you notice blood on your wife when the attacker left but before she ran to the phone?"

"No."

"Did you get any of your blood on the murderer?"

"I didn't notice any."

"Did you see any blood at all on the murderer?"

"No."

"Your witness, Mr. Dickson."

Somehow Greg would overcome this crazy idea that the killer had no blood on him.

"Mr. Luna, did Detective Crawley show you a photo line-up which included Ariel Levine?"

"Yes."

"Did you identify Ariel Levine as your assailant?"

Henry bit his lower lip.

"Mr. Luna, please answer the question."

"No. I . . . I picked someone else."

"How do you know?"

Henry gazed at his lap. "Detective Crawley looked disgusted. But I had already explained that my glasses broke so I could hardly see anything."

"If you could hardly see anything, then couldn't there have been blood on your attacker and your wife that you didn't see."

Henry's answer was inaudible.

"Please repeat your answer, Mr. Luna."

"Yes."

"No further questions."

Mara sighed. Mr. Luna's testimony hadn't hurt Ariel. But tomorrow Andrew Block would be the first witness.

THIRTY-FOUR

"The State calls Andrew Block."

Mara watched the six-foot tall man with a medium build and dark blond hair walk to the witness stand. She was struck by how his physical characteristics matched Ariel's. When Andrew sat down and faced her, he looked to be in his early twenties, a few years older than Ariel. Neither Mr. nor Mrs. Luna had gotten a good look at their assailant's face. He was behind Mrs. Luna during the attack, and Mr. Luna's glasses had fallen off.

In the scenario that appeared before her, Mara envisioned Andrew Block killing Mrs. Sorento, running out of Lingerie for Life, zipping off his bloody jogging suit and tossing it into the trunk of his car. He sees the parked Land Rover and writes down its license plate number. He runs back into the store and pretends to help so that he has an excuse when his prints, hair and skin particles are found there. The scheme depended on Ariel being at the shopping center for some innocent purpose and on Andrew having a motive for killing Mrs. Sorento.

Maybe something in Andrew's testimony would confirm Mara's theory.

Sissy's questions established that Andrew was a twenty-four year old chiropractor who on November 24, 2000, shopped at a Kroger Super Market, which was in the same shopping center as Lingerie for Life.

"As I walked to my car, I saw a man running from the direction of the lingerie shop."

"Describe him."

"Late teens or early twenties, close to six-feet tall with blond hair."

"Did you see his face?"

"He looked at me and then put his head down and ran to a dark colored Land Rover. I got in my car and went down the aisle where it was parked. As he backed out, he had to pull along side my car so I saw his face again."

"When did you get the license plate number?"

"As he drove off, I turned around and saw it, grabbed the Kroger receipt from my shirt pocket and wrote it down."

Sissy introduced the receipt into evidence and Andrew read its time stamp of 4:01.

Andrew couldn't have been in Kroger and committing the murder at the same time. Did the receipt have a date stamp on it...?

"How sure are you that you wrote down the license plate number correctly?"

"One hundred percent sure."

"What happened next?"

"I parked my car and ran into the store."

"Dr. Block, did you notice any blood?"

"Not until I turned Mrs. Sorento over. She was dead. I insisted Mrs. Luna lie down. Detective Crawley thinks I saved her life." Andrew sat up straighter.

"Did you have an opportunity to identify the man fleeing from the lingerie shop?"

"I went to the police station where Detective Crawley showed me the pictures of six men and I told him that one looked familiar. Then he showed me a video tape, and again I saw a man who looked familiar."

"Was it the same man?"

"Yes."

"How sure were you of your identification?"

"Eighty percent."

"Is the man you identified in the courtroom?"

Andrew pointed at Ariel. "It's the defendant."

"No further questions."

Greg stood up and rubbed his hands together.

"Mr. Block . . ."

"It's Dr. Block," Sissy said.

"Your Honor. . ."

"Ms. Kleinman, you know better than to interrupt Mr. Dickson's cross-examination. Though your point is well taken."

Mara shook her head. The judge was going along with Sissy's attempt to give Andrew Block more credibility by having the jurors think of him as a doctor.

Greg addressed the witness. "Did you just testify that the man you saw running from the direction of the lingerie shop had blond hair?"

"Yes."

"Does Ariel Levine have blond hair?"

"No, but I identified him on the basis of his face."

"How long did you see that face when the man was running?"

"For a second or so."

"When his car was passing yours?"

"For about two seconds."

"In those fleeting seconds did you see blond hair?"

"I thought so. Maybe it was light brown."

"That's not what you said right after you saw him, was it?"

"No."

Greg was making his points well, but when Mara looked at the jurors, one was blowing her nose, another yawning and the rest were expressionless.

"When you saw Ariel's photo, you said he looked familiar."

"Yes."

"Could that be because you saw him before?"

"I never have."

"Approximately two months before Mrs. Sorento's murder were you at the office you share with Dr. Daryl Freed when Ariel's father Simon Levine came to show Dr. Freed how to use software he'd sold him?"

"That's probably so."

"Do you remember that Ariel was sitting in the waiting room when you left the office?"

"No, I don't remember seeing him. If someone had introduced us, I'd remember."

"I'm not asking if you were introduced, I'm asking if you saw him."

"Not that I recall."

Mara gripped the wooden bench. Andrew had to be lying.

"When you left the building with Dr. Freed, did you notice a dark Land Rover parked near his car?"

"I . . . I might have."

Though Greg was trying to establish that Andrew identified Ariel and the vehicle because he was familiar with both, Mara had a different interpretation. Andrew had seen Ariel, knew he resembled him and had written down the Land Rover's license plate number that day as part of a premeditated plan to kill Mrs. Sorento and frame Ariel.

But what motive could Andrew have for killing her?

Mara returned her attention to Greg.

"Is it your testimony that you saw the license plate of the dark colored Land Rover as it was driving away from you and that you had to turn your head to look out your back window to see it?"

"Yes, but I saw it clearly."

"How much time did you have to look at it?"

"A second or so."

"Yet, with all those impediments to being accurate, you still claim you couldn't have made a mistake?"

"Anything's possible, but . . ."

"Let's turn to your time in the store. You testified that you didn't see any blood on Mrs. Luna and yet you had her lie down. Why?"

"By then she'd been running around the store and was bleeding."

"When you rushed into the store, who caught your attention, Mrs. Sorento lying on the floor or Mrs. Luna?"

"Mrs. Sorento."

"Then isn't it possible you didn't notice the blood on Mrs. Luna because you weren't paying attention to her?"

"Anything's possible, but I think I would have noticed."

"Then you're not sure."

"Objection, argumentative."

"Sustained."

"No further questions."

"We're going to take a lunch break. Be back at 1:30," Judge Mason announced.

When the courtroom cleared, Mara asked Greg, "Was there a date stamp on Block's Kroger receipt?"

"It was smudged, illegible."

"I've got to talk with you."

"Come to my office with Mr. Levine and Ariel."

Once there Mara set out her theory on how Andrew Block could have planned to kill Mrs. Sorento and frame Ariel. "Block

214

doesn't have an alibi. He could've been in Kroger any day at 4:01."

Ariel became animated. "If he were really quick and no one was near him in the parking lot, he could have taken off his bloody jogging suit and put it in his trunk with no one seeing him."

"He has no motive," Simon responded.

Mara glared at her former husband. "Neither does your son."

"But they do have Ariel's letter to Dov Lieberman and Sissy may get in the notebook testimony," Greg said.

The attorney broke the silence, which followed. "Mrs. Levine's ideas will help me in cross-examining Detective Crawley. She's thought of things he should have checked into if he'd done a thorough investigation."

***

Oracio Crawley sat in Judge Mason's courtroom looking forward to testifying. He'd worn his best suit, a dark gray, and had set off his white shirt with a black tie sporting thin gray and white stripes. When Sissy called his name, he straightened his back and shoulders and walked to the witness stand.

Through her questions and his answers, Sissy established that Oracio had been on the Houston Police Force eighteen years and was the detective in charge of the investigation into the lingerie shop murder. He told the jury about coming into the store and finding Mrs. Sorento dead, the unconscious Mrs. Luna with multiple stab wounds and the distraught Mr. Luna with wounds Dr. Block insisted had to be treated. Sissy led him through an explanation of how the crew from the lab collected specimens and fingerprints. He related how Mr. Luna and Dr. Block gave him almost identical descriptions of the attacker and how both Mrs. Luna and Dr. Block identified Ariel Levine.

"When Ariel was arrested at the airport in Guatemala, was he about to board a flight to Mexico City?"

"Yes."

Oracio could tell by Sissy's hint of a smile that she was happy with his testimony. Greg Dickson never looked at him, just took notes while he was testifying.

The attorney rose to cross-examine him.

"Detective Crawley, please tell us about all the witnesses who either didn't identify Ariel Levine or who identified someone else."

215

Mr. Luna had probably testified about not being able to identify Levine. But did Dickson know about the other two?

"Mr. Luna's glasses broke during the attack so he had trouble making an identification."

"Did he pick someone else in the line-up?"

"Yea, but the guy couldn't have done it because the other people in the line-up came from the jail."

"Do you know what time the person Mr. Luna identified arrived at the jail?"

"No, but he would have been there a while because he was already processed."

"But you can't say for sure that he was in jail before the murder was committed."

"No."

"Was he the same man the manager of Discount Delight identified when she saw the photo line-up?"

"I don't remember. When the identification's wrong, we don't keep records of who was identified."

"So if the identification's not what you want, you ignore it?"

"Objection, argumentative."

"Sustained," Judge Mason intoned.

Oracio took advantage of Greg's momentary pause. "Anyway, it was someone she saw hours before in her store."

"But aroused her suspicions to the extent that she called you?"

"Yeah, the woman was a real attention seeker."

"Did you try to find the suspicious man she told you about?"

"No, it was days later." Oracio immediately regretted his words. It made him look lazy that he hadn't canvassed the shopping center right after the murder. But he'd known the night of the crime he had his killer.

"Did the postal worker who saw someone run from the lingerie shop identify Ariel Levine from the photo line-up?"

"No."

"Did you make a note of that?"

"No, we don't keep records of non-identifications."

"Describe Ariel Levine."

The attorney was trying to trick him over the way the attacker was described as having blond or dirty blond hair when Ariel's hair looked darker.

"Late teens or early twenties, about six feet, medium build, 170 to 180 pounds and dirty blond hair at the time of the attack."

"Describe Andrew Block."

Oracio had been had. Except for a slight difference in the age, his description of Andrew would be identical to that of Levine.

Sissy saved him. "I object. That question has no relevancy."

"Your Honor, I'm just trying to point out how numerous people share that identification."

"Your Honor, he's arguing his case," Sissy said.

Judge Mason addressed the jury. "You are instructed to ignore Mr. Dickson's remark."

The judge glared at Dickson. She reminded Oracio of a schoolmarm about to send an incorrigible student to the principal's office. Oracio glanced at the jurors who were looking at the judge.

"Detective Crawley, when you entered the lingerie shop, where did you see blood?"

"On the floor, the counters, lots of places."

"With all the evidence collected at the scene, did any of it connect Ariel Levine to the crime?"

"No."

"If you didn't find any of Ariel Levine's fingerprints in the store, whose did you find."

"Mrs. Sorento's, Mr. And Mrs. Luna's, Dr. Block's, lots of unknowns."

"Did you consider Andrew Block a suspect after his prints were identified?"

"No. He had reason to be there, and, besides, he had an alibi. His Kroger receipt showed he was at the super market at 4:01 when the murder took place."

Dickson handed him the receipt. "Can you read a date?"

"No."

"Did you return to Kroger to verify he'd been there at 4:01 the day of the murder?

"No."

"Would you agree that all we really know is that Andrew Block was in Kroger at 4:01 some day, but not necessarily the day of the murder?"

"I guess so."

"Do you believe you conducted a thorough investigation?"

217

"Yes."

"Yet, you didn't investigate the man Mr. Luna identified as his attacker, didn't try to find the suspicious man identified by the manager of Discount Delight and didn't check out Andrew Block's alibi, did you?"

"Those were all rabbit trails."

"Please answer the question."

"No."

"When you brought Ariel Levine back to Houston, did he tell you he was meeting his father in Mexico City so they could return to Houston together?"

"That's what he claimed."

"No further questions."

As Oracio left the stand, he averted his eyes from Sissy, sure he'd disappointed her. But when he looked at the jury, he saw two men, one Anglo and one Hispanic, smiling at him.

Oracio returned their smiles. He remembered what Sissy had told him before he testified at his first trial.

People want to believe the police.

THIRTY-FIVE

Judge Mason looked at the prosecutor. "Ms. Kleinman, do you want to call one last witness today or start with him tomorrow?"

"Your Honor, we have another of Houston's finest waiting to testify. His time is too valuable to have him come back."

Sissy turned to the jurors. "The State calls Glen Healy."

The tall detective, who looked to Mara to be about thirty, patted down his cowlick as he walked to the stand.

He testified he'd been Oracio Crawley's partner for six months when the murder occurred. "He was the lead detective in the investigation. I always learn a lot from him."

"Did Detective Crawley do everything by the book—at the crime scene, at the house, at the station?"

"Absolutely."

"Please tell the jury about the important task he gave you after the murder."

"He had me drive the distance between Lingerie for Life and Levine's father's house and time it."

"How long did it take?"

"Seven minutes and fifty-two seconds."

Mara shook her head. It couldn't have taken that little time, especially since around Thanksgiving they were doing road repairs adjacent to the shopping center.

"So Ariel Levine could have made a round trip from his father's home and the shopping center in approximately fifteen minutes, hardly enough time for his absence to be noticed."

"Objection. Leading the witness."

The judge yawned. "Sustained."

Sissy looked at Greg. "Your witness."

"At the time of the murder, there was construction on the road bordering the shopping center. On the date you did your test run, was there still construction?"

"Objection. Mr. Dickson is referring to a fact not in evidence."

"Your Honor, the defense presents as an exhibit a copy of the *Weekly Bulletin* dated the day of the murder which contains an article by Loretta Sanchez reporting on how the construction on Baylor Street was having a negative effect on the stores in the shopping center."

How ironic that something Loretta Sanchez had written could help Ariel.

Judge Mason looked at Sissy, as though waiting or her to object. When she didn't, the judge intoned, "Admitted."

Greg resumed his questioning. "Was there any construction the day you tried to recreate the trip?"

"No."

"There are three possible routes someone driving between the shopping center and the Levine's house could have taken. How did you choose the one you did?"

Glen hesitated. "It's the one Detective Crawley told me to take."

"Since part of the route was on Baylor Street, wouldn't you have been considerably slowed down if you'd taken that trip on the day of the murder?"

"I have no way of knowing."

"That's right. You don't."

Glen blushed.

Mara clasped her hands. Greg was doing a good job but he might turn Glen hostile.

"What was the speed limit on the streets you took?"

"Thirty-five miles an hour."

"How fast did you drive?"

"Never over thirty-nine miles an hour."

"So you drove over the speed limit."

"There's a common belief that the police won't ticket you unless you're going at least five miles over the speed limit, so I never went more than four miles over it."

"If you had driven the speed limit and been slowed down by construction, wouldn't the time it took to make the trip have increased?"

"I guess so."

"When you were at the crime scene, did you see a lot of blood?"

"Yes."

"When you were at Mr. Levine's house the night of the murder, did you look inside the Land Rover?"

"I just glanced at the inside. I didn't open the door."

"Did you notice any blood?"

"No."

"Do you know that not even a trace of human blood was found when the police laboratory went over the vehicle?"

"Yes."

"Assuming it's even possible, how long do you think it would take someone to clean out a bloody vehicle so that there wasn't even a microscopic trace of blood in it?"

"Objection," Sissy roared.

"Sustained," the judge ordered as she brought down her gavel so hard it startled Mara.

"Your Honor," Greg said, "I'll be presenting a blood splatter witness who will testify that blood would have had to have gotten on the killer and been transferred to the car, and two others who will testify Ariel was playing basketball at 4:30."

"Your Honor, he's arguing his case."

"I've had it with you, Mr. Dickson. You won't use my courtroom for your theatrics. Any more of that, and I'll hold you in contempt."

"But, Your Honor, I was just . . ."

"No more out of you."

All the jurors sat up straight and looked from the judge to Greg Dickson.

Mara's eyes welled will tears. The jury wouldn't remember the points Greg had made on his cross-examination.

The judge's dressing him down was all that mattered.

THIRTY-SIX

Mara turned over and looked at the luminous dial of her clock radio. It was after midnight, but her mind was too active for sleep. Dov Lieberman would be on the stand reading from the letter in which Ariel claimed he wanted to slit the throats of sand nigger bitches. Then if Judge Mason allowed Ava Branson's testimony about the notebook seized from Ariel, the jury would again hear that Ariel had a fantasy about killing women.

Mara guessed Ava Branson's motives. The young police officer knew she could get ahead by saying whatever she was told to by Crawley or Kleinman. But what about Dov Lieberman? He was Ariel's friend. Why would he turn on him? He had to understand the context in which Ariel had written the letter three years before. If he didn't, and truly believed it showed Ariel had an emotional problem, why hadn't he brought the letter to her attention?

But to just keep it? It made no sense. The only letters Mara had ever saved were those from boyfriends when she was an infatuated teenager. She remembered how Dov frequently hugged Ariel, put his hands on him. Could Dov have been romantically interested in Ariel and felt rejected when he realized her son didn't return those feelings? All she could do was speculate. Dov had refused to let Greg Dickson's investigator interview him.

A sleep deprived Mara suppressed a yawn the next morning as Sissy called Dov to the stand. When he walked past her, Mara saw his jutting jaw and hooked nose in profile.

Sissy's questions established that Dov was twenty-two, an Israeli citizen and Ariel's life long friend.

Sissy had Ariel's letter introduced into evidence. Dov identified it as having come from Ariel and bearing his signature. He'd even saved the envelope which bore the return address.

"Please read the paragraph which concerned you."

Dov took the missive from Sissy's outstretched hand.

222

"I'm much more violent than you'd ever guess," Dov read. "If I was in Israel I'd slit the throats of their women. Maybe I'd better have a knife ready in case I luck out and find some sand nigger bitch here in Houston."

One African American female juror put her hand to her mouth and the other placed her palm on her chest. The male African American juror sat up straighter.

"Isn't sand nigger a pejorative term for Arabs?" Sissy asked Dov.

"Yes."

"Then why were you concerned that Ariel Yitzhak Levine, who was born in Israel and has dual Israeli/American citizenship, wanted to kill Arabs?"

Dov leaned forward. "He knows we Israelis don't slit the throats of Arab women. We fight their men in battles or when they're about to attempt a suicide bombing."

"What did you do because of your concern?"

"I visited Ariel a few weeks ago and begged him to get help."

"What happened?"

"He refused."

"Is that when you came to my office?"

"Yes, I didn't want him to hurt anyone else."

"No further questions."

Greg stood. "When did Ariel write that letter?"

"Three years ago."

"What had happened in the Israeli neighborhood he grew up in just prior to his writing it?"

"A suicide bomber attacked. The terrorist and six Israelis were killed."

"And weren't other of Ariel's neighbors and friends horribly maimed? Faces torn apart, third degree burns, body parts severed."

"Yes."

"Were you angry when that happened?"

"Sure."

"Yet, you waited three years to discuss the letter with Ariel. Is it because at the time Ariel wrote it, you understood he was writing with the same anger and frustration you felt?"

"Objection, leading the witness."

"Sustained."

"How do you think Ariel felt about the suicide bombing in his old neighborhood?"

"Enraged at the Arab who did it, so why mention going after some innocent woman in Houston?"

Mara suppressed a gasp. Sissy must have anticipated Greg's question and rehearsed Dov's answer with him.

"If you actually believed that, why did you wait three years to bring the letter to anyone's attention?"

"It wasn't until after Mrs. Sorento's throat was slit and Ariel was arrested that I was sure my fears were justified."

Mara's heart beat rapidly. Greg was doing more harm with his cross-examination than Sissy had done with her questioning.

A glimmer of a smile crossed Sissy's face.

"In the three years since Ariel's old neighborhood was bombed, has he written you any other letters mentioning violence?"

"No."

"No further questions."

Two female jurors averted their eyes when Ariel glanced in their direction.

Judge Mason addressed the jury. "The attorneys have presented me with briefs which contain written arguments about whether a certain witness may testify. Now they're going to make their oral arguments, which the jury may not hear. You're excused until one thirty."

As soon as the jurors filed out, Judge Mason asked Sissy, "What is Officer Branson going to testify to?"

The judge's question told Mara she hadn't read the briefs.

"That at the time she arrested Ariel Levine for having beer on a high school campus, Officer Branson looked through a notebook in his backpack to see if any marijuana or LSD was hidden within its pages. Instead she saw images of knives and read the page they were on. That's when she learned about Levine's fantasy of slitting a woman's throat."

"Your Honor," Greg said, "the seizure of the notebook constituted an illegal search under the Fourth Amendment. Once Officer Branson saw no drugs were hidden within its pages, she had no right under the Fourteenth Amendment to read the private writings of the defendant. Since the prosecution claims the writings are incriminating, they're admitting that to let them in would be a violation of the defendant's Fifth Amendment right against self-incrimination."

Greg was making an excellent case, but it was Judge Mason he had to impress and the judge, her head bent, wasn't allowing him to make eye contact.

Judge Mason looked up when Sissy spoke. "Your Honor, there were exigent circumstances both for the search for drugs and the need to make sure there was no immediate threat to anyone once Officer Branson saw the depictions of knives. Further, we're dealing with motive, not self-incrimination."

"Your Honor, the assistant district attorney wants the jury to convict Ariel Levine, not because he committed murder, but for juvenile thought crimes. It's prejudicial for the jury to hear Officer Branson's testimony."

"I'll take it under advisement. Be back here at one fifteen for my decision."

"Your Honor," Greg said, "please also consider that since the notebook no longer exists, there is no physical evidence to back up what Officer Branson is going to testify to, so we can't meaningfully challenge something that could be made up."

"I trust the jury to decide on Officer Branson's veracity," Sissy responded.

The judge nodded.

So Mara wasn't surprised when Judge Mason ruled that Ava Branson could testify.

On the witness stand the officer looked mousy. Her dull faded brown hair hung behind her ears and her bangs slanted to the left. After being sworn in, she clasped her hands together and chewed on her lower lip.

Once Sissy established that Ava, as a member of the Houston Independent School District Police, had caught Ariel with beer on campus, the assistant district attorney asked the officer why she'd looked though the notebook.

"Marijuana or LSD could have been between the pages."

"What did you find instead?"

"A page with drawings of knives."

"Did you read that page because you were concerned someone

could be in imminent danger?"

Greg was on his feet. "Objection, leading the witness."

"Sustained."

"Why did you read the page?"

"I thought someone could be in imminent danger."

"What did it say?"

"It said over and over, 'Let's slit the bitches' throats.'"

All the jurors were sitting up straight, looking at Ava.

"Were you upset enough to ask the defendant about it?"

"Yes."

"What happened?"

"He smirked and said it was no worse than rap lyrics."

"What did you do with the notebook?"

"I marked the page and gave it to his mother."

Mara gasped. There'd been no marked page, but with the notebook gone, she couldn't prove that.

"No further questions."

Greg stood. "Officer Branson, did you write anything in your report about the notebook?"

"No."

"Even though it concerned you that much?"

"That's why I marked the page when I gave it to the mother."

"So we have no notebook and nothing else in writing to confirm your memory of three years ago?"

"You don't forget something like that."

"Had you ever seen Ariel Levine's handwriting before that day three years ago?"

"No."

"Did you know that other people besides him had written in the notebook?"

"Objection, the question is not based on any evidence before this court."

The judge brought down her gavel. "Sustained."

Greg continued. "You testified that the subject of rap lyrics came up when you discussed the page with the defendant."

"Yes."

"Didn't he, in fact, tell you that those were rap lyrics you'd just read?"

Ava looked over at Sissy who rose immediately. "Objection,

argumentative."

"Sustained."

"But Your Honor . . ."

"Sustained," the judge said in a louder tone.

"Are you familiar with rap lyrics, Officer Branson?"

"Yes."

"Is it possible that's what you were reading?"

"I guess so, but I doubt it."

"But you can't be sure?"

"No."

"No further questions."

Mara took deep breaths to stop hyperventilating. If she fainted, the jury would realize just how devastating she thought the last two witnesses had been.

***

Sissy got home to find a note from Dennis saying her dinner was in the microwave and that he'd taken the girls to a movie.

She shouldn't be so hard on her husband. He was a good cook, a good baby sitter and, when there was time, a satisfactory lover. He'd be an asset during the campaign, keeping their daughters' lives under control while she was electioneering.

Sissy put her empty plate in the sink and walked through the hall to their bedroom. Her briefcase was full, and she had more exhibits to take to the trial tomorrow. She went to their closet and found an old small suitcase on wheels. It would do. She moved the carry-on bag resting on top of it and pulled out the black case, which they hadn't used in years.

She put it on top of their bed, sat down next to it and unzipped it. She found a three subject notebook. Sissy opened it towards the middle and saw today's date with a blank space for the time she'd arrived home and a notation in Dennis's handwriting about how he'd comforted Paige who was disappointed that her mother wasn't there and that he'd made dinner for his daughters and taken them to the movies.

Sissy went back a few pages and saw a notation about how her missing Paige's soccer game had upset both Paige and Holly.

Half the notebook was filled with similar notes going back almost a year.

Sissy had worked unceasingly to get to the brink of the position and prestige she'd always wanted, and her traitorous husband was trying to turn her efforts against her.

She looked up as Dennis entered the room.

"That's mine," he said.

"You bastard."

"Every word is true."

Holly came into her parents' bedroom. "What's going on?" Her father looked at the notebook. Holly grabbed it from Sissy and ran out.

"Get back in here and give that to me."

Sissy got off the bed to go after her daughter.

Dennis moved in front of her. "Keep the children out of this."

"You're the one who put them into it."

"I just want custody of them. You can have everything else."

"How magnanimous when everything we have is because of me."

Holly rushed back into the room without the notebook. "I'm fourteen and can choose who I live with, so I'll be with Dad."

"You'll live without your sister because I'll get custody of her."

"Who'd give you custody?"

"Any judge I go before. They all know me."

"An ugly custody battle will cost you enough votes to lose the election," Dennis said.

"I'll lose the election, but I'll have Paige."

"Will she, Dad?"

"I don't know, honey."

Sissy had him now. "The price of ruining my campaign for District Attorney is separating your daughters."

"Don't let her, Dad."

Dennis looked from Holly to Sissy. He took a deep breath. "Let's cut a deal, Sissy."

"Like what?"

"We stay married throughout the campaign. After you're elected District Attorney, I'll file for divorce, and you give me custody without an ugly court battle."

Sissy thought of Paige, cute and cuddly, and about how she'd miss her dad and her sister and the soccer games Sissy would never be able to take her to. Sissy couldn't do that to her precious little one. But Dennis didn't know that.

"You'll give me unlimited help throughout the campaign."

"Right."

"I'll get the kids every other weekend."

"Yes."

"No, Dad, I don't want to be with her."

"She's your mother, and this is the best we can do."

"But, Dad, if she loses the election, she might still want Paige."

"Don't worry. As soon as I get Levine behind bars, the election's mine."

THIRTY-SEVEN

"Mom, do you think the jury believes I'm a blood thirsty killer?"

If only Mara could keep the *Houston Post-Gazette* away from her son. Its feature story that morning ran under the banner, "Levine's desire to slit women's throats highlighted by two witnesses." Hopefully the jurors were honoring their vow not to read news accounts of the trial.

"Things will look better once we put on our witnesses. Patricia Lansing, the memory expert, is scheduled first, right after the prosecution finishes."

The day started with Sissy Kleinman calling Tim Wyeth, head of the police crime lab to the stand. The black suit the hunched figure wore hung on his small frame and emphasized the pastiness of his skin, giving his face a ghost like appearance. The witness coughed and wheezed as he was being sworn in.

He testified that the only blood found in the Land Rover was a small amount from an animal, likely a dog.

"What did you find on both the steering wheel and on the handle on the passenger's side of the front seat?" Sissy asked.

"Eight white fibers."

Sissy looked at the jurors and then back at her witness. "Were they consistent with those from bras sold at Lingerie for Life?"

"Yes."

"Could they have been transferred to the steering wheel when someone who'd been in the shop drove off in the Land Rover?"

"Objection."

"Withdrawn. Your witness."

Greg began his cross-examination. "Wouldn't those eight fibers be consistent with bras sold in stores across Houston?"

"Possibly. But we only checked them against those from Lingerie for Life."

Her son hadn't brought those fibers into the Land Rover. They must have come from Virginia's bras. Yet, she hadn't offered to testify. Mara glanced at Simon who was staring at the floor.

"Did you find blood on the outside door handle or the steering wheel, places a killer with blood on his hands would have touched?" Greg asked.

Sissy leapt to her feet. "Objection, assuming information not in evidence."

"Sustained."

"Hypothetically, Mr. Wyeth, if a killer had blood on his hands, would you expect to find some traces on the outside door handle and on the steering wheel?"

"Yes."

"Hypothetically, if a killer had blood on his clothes would you expect to find some on the seat which those clothes touched?"

When a hacking cough prevented Wyeth from answering, Sissy ran up to the witness stand with a glass of water.

Greg said, "Your Honor . . ."

The judge peered at him. "It was a mission of mercy. But, Ms. Kleinman, you know better than to interfere with Mr. Dickson's cross-examination."

"Yes, Your Honor."

Two of the jurors smiled at Sissy as she returned to her seat.

Greg asked the question again, and Wyeth replied that based on the hypothetical he would expect to find blood on the seat.

"Did you analyze the 911 tape of Mrs. Luna's call?"

"No, 911 tapes are destroyed within thirty days, and we didn't request it until you asked about it."

"So we had no chance to prove the killer's voice wasn't Ariel's, did we?"

"Objection."

"Sustained."

"What were the results when you tested the skin under Mrs. Sorento's fingernails?"

"DNA tests were inconclusive."

"Why weren't the specimens given to the defense so we could have our own analysis done?"

"We'd thrown them away."

Mara's hand went to her throat.

"What happened to the bloody palm print the police lifted from the store's counter?"

"We can't find it."

"So, as with the skin, the defense had no chance to analyze it to prove it had no connection with Ariel Levine, but with the actual murderer instead."

"Objection."

"I'm warning you, Mr. Dickson," the judge boomed.

"No further questions."

Even if the jurors ignored the implication of the missing evidence, surely the lack of blood in the Land Rover had to have impressed them.

Sissy admitted the photo of Mrs. Luna's knife wounds into evidence and called Arturo Cruz to the stand. The copper brown coloring of his face was set off by thick black hair. He spoke in heavily accented English as he answered Sissy's questions which established he was thirty-one, a native of Columbia and had been a fifth year surgical resident when Mrs. Luna was brought to Ben Taub Hospital on November 24, 2000. When he described the damage to the patient's colon, stomach and lungs caused by her knife wounds, a woman in the second row of the jury box wrapped her arms around her mid section.

"During surgery I found a large amount of blood in the sac around her heart."

"What was the effect of the bleeding around the heart on the rest of her body?" Sissy asked.

"She was in shock so her blood pressure was very low so her blood wasn't perfusing. It wasn't reaching the organs."

"Then it's possible there was no blood on her when the killer left the store?"

"That is correct."

"Pass the witness."

Somehow Greg had to disabuse the jury of that crazy notion.

Her son's attorney stood. "Dr. Cruz, do you know how many units of blood Mrs. Luna lost before she arrived at the hospital?"

"No."

"Considering she had twelve knife wounds, would you surmise there would have been significant blood loss?"

Arturo Cruz crossed his arms in front of his chest. "No major arteries were cut."

"Don't people bleed from veins and minor arteries?"

"Yes, but you can cut someone who's in shock and have no bleeding."

"Since Mrs. Luna walked around and dialed a telephone for several minutes after being injured, wouldn't that indicate she was not in immediate shock?"

"I guess so."

"How much blood did you see on her when she first came into the emergency room?"

"That's not what I paid attention to. I had to figure out what we needed to do to save her life."

"Did you consider that emergency medical technicians had treated her and perhaps stopped the bleeding before you saw her?"

"I didn't think about it. She was in shock. No major artery was spurting blood so all I cared about was figuring out where the internal bleeding was coming from, so I could save her life."

"Since she had twelve stab wounds and her activity right after being stabbed indicated she was not immediately in shock, do you believe if you had been looking for signs of external bleeding, you would have seen them?"

"It's possible."

"No further questions."

Mara bit her lower lip. Sissy had done a remarkable job of preparing Dr. Cruz to testify. Even with Greg's cross-examination, the jurors could believe the killer had left the store with no blood on him.

THIRTY-EIGHT

As they left the courtroom, Simon whispered to Virginia, "Those bra fibers are the only connection between Ariel and the murder scene. That's what the jury needs to convict him."

Virginia turned towards him, her face pale.

"What's wrong?" he asked.

"I'm a bit nauseated." She put her hand to her mouth and ran into the ladies' room.

Simon waited outside the door. After a few minutes he considered going in but then saw a policewoman. "Could you check on my wife? I think she's ill."

Just then Virginia walked out. "I'm fine now."

"I'll get you right home."

"No. We need to go to Greg Dickson's office."

"Why?"

"I've been thinking. You were right. Some new bras did fall out of a bag when I brought them home in the Land Rover."

"I knew it. Let's go."

Simon paced in Greg's waiting room until the attorney was off the phone and escorted them into his office.

"Tell him, Virginia," Simon said.

Virginia ran her fingers through her hair. "Shortly before the murder, I bought new bras. They were in a bag in the front seat of the Land Rover, and when I came to sudden stop, they fell out."

Greg rested his chin in his hand and looked at Virginia. "Do you have a receipt to prove you bought them or perhaps an old credit card bill?"

"I paid cash."

Greg pursed his lips. "That's a shame. It makes the story less believable."

Simon put his arm around Virginia. "My wife is not a liar."

"You've seen Sissy in action. You know she can make her look like one."

Virginia shuddered.

"Where did the bras land when they fell?" Greg asked.

"I think on the floor."

"The fibers were found on the steering wheel and the handle on the passenger's side of the door," Greg said.

Simon glared at the attorney. "Virginia put the bras back in the bag so she had the fibers on her hands when she held the steering wheel."

"And the ones found on the door handle?" Greg asked.

"Virginia must have opened it to let someone in on the passenger side. It could have been me."

"You can have any lab do an analysis of my bras. The fibers will match."

"We'll do that immediately, to lay the predicate for you testifying."

"Okay," Virginia said in a barely audible tone.

***

More than half of the large pizza Mara had picked up on her way home remained. She didn't encourage Ariel and Benjie to eat. Who could be hungry after everything that had happened in court that day?

"Let's shoot some hoops," Benjie suggested to his brother.

"Nah. I'm tired. I'm going to bed early."

"You'll sleep better if I wear you out."

Ariel hesitated. "Okay. Just let me change." He left the table and headed up to his room.

Benjie looked at Mara. "He's going to prison, isn't he?"

"Things look bad because only the prosecution has put on its case. Once we have our chance . . ."

"I think about Ariel being in that tiny space behind bars, having to crap in the same area where he sleeps. He'll never eat another decent meal or go out to the movies or to a Rockets game. And forget about dating or even seeing his friends and family except for a little while once a week if anyone except us even bothers to visit."

"Benjie . . ."

"He's always been there for me. When I was little, he let me tag along; when I didn't have my license, he drove me everywhere; when I had guy questions, he answered them."

Mara went to her son and put her arms around him. "What will I do without Ariel, Mom?"

THIRTY-NINE

Looking at the burnished wood of the judge's bench and the seal of the State of Texas on the wall, Mara could never have imagined being in court under these circumstances. She was suppose to be at the defendant's table, helping her client get justice, not sitting helpless while her son was weighed on the scales of justice. Odd that she'd never thought the depiction of justice as blind could mean someone's innocence might go unseen.

Judge Mason entered the courtroom and addressed the jurors. "Because of our late start due to my judicial conference, I'm afraid we'll only have time to hear one witness today."

Sissy rose. "The State calls Dr. Abraham Cohen."

A man with a wine colored birthmark covering most of his right cheek and part of his forehead walked to the witness stand with his shoulders back and his chin up.

Mara had been surprised when she'd learned Cohen was to be Sissy's witness, but Greg had reassured her. "I've read his brief medical report. He says the seizures are questionable but since he prescribed Dilantin, an anti-seizure medicine, I'll get rid of any doubt when I cross-examine him."

"Dr. Cohen," Sissy began, "please tell the jury about your education and training."

"I graduated third in my class at the University of Texas, first in my class at Baylor Medical School and did my neurology residency at Harvard."

"Why did the defendant visit your office?"

"He claimed he'd had seizures when he was in Guatemala."

"Are those the seizures that supposedly kept him in Guatemala after his family located him, and before he was apprehended there?"

"Yes."

"What was your medical opinion?"

"That at worst he'd had a couple of fainting spells. Probably

237

hadn't eaten enough."

"Would that be a reason for him to stay in Guatemala?"

"No."

"Your witness, Mr. Dickson."

"Dr. Cohen, was it your medical judgment to continue prescribing Dilantin, a drug used by patients with seizure disorders?"

"Yes."

"Surely you wouldn't have prescribed it unless you had reason to believe Ariel needed it."

"You have to go by the history the patient gives. He claimed he'd lost bladder control during one of his spells."

"That's a sign of a seizure as opposed to fainting, isn't it?"

"Anyone who goes on the Internet can find that out."

Why hadn't Simon warned them about how hostile Cohen was? Mara glanced at her former husband who was gazing at his lap.

She returned her attention to Greg.

"The doctor who saw him in Guatemala diagnosed seizures and also prescribed Dilantin, didn't he?" her son's attorney asked.

"That's what the father told me, but I had no medical records to go by."

"You also diagnosed a seizure disorder and prescribed Dilantin."

Dr. Cohen's birthmark took on a purple hue. "I had no choice. If I hadn't, he could have faked a seizure and sued me for malpractice."

***

Greg looked over his desk at Simon, who sat between his former wife and an expressionless Ariel. "Mr. Levine, did you have any hint Dr. Cohen would be so antagonistic?"

"At the end of our visit, I overheard him on the phone. He told someone Ariel had shamed Houston Jewry. But I never thought he'd be so unfair."

Greg closed a manila folder. "This changes our plans. We'll need you to be our first witness to counteract the notion that Ariel stayed in Guatemala, not because he was sick, but to evade the law."

Simon turned towards his son who stared straight ahead. The boy's life depended on his testimony. If he failed, Ariel would be penned up with the most violent dregs of society, always in danger. And each day he survived would be a day without hope for any part of a normal life—marriage, children, the chance to realize his potential. A completely wasted existence.

"Don't worry, Mr. Levine, I'll woodshed you—rehearse all the questions I'm going to ask and the ones I think Ms. Kleinman will."

"That seems like a big gamble," Mara said. "If Kleinman trips up Simon, it'll reinforce the notion Ariel fled. Maybe we should stick with Patricia Lansing, the identification expert, as our leadoff witness."

For the first time in years Simon thought Mara was right.

"Don't forget that to support Simon's testimony, we have the tape of District Attorney Reardon saying Ariel could leave the country. I'll call him as our last witness. Also, there's a scheduling issue. Ms. Lansing can't make it here in time to open Ariel's defense."

Mara frowned. "When will you have a chance to prepare her?"

"That's not necessary. She's testified so many times she knows what to say."

"Every case is different," Mara said.

"You worry too much, Mrs. Levine."

***

The next morning Judge Mason looked down from the bench. "Ms. Kleinman, do you have any further witnesses to call at this time?"

"No, Your Honor, the State rests."

"You may call your first witness, Mr. Dickson."

"I call Simon Levine to the stand."

Simon rose, wiped his palms on the pant legs of his new suit and walked to the front of the courtroom.

He took his seat in the witness box and studied the jury, the twelve people who would decide the course of his son's life. He was struck by how bored they seemed. They yawned, studied their fingernails and glanced his way with half closed eyes. Was it already too late? Had the prosecution used up all their interest? Or was he fooling himself that the jurors wouldn't notice if his testimony condemned Ariel?

Simon's answers to Greg's questions established he was Ariel's father, that Ariel had lived in Israel until he was nine and that his son had dual American/Israeli citizenship.

"Why did Ariel go to Israel last December?"

"To join the Israeli Air Force."

"Was he under arrest?"

"No. The police hadn't questioned him since the night of the tragedy. District Attorney Reardon Jones said there were no restrictions on Ariel leaving the country."

"Why did Ariel come back to Houston?"

"He found out his eyesight was too poor for him to be a pilot."

"Why did he leave Houston again?"

"We feared for his safety. We got hang-up calls, dead flowers on our doorstep and then our dog was poisoned. We were afraid they'd come after Ariel next." Simon's eyes filled with tears. He clasped his hands so they'd stop shaking.

"Did he leave immediately?"

"No, not until District Attorney Reardon Jones gave him permission to go."

"What were his plans?"

"To take a six month backpacking trip, like Israeli boys do before they go into the armed forces. I did it at his age."

"Why didn't you know where he was going?"

"He and I had words just before we got to the airport so he left the car without telling me."

"Were you surprised when he didn't contact the family?"

"No. He's never been much for writing or calling home."

"When did you hear from him?"

"He called from Guatemala after he had two seizures."

"Did you tell him then about the indictment?"

"No. I was afraid it would upset him, make him have another seizure."

"What did you do?"

"I went to Guatemala and took my son to a doctor. He started Ariel on Dilantin to stop the seizures but said he'd have to do blood tests in a week to know if Ariel was on the right dose."

"Why didn't you bring him back immediately instead of waiting for the results of the tests?"

Simon's voice cracked. "He could have had a seizure on the

240

plane and died."

"When the doctor said it was safe for him to fly, what did you do?"

"I asked you to arrange with District Attorney Reardon Jones to have him surrender, and I made plans to meet him in Mexico City so he wouldn't return to Houston alone."

"Is that what happened?"

Simon took a deep breath. "You and the District Attorney arranged the surrender. But it didn't happen as planned because Ariel was arrested at the airport in Guatemala City on his way back to Houston."

Greg spoke the words Simon dreaded. "Your witness, Ms. Kleinman."

Sissy approached Simon with the hint of a smile and a slight nod.

"You testified your son didn't pass the vision test to be an Israeli pilot."

"Yes."

"Why didn't he take the eye exam in Houston and send the results to Israel, saving himself a trip?"

"I . . . I never thought of that."

"If he really wanted to join, couldn't he have taken a non pilot position?"

"Yes, but . . ."

"But he really came home, not because he was denied being a pilot, but because he thought the police had lost interest in him."

Greg jumped to his feet. "Objection."

"Withdrawn."

"Can anyone outside your family testify to the phone calls and flowers and dog problem that supposedly scared you into sending Ariel away again?"

"No, but . . . "

"Did you report them to the police?"

Why hadn't Dickson asked him that question and prepared him to answer it? Simon couldn't think quickly enough of how to explain it, so all he said was, "No."

"Do you expect this jury to believe it's perfectly normal for a nineteen year old to be gone months without getting in touch with his family?"

"It's true with Ariel."

"Did he fail to contact his family because he learned about the indictment and didn't want anyone to be able to find him?"

"Of course not. I broke the news to him in Guatemala City after he was on the anti-seizure medicine."

"What's the name and address of the doctor you took him to in Guatemala?"

"It was something like Martinez-Costello or Costello-Martinez. I . . . I don't know the address. A cab took us there."

"Can you provide any medical records from the visit?"

"No, they're in Guatemala."

"How convenient."

"Objection."

"Withdrawn."

"How long did you wait to tell Mr. Dickson or the authorities you'd located Ariel?"

"I told Mr. Dickson when the blood tests were back, and I knew Ariel could travel."

"Was that over a week?"

"Yes."

"Did you spend that week trying to convince Ariel to come back to Houston?"

Simon raised his voice. "Absolutely not. Ariel wanted to return and clear his name."

"Why didn't he plan to come straight home, rather than stopping in Mexico City, where it's easy to get a visa to Israel?"

"Objection," Greg roared.

"Withdrawn. No further questions."

Simon left the witness stand and walked past Ariel.

His son averted his eyes.

***

Sissy decided to ask just one question when she cross-examined the nerdy looking fiber expert Greg Dickson had on the witness stand. He was testifying that the fibers found in the Land Rover were consistent with those from Virginia's bras.

"Can you say positively that those fibers came from Virginia Levine's bras?"

He replied in his squeaky voice, "No, but . . ."

"Thank you."

242

Greg called Virginia as his next witness. Sissy studied her as she walked to the stand. She looked like she'd gotten ready to testify by having her hair coifed, her nails manicured and her new suit altered to fit her perfectly maintained body.

Virginia was giving the jury a story about her new bras falling out of a bag and her picking them up, getting fibers on her hands which she transferred to the steering wheel and onto the passenger door handle when she opened the door for Simon.

Greg finished questioning his witness, and Sissy began her cross-examination.

"Can you provide the jury with a receipt for those bras?"

"No. I paid cash and didn't save the receipt."

"At what store?"

"Macy's."

"Did you have them check their records and give you a duplicate receipt?"

"I . . . I didn't know they could do that."

"So we don't have a receipt. Can you describe the saleswoman you bought them from?"

"I don't remember. I've seen lots of salespeople."

"Of course, with all the shopping you do."

"Objection," Greg bellowed.

"Withdrawn." Sissy paused. "But she must have been pretty incompetent."

"I don't understand."

"When I buy bras the salesclerk wraps them in tissue paper, and once they're securely inside the bag, closes it. Is that what happened when you bought the bras in question?"

"I wasn't paying that much attention."

"If it happened that way, don't you think it would be almost impossible for the bras to fall out?"

"Objection. Ms. Kleinman is assuming facts not in evidence."

"Withdrawn." Sissy watched Virginia rub her hands together, and then asked, "If the bras fell on the floor, why weren't any fibers found on the car's carpeting where they would have landed?"

Virginia opened her mouth, closed it and looked at Greg Dickson. Sissy could hardly believe her opposing counsel hadn't anticipated that question and told his witness how to handle it.

"I used a hand held vacuum on the carpet when I cleaned out the interior," Virginia said.

"So you cleaned out the car well enough to remove the bra fibers from the carpet but not from the steering wheel or door handle?"

"I guess so."

"You testified you transferred bra fibers to the door handle when you opened the door for your husband?"

"Yes."

"How could you have reached across that big Land Rover of yours and opened the door?"

"I . . . I must have taken off my seat belt and then opened the door."

Sissy glanced at the jury. They knew Virginia was a liar.

FORTY

The courtroom doors opened.

Mara turned and saw a middle aged woman with bleached blond hair who was outfitted in a canary yellow suit, its skirt ending six inches above her knees.

She waved at Greg. "I made it."

The jurors looked at her, none smiling.

"I call Patricia Lansing to the stand," Greg said.

Mara was still disturbed that Greg had spent no time preparing this witness before her appearance. But once she began testifying, Mara understood why he hadn't felt the need to. Through his questions the jury learned about Patricia's credentials as an identification and memory expert. She'd written five books and her articles had appeared in twenty-six journals. She'd taught FBI and Secret Service agents as well as police officers. She quoted from one Department of Justice study showing that of forty convicted people who were later exonerated, thirty-six had been found guilty because of mistaken eye witness testimony and another report illustrating that by using a photo identification, the chance of a false identification rose by twenty per cent.

Their witness had to be impressing the jurors, but two in the back row and one in the front had lowered their heads, making Mara suspect they were dozing.

"Tell the jury about unconscious transference," Greg said.

"It occurs when you've seen someone in one situation and you confuse him with someone you've seen in another."

"So if a witness saw someone in a chiropractor's waiting room and then identified him in a photo line-up, it might be because of this confusion?"

"Certainly."

"Objection. Block denied seeing Levine before."

"Sustained. The jury will disregard the witness's answer."

"Could unconscious transference occur if a witness saw

245

someone in a photo line-up and then saw him again in a video line-up?" Greg asked.

"That's a likely place for it to occur."

Greg's next sequence of questions and Patricia's answers established that when people saw a series of letters or numbers, such as on a license plate, and then wrote them down, they were likely to make mistakes in remembering those at the end of the series.

Sissy smirked as she rose to cross-examine Patricia.

Mara touched her neck and realized she'd forgotten to wear the chasma.

Sissy began her questioning. "In one of those famous articles you cited for Mr. Dickson, didn't you complain about judges who wouldn't allow your testimony because they think it's junk science?"

A deep pink hue rose from Patricia's neck to her cheeks. "Only two judges have ever refused to let me testify. They claimed the attorneys didn't lay the predicate for the scientific basis of my testimony. No one has ever called my work junk science."

"Those attorneys would have to be defense attorneys since you've never testified for the prosecution, have you?"

"The prosecution wouldn't challenge their own eye witnesses."

"Your Honor," Sissy said, "please instruct the witness to answer 'yes' or 'no.'"

"You are so instructed."

"Have you ever testified for the prosecution, Miss Lansing?"

"No."

"How much are you charging the defense?"

"Twelve thousand dollars."

Sissy walked to the prosecution's table and picked up a book. "I enjoyed your chapter on famous criminals you've met."

Patricia smiled.

Sissy handed the book to the witness. "I've turned to the part where you wrote about the time you spent with Ted Bundy. Please read the sentence I highlighted."

Patricia looked at the page but didn't speak.

"Read it," Sissy commanded.

"Ted Bundy is one of the cutest guys I've ever met."

"No further questions."

FORTY-ONE

Mara had looked forward to the testimony of Jim Johnson, the Land Rover dealer. With him coming right after Patricia Lansing the jury would understand how easily Andrew Block could have written the license plate numbers down wrong. Now all the jurors would remember about Patricia was that she thought mass murderer Ted Bundy was cute.

As soon as Jim was sworn in, he moved his hand to his head in an unsuccessful effort to rearrange some remaining hair over his bald spot. He patted his moustache and looked at his hands as though checking his manicure.

Greg had the car dealership's record book entered as an exhibit. "How many dark colored model year 2000 Land Rovers did your dealership sell?"

Jim cleared his throat, making a noise reminiscent of a bleating sheep. "Six, four black and two dark blue."

"Did you provide the license plates for those vehicles?"

Jim cleared his throat again. "Yes."

"What was the license plate on the Land Rover sold to Mrs. Virginia Levine?"

Jim pointed to an entry in the record book. "PBD164."

"Did the license plates on the other five dark colored Land Rovers also all begin with PBD1?"

"Yes."

"So except for the last two numbers, those plates were identical to that on the Levine Land Rover?"

"Yes."

"No further questions."

Sissy began her cross-examination by having Jim Johnson read the names and addresses of Virginia Levine and the other five Land Rover owners.

"Does any of them, except Virginia Levine at whose house Ariel Levine was staying on November 24, 2000, live in the vicinity of West and Baylor, where Lingerie for Life is located?"

"No."

"No further questions."

***

Their next witness was the blood splatter expert Matthew Cavazos. What could go wrong when he testified?

The judge called a twenty minute recess. The Levines, Greg and Matthew Cavazos went to the court clerk's office. Greg closed the door and introduced their expert, a tall, long faced man whose gray hair didn't completely extinguish strands of black, which had once been predominant. The top button of the striped blue and white shirt he wore under his sport jacket was unbuttoned, revealing a small cross on a silver chain.

Greg excused himself to make a phone call.

Matthew put his hand on Ariel's arm. "I'm sorry you're going through this. I know there's no way you could have committed that murder and not gotten blood on you."

Matthew's unhurried soft speech calmed Mara. "It's so good to hear someone objective say what I've always known in my heart."

"A parent knows a child. There's no way I could ever have believed my son capable of a vicious act."

"How old is your boy?" Mara asked.

"I lost him in a car accident when he was twenty. I think about him every day."

Mara had caused this kind man to remember the worst possible pain. "According to Jewish tradition, the loss of a child is considered a tragedy in such a special category, that even if a person never recovers from it, no one has the right to question his faith in God."

"Thank you. That's a comforting thought."

When the recess ended, Greg called Matthew to the stand.

The jury had to be impressed with their expert's credentials. Greg's questioning revealed that Matthew had worked in the San Antonio Police Lab for twenty-eight years during which time he'd visited over 700 crime scenes. He was the lab's chief forensic chemist when he'd retired a year ago. Since then he'd testified for both the State and various defendants.

Matthew, having been part of the San Antonio Police Department, might know about the collection methods of Lucky

248

Lazarus, the gambler to whom the victim's son was indebted. Mara would ask him later.

Greg handed their expert the picture of the crime scene taken by the police.

"In twenty-eight years I never saw a scene this bloody where the perpetrator left without having blood transferred to him."

"Is there anything about the crime itself that makes you feel blood must have been transferred to the killer?"

"He stabbed one victim twelve times while his body was pressed against hers."

"Assuming the killer got blood on him, would you expect it to be transferred to his vehicle?"

"Yes, on the door handle, the steering wheel, the seat."

"How easy is it to get blood out of a car so that not even the most minute trace would be left for a forensic chemist to analyze?"

"Almost impossible."

"Your witness, Ms. Kleinman."

"Your Honor, considering it's almost five o'clock, and I'm sure the jury wants to get home a little early for the weekend, I'd like to begin my cross-examination Monday morning."

The jurors smiled. Mara wondered whether Sissy's goal had been to ingratiate herself with them, to give herself more time to prepare or whether she wanted to inconvenience their San Antonio witness. Probably all three.

When the spectators left, Matthew went to the defense table and spoke to Ariel. Mara was sure he believed the words of encouragement, which brought a smile to her son. But this afternoon was Matthew's first time in the courtroom so he didn't know what had gone on before. The impact on the jury of Andrew Block's identification of Ariel and his being 100% certain he'd written down the correct license plate number hadn't been affected by the discredited Patricia Lansing. And as good as Matthew's testimony had been, Sissy's cross-examination would create doubt in the jurors' minds.

Sissy was well on her way to getting the ninety-nine year prison sentence she sought. Since the crime had been committed with a deadly weapon, Ariel would have to serve one half of that sentence, forty-nine and one-half years, before he was eligible for parole. He'd be seventy years old. Mara would be long dead. Would they let him come to her funeral? He wouldn't be able to sit shiva for her, to spend the seven days after her death being at home, saying prayers, accepting condolences. Would anyone except Benjie visit Ariel in prison after Mara and Simon were gone?

Those thoughts were still with Mara as she walked to the parking lot with Ariel, Simon, Greg and Matthew. When Matthew stopped at a white Land Rover, Mara found it ironic that he owned the vehicle she'd come to hate.

She glanced at its license plate, and read it as PBD148.

The first four characters on the plate were the same as on the Land Rover the killer drove. The same first four as on Virginia's.

She looked at their witness, the man who'd been so kind to Ariel.

She had to be out of her mind if she thought he could be the killer.

Besides, his vehicle was white, not black.

She had to get a grip.

She looked at the license plate again.

It was DBP148.

"My God, that's it," she gasped.

The four men stopped talking and looked at her. She pointed at the license plate. "Block transposed the first and third letters, like someone under stress or someone dyslexic would do. He actually saw DBP164."

Simon and Ariel crouched down and studied the license plate.

"You bought your Land Rover in San Antonio where you live, didn't you?" Mara asked Matthew.

"Yes."

Mara turned to Greg. "Lucky Lazarus runs his gambling operation out of San Antonio."

"Let's go to my office," Greg said.

FORTY-TWO

They sat around the table in Greg's conference room. "Don't get too excited about this, Mrs. Levine," the attorney said. "The odds that Lucky or one of his associates has a Land Rover with a similar license plate to Virginia Levine's are highly improbable."

"Not as improbable as you might think," Matthew replied. "When I bought the car from my neighbor who owns the dealership, he teased me about how he was glad to be selling one to a former cop. Seems Land Rovers had become the vehicle of choice of what he termed 'a certain San Antonio element.'"

Mara raised her voice. "We've got to find out whose car has the license plate DBP164."

"I'll call my neighbor. If he sold a Land Rover that got that license plate, he'll give me the name and I'll check the owner out with one of my police buddies."

"Wouldn't it be quicker to call the Department of Public Safety?" Mara asked.

"The law no longer allows private citizens to get that information from them," Greg replied.

Mara addressed Matthew. "Couldn't you have one of your police contacts get it for us?"

"That's not fair of you to ask," Greg said. "It could cause problems for Mr. Cavazos."

"I'll get you the information one way or another," Matthew assured Mara.

He left to use the phone in Greg's office.

"If only this would end it all," Ariel said.

Had Mara raised Ariel's hopes for nothing? If Matthew couldn't get the information or if her idea about the license plate didn't pan out, the likelihood of his conviction would confront her son. Somehow she'd have to help him face that possibility.

It was over an hour before Matthew returned. "The owner of a dark green Land Rover, license plate number DBP164 is Ivan

Verkonovitch, a twenty-five year old known associate of Lucky Lazarus."

Mara and Ariel hugged.

Simon sat with his mouth open.

"Mrs. Levine, this does not get Ariel off the hook," Greg said.

Mara pointed her finger at the attorney. "I'm tired of your negativism. We know the victim's son hasn't paid off his gambling debts to Lazarus."

"There's no way to prove that."

"You've got a guy the right age and an almost exact match on the license plate."

"Sissy has two eye witness identifications of Ariel and an exact match on the license plate."

"Surely she wants to convict the right person."

"All she cares about is winning. I'll talk to her but the best we can hope for is that she'll agree to a short recess in the trial while the police investigate."

***

Sissy was sitting at her desk taking notes on a yellow legal pad, working on her cross-examination of Matthew Cavazos when the phone rang. Upon hearing Greg Dickson's voice, she smiled. He must want to talk about a plea bargain. She'd play with him, but in the end, unless his client agreed to fifty years, she'd go for her win at trial.

"Remember how I told you Luis Sorento hadn't finished paying off his gambling debts to Lucky Lazarus?" Greg said.

"Detective Crawley assured me they were taken care of."

"Turns out a twenty-five year old known associate of Lazarus owns a Land Rover with a license plate number DBP164."

Sissy had heard about how brutal Lazarus' henchmen could be. But she was on the verge of convicting Levine.

"Unless you're about to tell me you have proof this guy did it."

"With a short recess I should be able to."

She'd look incompetent, unfit to be District Attorney, if someone else turned out to be the killer.

"You've got the weekend."

"I need more time and the cooperation of Detective Crawley."

"He's his own man," Sissy said.

She hung up and dialed Oracio Crawley's number.

252

***

Greg walked into the conference room with the news he'd told them to expect. Sissy opposed the recess, and without her agreement, Judge Mason would almost certainly deny one.

They had only this weekend to prove Ivan was the killer.

"Once the San Antonio police get a search warrant and seize the Land Rover, how quickly can they test it?" Mara asked Matthew. "Even after all this time, do you think there'd still be some microscopic blood in it?"

"I'm almost sure there would be, but the Houston police have jurisdiction over the case. Unless they request help, no one in San Antonio can act."

"I talked to Detective Crawley. He refused to reopen the case," Greg said.

"That bastard," Ariel shouted. "I'm here because he tricked me into cooperating. Now he won't do anything to help me. I hope he rots in hell."

"Get your investigator to San Antonio now," Mara ordered Greg.

"He can take pictures of the Land Rover and its license plate and of Ivan himself, who you're assuming resembles Ariel, but he can't bring us the kind of evidence you alluded to." Greg hesitated. "And it will be difficult to get Judge Mason to allow him as a witness."

"But my life is at stake," Ariel said.

The room fell silent.

"I'm going to the press," Mara announced. "Shondra Nandagiri at the *Post-Gazette* has written one sympathetic article about Ariel. She'll jump at this."

"Don't be a fool," Simon yelled. "You'll alert the killer. He could flee, get rid of his Land Rover, the knife, if he still has it."

But it was Mara who fled, bolting out of the conference room, running down twelve flights of stairs and onto the street.

***

Mara didn't know where to go or what to do. She crossed the street, walked around the block and found herself in front of the Alley Theatre. Its marquee announced the production of Agatha Christie's Ten Little Indians.

Judith Groudine Finkel

In all the mysteries Mara had read or seen, the detective discovered the guilty party, proved he did it and insured justice prevailed.

They knew who had murdered Mrs. Sorento, but they couldn't prove it.

They needed time to do that.

Sissy had refused to give it to them.

They needed Detective Crawley's cooperation.

Sissy could get that.

Without both, her innocent son would go to jail while the killer remained free.

There had to be something Mara could do.

She headed purposefully towards a tall white brick building blocks away.

FORTY-THREE

Mara opened the door to Sissy Kleinman's office.

The assistant district attorney stopped writing on a yellow notepad, her pencil poised in midair. "You shouldn't be here, Mrs. Levine. I can't do anything for your son."

She moved her hand closer to the telephone.

To call security?

"You still want to be elected District Attorney, don't you?"

"You're making no sense. You'll have to leave."

"When I leave, it'll be to go to the *Houston Post-Gazette* where I've got a sympathetic reporter ready to write a story about an assistant district attorney who'd rather convict an innocent boy than take on a crime boss and one of his lackeys."

"You won't," Sissy said. "That would only alert the guy you're sure did it."

"Dickson's investigator is in San Antonio ready to tail him, so we'll have pictures when he cleans out the Land Rover or gets rid of it and the knife. There'll be a great follow-up story run with those photos about the results of your failure to cooperate."

"If he did it."

"If he didn't, I'm no worse off. But if he did, you are."

Sissy snapped her pencil in two.

Mara moved closer. "Why don't you turn yourself into a hero instead?"

Sissy stared at her visitor.

"You can take credit for noticing Matthew Cavazos's license plate and checking out your hunch that it could mean Block had mixed up the first three letters. Caring as you do more about justice than winning, you got Detective Crawley's cooperation and that of the San Antonio police." Mara laughed. "It's a great story."

"It could take days to figure out if Lazarus's thug did it."

"Oracio Crawley and Judge Mason will do whatever you say. Ask for a recess. They can be heroes, too."

"And if he didn't do it?"

"You're still a heroine for turning over every stone to get to the truth. And you still convict my son."

"I need to be sure of that. If by next Thursday morning there's no proof Lazarus's guy did it, Ariel agrees to a plea bargain. Fifty years."

Mara had this one chance to prove her son innocent. Otherwise, Sissy would get her conviction along with a ninety-nine year sentence. The fifty years Sissy was asking for would make Ariel eligible for parole in twenty-five years. Mara would still be alive when he was released. She could renew her relationship with him.

Mara swallowed. "You've got a deal."

"Which I'll deny we ever made and make you look like a crazed mother if you claim it happened."

"I know better," Mara said.

"I'm sure you do, and I'm sure you wouldn't agree unless you knew you could convince Ariel to accept my offer."

Mara's stomach clenched.

Sissy glared at her. "I have contacts in the Institutional Division of the Texas Department of Criminal Justice. They decide which prison Ariel goes to. And I'm friends with every warden in Texas. They'll give Ariel any cellmate I ask them to."

***

Oracio had been surprised when Sissy insisted he come to her office, that she couldn't talk to him on the phone.

Then he'd figured it out. It was Friday night with no one else around. She wanted to jump his bones. He smiled and crunched a couple of breath mints.

Sure enough, when he arrived, Sissy had her jacket off, revealing a clinging white sleeveless number. She told him to close the door. When he sat down and she moved from behind her desk to sit next to him, he decided to let her make the first move. He'd always wanted that kind of woman.

"I'm afraid I was a little hasty when I told you not to reopen the Levine case."

Sissy was pretending she'd asked him here for a business reason. She had her pride.

"I've been thinking about it," she said. "If it turns out this thug

256

in San Antonio did it, both our careers are hurt."

Sissy really did want to discuss business, and very serious business at that.

"If we don't cooperate, they never find out if someone else did it," Oracio said. "The San Antonio police will stay out of this unless I ask for their help."

"They've threatened to go to the press. We both could look bad."

Oracio saw how this was playing out. He'd be the one who'd look bad. Sissy's case was based on evidence he had or hadn't brought her. His poor investigation would be blamed.

He stood up. "I gave you the right man."

Sissy put her hand on his arm. "You're the one who figured out it could be someone else and insisted we look into it."

"What do you mean?"

"You saw Matthew Cavazos's license plate, realized Block could have transposed the letters, asked me to get a trial recess so you could investigate further."

"If it doesn't pan out, I'm the fool who made you get a recess for nothing."

"All right. We'll wait to decide which one of us is responsible for the San Antonio investigation after we get the results. If it comes up with nothing, it was my idea."

The rumors about Sissy running for District Attorney must be true. She had to prevent any bad publicity.

"I'll call the San Antonio police. But if you double cross me, forget about being District Attorney."

***

As she walked the nine blocks to Greg Dickson's office, Mara couldn't believe she'd gambled twenty-five years of her son's life.

When she arrived, Ariel ran to her. "Where were you? We were worried. Kleinman called and gave us until next Thursday morning. Isn't that great?"

"I took a walk. I had to get away for a bit."

Simon, Greg and Matthew looked at her but said nothing.

"What happens next?" she asked Greg.

"Right now there's not enough evidence to get a search warrant for Ivan's Land Rover, so the San Antonio police are going to follow him in unmarked cars, figuring he'll disobey some traffic law. Once they have an excuse to stop him, they're hoping they'll see something in the Land Rover which gives them a reason to search it and then impound it."

The odds of all that falling into place were next to nothing.

Mara gazed at her smiling son. When the time came, how could she tell him what she'd done?

FORTY-FOUR

Saturday afternoon Oracio sat in an unmarked car with Jesse Benz, a San Antonio rookie cop. They'd parked around the corner from Verkonovitch's two story Victorian house in the King William District, south of downtown on the banks of the San Antonio River. Ivan's dark green Land Rover was visible on the side drive.

"So, Jesse," Oracio mused, "we've got a Russian immigrant, living in the formerly German area of the overwhelmingly Hispanic city of San Antonio. Only in America."

"Right." Jesse returned to one of his crossword puzzle books. For the next six hours the taciturn rookie worked through three of them and periodically reported into the station while Oracio silently cursed the monotony of surveillance duty.

At nine o'clock Ivan pulled the Land Rover onto the street.

Oracio and Jesse followed at a distance. Ivan led them on the short trip to the Paseo Del Rio, where the river was surrounded by hotels, restaurants and shops as well as tourists lined up to take short cruises along its banks in open topped barges.

Ivan gave his Land Rover to a valet at the Hilton Hotel.

An hour and a half later he exited the building with a tall blond woman in a short black dress. Valets delivered the Land Rover and a red Mazda convertible, which the woman entered. She followed Ivan, who drove slowly, likely in an effort to make sure she didn't lose him.

"Well, so much for giving him a speeding ticket," Jesse said.

By the time they arrived at Ivan's house, two officers were waiting in another unmarked car to relieve them.

Sunday afternoon when he went back on duty Oracio learned that Ivan hadn't left the house again on Saturday night but had driven to church and back that morning.

While Oracio and Jesse watched, a pizza delivery truck stopped at Ivan's, and the blonde came to the door for the food.

Oracio went off duty Sunday night without having seen Ivan that day.

*　*　*

Monday morning Sissy had to deal with Luis and Angelina Sorento. She'd tell them in the privacy of her office about the impending trial recess so the volatile Luis didn't make a scene in the courtroom when it was announced.

When they walked through her door, Luis surprised her with a smile. "You've got the bastard. I can tell the jury thinks he's guilty."

Angelina, looking dowdy in a brown plaid shirtdress, sat down next to her brother in front of Sissy's desk.

"We have to make sure the conviction sticks once we get it," Sissy said.

"Why wouldn't it?" Luis asked. "The judge acts like everything you do is right."

"It appears she's going to call a recess until Thursday."

"Why?" asked Angelina, her dull gray eyes studying Sissy.

"There's a thug in San Antonio, Ivan Verkonovitch, who has a Land Rover with almost the same license plate number as the one Dr. Block wrote down. The police there say he pretty much matches the killer's description, right size and weight and blond hair. Judge Mason will want to give the police a little time to establish it's not him. Then we'll get on with the trial."

Luis bit his bottom lip.

"What kind of thug?" Angelina asked.

"He works for a gambler - Lucky Lazarus."

Angelina rose and looked down at her brother. "You told Mama you'd paid all your debts and stopped gambling. That's why she let you move back into the house."

"They . . . they were all . . . almost paid off."

"That's why you want to sell the shop. So you can pay off the rest of them. They knew you'd do that if she were dead."

"I never thought they'd hurt Mama. Maybe me, but never her." Luis spoke so softly it seemed as though he were talking to himself.

"You killed Mama," Angelina screamed. She lifted her large vinyl purse and hit Luis's head over and over again, yelling, "Mama," with each blow.

The metal clasp smashed into his forehead. He started bleeding, but stayed seated and accepted more. When Angelina collapsed into her chair, crying, Luis left Sissy's office.

***

Sissy rushed into Judge Mason's chambers. The judge was seated at her desk and Greg Dickson sat in a chair in front of her. Sissy looked at her watch and apologized for being five minutes late. She'd taken the time to find a secretary to call a cab for Angelina and agree to sit with her until it arrived.

"Mr. Dickson suggested you be the one to explain this highly unusual request for a recess until Thursday morning."

Sissy told the judge about the possibility that a San Antonio thug was responsible for Mrs. Sorento's murder. "While I believe no proof will turn up through this investigation, still I wouldn't want the public to lose faith in the judicial process by learning about this, and thinking we'd ignored it."

The judge looked at Sissy. "I'll instruct the jury to not discuss the case or watch or read reports of it during the recess. But you realize that if even one of them disregards my instructions, any conviction you got would be overturned on appeal."

That's why Sissy had struck the plea bargain with Mara. There'd be no conviction to overturn, just an agreed upon fifty year sentence for Judge Mason to approve.

"I trust they'll follow your instructions."

"Has District Attorney Jones agreed to the recess?" the judge asked.

"He's given me full authority over this case."

"Do you expect me to give the investigation as the reason for the recess?"

"Please don't, Your Honor," Greg said. "That would tip off the suspect."

***

When Mara entered the courtroom, she noticed the absence of Luis and Angelina Sorento. Sissy must have told them privately about the impending recess. Mara hoped she'd stressed they weren't to discuss the reason and thereby alert Ivan Verkonovitch.

Matthew Cavazos was also absent. He'd returned to San Antonio, ready to call Mara the moment the police made a move on their suspect.

No call had come.

Everyone rose when Judge Mason entered the courtroom.

"You may be seated. Ladies and gentlemen of the jury, I'm going to make an announcement for which I apologize in advance as I know it's going to inconvenience you. I'm recessing this trial until Thursday morning. During that time you may return to your normal activities, such as work, but you still may not discuss the trial, read about it or watch or listen to news reports concerning it. You'll return here Thursday to continue your duties as jurors."

Judge Mason exited to a rising murmur from the spectators. The bailiff ordered everyone to leave the courtroom quietly.

Once outside, Norty Walsh approached Mara. "What's going on?"

"No comment," Greg replied.

The reporter went over to Sissy who gave the same response.

"You're making a mistake," Norty said. "All the press will have to work with is speculation."

As Mara and Ariel watched the local news at noon, Mara was surprised at how accurate that speculation was.

News anchor Charles Walen intoned, "Judge Denise Mason gave no reason for the recess but our legal expert Professor Harvey Slocum of South Texas College of Law has some thoughts on the situation."

"Yes, Charles, I do. If we were dealing with something simple like illness or scheduling problems, the judge would have been forthcoming."

"Why the secrecy?"

"It makes me think they have another suspect."

"Why wouldn't Judge Mason want the jury to know?"

"It could tip off the suspect. Also, if the suspect doesn't pan out, and the jury comes back to hear the case against Levine, they might figure if even the police thought it could be someone else, how can they convict? But if they don't know that's the reason, the way the trial's been going, a conviction, or a plea bargain are good possibilities."

"Why would anyone think I'd plea bargain?" Ariel asked.

Mara didn't answer her son. She couldn't even look at him.

Ariel didn't seem to notice. "What worries me is that the real murderer will figure it out and be too careful to get caught."

With no call from Matthew Cavazos, Mara shared that fear.

FORTY-FIVE

On his Monday afternoon surveillance shift Oracio was paired with Craig Orland, an overweight, about to retire, thirty-five year veteran of the San Antonio police force. Their car was across the street and up the block from Ivan's house, his Land Rover perched on the side drive. They'd learned from the previous surveillance team that Ivan had left his house just once, walking out in his robe to pick up his newspaper.

"Lazy son of a bitch," Craig observed before filling the next two hours with more than Oracio wanted to know about his retirement plans. Oracio became an expert on the construction of Craig's lake cabin, the bargain he'd negotiated on his fishing boat and the special features of his fishing rod.

Oracio was yawning when Craig said, "The tan Ford that stopped across from Ivan's house ten minutes ago is still there and the driver hasn't come out."

"Could he be one of your guys?"

"I doubt it, but I'll call in just in case."

Before Craig did so, Ivan walked out of his house and opened the door to the Land Rover.

The man in the car ran over to him.

The guy looked familiar to Oracio but he moved quickly and then stood across from Ivan with his back to the detective.

The two men talked and then gesticulated as though arguing.

Ivan leaned into the Land Rover, pulled something out and showed it to the other man, who sprinted towards his Ford yelling, "No."

Oracio and Craig simultaneously left their car.

"Police, drop the knife," Craig yelled.

Ivan turned around. "I wasn't going to hurt him. I'm just showing him a knife he wants to buy."

"Drop it and then we'll talk," Craig said.

Ivan hesitated.

Oracio aimed the gun at his chest.

Ivan let the knife fall.

A pale Luis Sorento spoke. "He showed me the knife and said just before he used it on my mother, he told her, 'You can thank your son for this.'"

***

Ariel sat on Mara's right and Benjie on her left as they watched the televised news conference at which Sissy Kleinman and Oracio Crawley announced the charge of murder against Ivan Verkonovitch.

When it ended, the family would leave for the celebratory dinner Simon and Virginia were hosting at Dominic's. Her former husband had told Mara to invite Josef.

On the screen a smiling Sissy spoke. "When Sergeant Crawley saw Mr. Cavazos's license plate in the parking lot, he realized how easy it would have been for Dr. Block to have transposed the letters at the beginning of the fleeing Land Rover's license plate."

"That's a crock," Benjie said, "Mom's the one who figured it out."

"Doesn't matter. We've got Ariel home with us."

Sergeant Crawley looked like a puffed up penguin. "As soon as I brought it to Ms. Kleinman's attention, she acted."

"Now that's a real crock," Ariel said. "She refused to do anything. Then Mom took off and by the time she got back, Kleinman was ready to cooperate."

"How'd you do it?" Benjie asked.

Mara, still overwhelmed by the knowledge that the deal she'd cut with Sissy could have destroyed Ariel, didn't respond.

"Sissy Kleinman put justice first," District Attorney Jones said. "The public can't ask for anything more."

"Does that mean you're going to support her to take over your job once you retire?" a reporter asked.

"I'd leave the position happily if I knew she were my successor."

"I can't believe it," Benjie said. "Crawley and Kleinman tried to railroad Ariel. Now he'll wind up with a promotion and she'll wind up District Attorney. It isn't fair."

Mara thought of something she learned in a long ago Sunday school class, in a course called "Sayings of Our Sages."

265

Judith Groudine Finkel

"Never envy evil doers their ill gotten gains," she told her sons.

Her hand went automatically to the chasma at her throat. There'd been enough evil in their lives that she had to believe there'd be no more.

ORDER EXTRA COPIES

TEXAS JUSTICE

A Legal Thriller

■■

Name: _____

Address:_____

_____

_____

Email: _____

\# of copies at $13.95 each: _____
plus $3.00 mailing and handling: _____
Florida residents add: $1.12 state tax: _____

     TOTAL: _____

EXCEPTION: If ordering four or more books,
        Total S & H: = $10.00

Please send check for correct amount to:
        Fireside Publications
        13539 SE 87th Circle
        Summerfield, Florida 34491

Or use Paypal to email address: **belois@comcast.net**

Please use this order blank or a facsimile.

ALSO AVAILABLE FROM FIRESIDE PUBLICATION

AN AGENT SPEAKS by Joan West: $9.98
A Primer for unpublished Authors

ENGELHARDT by Gisela Engelhardt: $9.98
From ideal childhood to horror in Hitler's
Germany to life in America.

BLESSED: MY Battle with Brain Disease $9.98
By Mary J. Stevens:
From Convent life to reintegration as a wife
and mother, all the while seeking a diagnosis
for her brain disease and learning to live with it.

BEYOND FOREVER: Past Life Experiences
By Taylor
Shaye $11.95
Shari searches through time for her soul mate.

THE COST OF JUSTICE $15.95
by Mike Gedgoudas
Legal thriller with an inside look at a State
Supreme Court

TITLE _____ _____

TITLE _____ _____

TITLE _____ _____

Include # of copies& price of each book. Add $3.00 S & H
Per book. Florida residents, add 7% per book for state tax.
EXCEPTION: If ordering 5 to 10 books to same address,
          Total S & H = $10.00.

          TOTAL DUE: _____
Please mail check for correct amount to:
      Fireside Publications
      13539 SE 87th Circle
      Summerfield, Florida 34491
Or pay by PayPal using email address: belois@comcast.net